The ULTIMATE NOSE PICKERS COLLECTION

Gordon Korman

Illustrated by Victor Vaccaro

Hyperion Paperbacks for Children
New York

For Jay Howard Korman,
the NEWEST EarthLing
—G.K.

For my Father, with
affection and admiration
—V.V.

Nose Pickers from Outer Space text © 1999 by Gordon Korman
Nose Pickers from Outer Space illustrations © 1999 by Victor Vaccaro

Planet of the Nose Pickers text © 2000 by Gordon Korman
Planet of the Nose Pickers illustrations © 2000 by Victor Vaccaro

Your Mummy Is a Nose Picker text © 2000 by Gordon Korman
Your Mummy Is a Nose Picker illustrations © 2000 by Victor Vaccaro

Invasion of the Nose Pickers text © 2001 by Gordon Korman
Invasion of the Nose Pickers illustrations © 2001 by Victor Vaccaro

Printed in the United States of America

First Hyperion Compiled Paperback edition, 2006
1 3 5 7 9 10 8 6 4 2
Library of Congress Cataloging-in-Publication Data on file.
Library of Congress Control Number: 2005931748
ISBN 0-7868-3740-3
Visit www.hyperionbooksforchildren.com

NOSE PICKERS from OUTER SPACE!

CONTENTS

Chapter 1
NERD ALERT

✷ DEVIN HUNTER'S RULES OF COOLNESS ✷

☞ **Rule 1:** Don't ever act excited—even when you're excited.

I kept saying it over and over to myself at the airport.

"What are you mumbling?" my mother asked me.

I didn't answer. That was because of ☞ **Rule 6: In public, NEVER show that you have a mother.**

It was one of the most important of my rules of coolness, along with ☞ **Rule 9: Broccoli is for losers,** and ☞ **Rule 27: Don't let anyone sew name tags on your underwear.**

But back to Rule 1. I didn't want it to show, but inside I was totally psyched. We were here to pick up my exchange buddy. That was a pretty big thing in our school.

Most of the fourth-graders signed up for the National Student Exchange Program. Your exchange buddy was a kid from another state. He or she would come to live at your house for a month, and go to school with you as a guest student.

Joey Petrillo already had a great exchange buddy, Cody. Cody was from Texas. He lived on a real ranch. He could rope and tie a calf in less than ten seconds. And Calista Bernstein's buddy, Wanda, came from California. She dressed like a supermodel and even wore makeup!

Come to think of it, all the exchange buddies had turned out to be pretty cool. That's why I was so excited about meeting Stan. Was he a star quarterback? A Nintendo master? A laugh-a-minute class clown?

Mom checked her watch. "Where could he be?"

Good question. All the passengers were off Flight 407. They were picking up their suitcases at the baggage claim.

Suddenly, the luggage carousel groaned to a halt. The lights flickered once, and then the whole airport went dark.

"Stay close to me," ordered Mom in the gloom. "It's a power failure."

The words were barely out of her mouth when the lights came on again. The carousel sprang back to life, and more luggage came down the slide. Out rolled a steamer trunk, a garment bag, two duffles, and a *person!* He tumbled down the chute, hit the carousel, and started circling like he was a suitcase.

TALK abOUT EXCESS baggagE.

I was so shocked that I broke Rule 6.

"Mom, did you see that?"

But she was looking the other way.

A shiny silver travel bag came down and bonked the guy on the head. He picked it up, jumped off the carousel, and landed at our feet.

What a nerd this kid was! He had a crew cut, and big thick glasses that made his eyes look like fried eggs. Worst of all, he was wearing a tie!

Didn't he know about ☛ **Rule 21: No ties?** His pants were too short! His sleeves were too long! I think his belt was up under his arms somewhere.

"Beat it, kid," I whispered. "I'm looking for my exchange buddy."

"You must be Devin Hunter," said the nerd with a little munchkin voice.

Oh no, I prayed to myself. **Please don't be Stan.**

He nodded, grinning. Even his teeth were nerdy. "I'm Stan."

Mom took his suitcase and smiled at him. "What's your last name, Stan? In the letter from the exchange program, there must have been a mistake. It looked something like Mflxnys."

He beamed. "That's me. Stan Mflxnys."

Mflxnys? I was going to have to introduce this guy around school. Everybody would think I had a mouthful of gravel!

"Welcome, Stan," said Mom. "The car's just outside—"

"Hold it!" I choked. "This could be the wrong Stan Mflxnys!"

5

It wasn't. He had all the papers to prove he was the right person.

"Thank you for hosting me," he said stiffly. "May the Crease be with you."

May the *what?*

My mom giggled. "Oh, Stan. You're so full of fun."

Fun wasn't the word I was thinking of. Try ***baloney***.

It wasn't fair. In a world of cool exchange buddies, I got the dweeb.

Chapter 2

STAN FROM PAN

When Mom put the suitcase in the trunk of our Honda, Stan tried to climb in there with it.

I stared at the guy. "Haven't you ever seen a car before?"

"Only in pictures," he told me, dead serious.

My mother laughed and laughed. "You're such a joker, Stan."

But I didn't think he was joking. I was starting to think he was crazy. "Where are you from, the Moon?" I asked.

He frowned at me. "There are no intelligent life forms on Earth's Moon. I, Stan, am from Pan."

"The letter said you were from Chicago," my mother put in.

"Right. Of course," Stan amended. "Pan is— outside Chicago."

I groaned. Stan from Pan. **I had to make up a new rule of coolness—something about your name rhyming with your hometown.** I'm against it. It sounds dumb.

When we got home, Mom and I showed Stan up to my room. All my stuff was pushed to one side so we could move in the extra bed.

"That's where you sleep," I told him. "You know, unless you prefer the furnace room or the garage or something."

"Don't be rude," Mom said sharply. "Stan, you get yourself unpacked. Then come and meet the rest of the family."

Mom and I started downstairs. Suddenly, I heard footsteps behind me. It was Stan!

I stared at him. "You're supposed to unpack first."

"Yes."

"So do it!"

"I, Stan, have completed the task."

"You're finished? No way!" I ran back up. My jaw dropped. Shirts hung in the closet; pants were folded in the drawer. A whole shelf of books sat on top of the dresser. There was a dartboard on the wall, and a bearskin rug on the floor. All this out of one small silver suitcase! And he did it in two seconds! **What was going on here?**

I checked out the clothes. They were all the same. I mean, identical. He had twenty black ties with white polka dots. Fifteen dress shirts. And—what was this? A Chicago Bulls basketball jersey—number twenty-three!

Hooray! Something normal! I grabbed it and ran down to the family room.

Mom was introducing Stan to my father, my older brother, Roscoe, and my kid sister, Lindsay.

I barged right in and waved the jersey in Stan's face. "You've got to wear this to school tomorrow! It's the only decent thing you own!"

"I, Stan, never wear that shirt," he said seriously. "It's a gift from a dear friend."

Roscoe put an arm around Stan's wimpy shoulders. "Awesome, you're a Bulls fan! Me, too. There's a game on tonight. We can watch it together."

"Acceptable," Stan told him.

Did you catch that? *Acceptable?* He talked like he'd swallowed a dictionary! But my

family didn't even notice. They thought he was great.

Even Fungus, our cocker spaniel, loved Stan. Fungus, who hates everybody, jumped up on his lap and barked at him. Stan looked right into our dog's eyes and barked back.

I don't have a rule of coolness about talking to dogs. I didn't think I needed one. But there was a whole woof-woof conversation going on!

All at once, Stan threw back his head and laughed.

"What's so funny?" I asked, disgusted.

"Fungus knows a lot of knock-knock jokes," he told me.

"He's a dog!" I said through clenched teeth.

He nodded. "With an excellent sense of humor."

KNOCK KNOCK. WHO'S THERE? WOOF.

It was after midnight when I finally figured out what was really wrong with that conversation. **Nobody had told Stan that our dog's name was Fungus!**

I went over to the other bed. Stan was snoring. Naturally, the dweeb couldn't snore like a normal person. The noise that came out of him sounded more like the hum of a microwave oven.

I shook him awake. "How did you know?" I demanded. "How did you know the name of our dog?"

"He told me," Stan mumbled.

"My dad? Roscoe?"

"No. Fungus."

And, no matter how hard I shook him, I couldn't wake him up again.

Chapter 3
EIGHTY·FIVE THOUSAND LIGHT·YEARS

☛ **Rule 11:** If you hang out with a dweeb, people are going to think you're a dweeb, too.

That was the problem with bringing Stan from Pan to school. It would take about five seconds for everybody to figure out that this was the biggest nerd in town.

So on the way to Clearview Elementary, I gave him a crash course in how to be cool.

"Listen, Stan," I said carefully. "This place is different from your school back in Chicago—"

"Pan," Stan corrected.

"Right. Pan. What I'm trying to say is this: around here, dogs bark at people. People don't bark at dogs. You don't want everyone to think you're—you know—a dweeb or something. You have to be cool."

"Not necessarily," he told me. "If I'm cool, I, Stan, can put on something called a sweater and warm right up."

All right . . . Plan B. "Stan, don't open your mouth at all. School rules. Mr. Slomin is big on quiet."

But as soon as I said it, along came Tanner Phelps and his exchange buddy, a real cool-looking kid with red hair and sunglasses that were mirrors.

"Hey, Devin, I want you to meet Sam Purvis. His soccer team was Minnesota state champs last year."

I burned with jealousy. Sam really was a fantastic soccer player. While we were talking, he was bouncing a ball off his head. I'll bet he could keep it up there for hours! I'll also bet he never barked at anybody's dog. Not once in his life!

"Hi, Sam," I greeted.

Both boys were looking at Stan, taking in the fried-egg eyes and the polka-dot tie.

"Aren't you going to introduce us to your buddy?" asked Tanner.

"Oh," I said. "This is Stan—" I dropped my voice and mumbled, "Mflxnys."

"Could you repeat that?" requested Soccer Sam. "It sounded like you just said 'Mflxnys.'"

My dweeb stepped forward. "Correct. Stan Mflxnys. May the Crease be with you." He shook hands with both of them. The soccer ball hit the ground and bounced away.

"Gee." Tanner's eyes narrowed. "That's a pretty weird name you've got there, kid."

Stan was surprised. "Really? Where I, Stan, come from, the phone book has a full page of us Mflxnyses."

"He's from Pan," I said quickly. "It's near Chicago. Stan's a big Chicago Bulls fan."

Sam looked interested. "How far is your house from the United Center where the Bulls play?"

Stan thought it over. "Not far. You make a left on Third Street, go down five blocks—"

Sam came a step closer. The twin mirrors of his sunglasses flashed in Stan's face. Suddenly, the dweeb's eyes crossed. "Approximately eighty-five thousand light-years," he finished in that munchkin voice.

The bell rang. It saved my life.

Class 4C was pretty crowded. We had our regular twenty-three kids, plus fourteen exchange buddies.

Mr. Slomin started the day by asking all the

visitors to introduce themselves. Sam gave a soccer demonstration. Wanda from Hollywood talked about the time she and her family ate next to Steven Spielberg in a restaurant. Cody made a lariat out of someone's jump rope and lassoed Mr. Slomin. It was pretty funny. But I couldn't enjoy it, because I knew Stan was up next.

"I'm Stan from Pan," said my exchange buddy. He almost had to talk around his tie. It was on so tight that it stuck straight up in front of his face. "I, Stan, am a very average youngster. My

hobbies are knitting, doing homework, going to the dentist, and cleaning my room."

I wanted to crawl under my desk.

Joey nudged me from behind. "I pity the poor jerk who has to be buddies with *that* nerd."

What could I do? I agreed with Joey. I pitied myself.

"My buddy is Devin Hunter," Stan announced. "I, Stan, first met him yesterday when he and his mother picked me up at the airport."

Mr. Slomin jumped to his feet. "The airport? There was a UFO sighting at the airport yesterday! Did you see anything?"

Mr. Slomin was totally into UFOs—unidentified flying objects. At first, it was fun to have a teacher who talked about visitors from outer space. But waiting for aliens can be pretty boring, especially when they never show up.

"I, Stan, observed nothing," said Stan.

UFOs weren't just a hobby with Mr. Slomin. He was nuts on the subject. It was enough to turn a normal adult into the weirdest teacher at school.

"Think harder," he urged. "From an airplane

you would have a perfect chance to spot a spaceship or a flying saucer."

Stan shook his head. "Sorry, Mr. Slomin."

But when Mr. Slomin was talking about UFOs, he was like a bloodhound. "What about your fellow passengers? You know, the other Pannites on the plane?"

Stan frowned. "Pannites? Oh, no, we're not called Pannites. People from Pan are known as Pants."

That did it. The whole class howled with

laughter. It came on a tidal wave, washing away all talk about UFOs.

Then, just when I thought things couldn't get any worse, I looked up at my exchange buddy. There he stood, in front of the whole class— *with his finger up his nose!*

Question: What could be worse than a nerd exchange buddy?

Answer: A nerd nose picker.

This bOOK is rEALLY ENGROSSINg!

Chapter 4
HAPPY 147TH BIRTHDAY

"Listen, Stan," I said at lunch. "You're not a very cool guy. I can live with that. But you've got to stop picking your nose. It's worse than just the uncoolest thing in the world. It's gross!"

Stan was outraged. "Pants are not nose pickers."

"I saw you!" I insisted. "The whole class saw you! You were up there to the second knuckle!"

Tanner and Sam plunked their trays down opposite us. Calista and Wanda took the seats beside them.

"Can anybody sit here?" giggled Calista. "Or is it just for Pants?"

"I'm *wearing* pants," added Tanner. "Does that count?"

"Please join us," invited Stan. "May the Crease be with you."

"The *crease*?" echoed Calista. "You mean the crease in your . . . *pants*?"

Everybody laughed, even Stan. I think the poor guy believed he was popular, instead of the laughingstock of the fourth grade. I'll bet my face was bright red.

"Well, I'm starved." I picked up my slice of pizza.

Stan picked up his, too. **And he took a big bite—*out of the paper plate!***

I started to choke. Before our horrified eyes, Stan munched happily until the plate was gone. Then he ate his napkin. He started to nibble at the plastic tray, but shook his head. "Stale," he decided. He wiped his mouth with his pizza and threw it in the garbage. "Delicious!" he burped happily.

"Oooh, gross!" exclaimed Wanda. "Stan ate paper!"

"Devin, where did you find this guy?" Tanner hissed. "He's a nut-job!"

I had to change the subject. I wracked my

brain. What does everybody love to talk about? And then it came to me.

"My birthday is next month," I announced loudly. "November twenty-seventh. I'll be ten. Double digits."

It worked!

"I'm already ten," said Calista. "It's no big deal."

"My birthday is on Christmas Eve," Sam piped up. "I hate that."

"It's better than July," put in Wanda. "All your friends are at camp. There's nobody around to come to your party." She pushed away her salad and popped open her makeup compact. She

dabbed at her nose with the powder puff. "How about you, Stan? When's your birthday?"

"Well, Wanda—" Stan turned to answer her and found himself staring into the mirror of her compact. His eyes crossed. "When the North Star passes through the constellation of Scorpio, I, Stan, will be 147."

Calista gave me a shove. "Devin—"

Like it was my fault that I got the worst exchange buddy of all time!

"He's just kidding," I mumbled. "He's a great kidder."

But deep down, I knew there was something very weird about this guy.

Chapter 5

THE GREAT
DISHWASHING MYSTERY

This called for drastic action, and I was just the guy to take it. I let Stan read my Rules of Coolness notebook. I'd never let anybody see it before. No one knew it existed.

I even added a few special rules aimed just at him: ☛ *Don't cross your eyes unless it's part of a joke.* And: ☛ *If homework is your hobby, shut up about it.* And of course: ☛ *No nose picking.*

It wasn't easy. Stan kept me on my toes making sure the rules were up to date. For example, Rule 44 started out: ☛ *Don't eat paper.* But Stan went after paper the way a dog digs in a flower bed. He couldn't help himself! I had to change the rule to: ☛ *Don't eat paper, cardboard, phone books, catalogs, packing cartons, or the mail.* And still there were teeth marks in my *World Book Encyclopedia*.

At school, Stan was a total loss. The kids called him every name you could think of: Stan-Pan, Pan-Stan, Stan from Pan the Panty Man, and Stan-Stan Moo Goo Gai Pan.

The nose picking jokes were the worst:

"Hey, Stan, if you find anything up there, I'll split it with you, fifty-fifty!"

"What are you doing—drilling for oil?"

"Shake hands? I don't think so!"

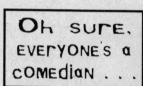

They laughed at him, which meant they were also laughing at me. While exchange buddies like Sam, Wanda, and Cody were welcomed like movie stars, Stan and I were treated like we smelled bad. I didn't get invited to Ralph O'Malley's party because nobody wanted a nose picker too close to the cake. To be honest, I couldn't blame them.

"Sorry, Devin," Ralph whispered to me in gym class. "I was kind of afraid he would eat the streamers."

What could I do? I added *streamers* to Rule 44.

Yeah, school was rough. But I have to say, home was worse. Nobody believed me when I told them how weird Stan was.

"But Mom, he's a nose picker!"

"Oh, stop it," she scolded me. "You've been mean to poor Stan ever since he arrived. Everyone has a couple of bad habits."

"Does everyone eat paper?" I challenged.

"Oh, come now," she scoffed. "A lot of people chew paper. It isn't very nice, but it's not the end of the world."

I was getting desperate. "He doesn't chew it! He *eats* it! It's his favorite food! He throws away his lunch and chows down on the bag! Yesterday I caught him sneaking the newspapers out of the recycling bin! He's crazy!"

Boy, was Mom ever mad! You'd think Stan was her real son, and I was the idiot who had come out of the baggage chute at the airport. She put me on dishwashing duty for the whole rest of the week.

Scraping plates and loading the dishwasher is the job I hate second most in the world. The worst is *un*loading the dishwasher and putting everything away. And I was stuck doing both for three entire days. I had to get out of it!

I found Stan in my kid sister Lindsay's room, playing Barbies with her. Every time I think he's hit the bottom of the dweeb ocean, he manages to sink a few more feet.

I took him aside. "Great news, Stan. Mom's put me in charge of the dishwasher. And I'm going to let you help."

"Don't do it, Stan!" cried Lindsay. "He's just using you to—*oomff!*" I quickly stuck my hand over her mouth.

"So, what do you say?" I asked Stan.

"I, Stan, will assist you," he declared like he was Superman, about to save the world.

It's a bird . . .
It's a PLANE . . .
It's SuperPicker!

Dinner was spaghetti with meat sauce, so the plates were covered in gunk. During dessert, I leaned over to Stan and whispered, "Let's make a race out of it."

As soon as Mom and Dad were gone from the table, I yelled, "Ready, set, go!" Then I sprinted down to the basement to hide while he did all the work. Okay, so I'm not such a swell guy.

But the next minute, I heard Roscoe taking him to watch the Bulls game on TV.

I rushed back upstairs. "No! No! No!" I dropped my voice to a whisper. "What about the dishes? The race?"

Stan beamed at me. "I, Stan, was victorious," he announced with pride.

"You mean you *won*? No way!"

He led me into the kitchen. The dishwasher was empty.

"Aw, Stan! You haven't even started loading it yet!"

He opened the cupboard. The dishes were sparkling clean and neatly put away. The glasses and cutlery were all in their places. The counter was clear, and the floor gleamed. Even the garbage had been taken out.

"But that's impossible!" I exploded. "The dishwasher alone takes half an hour! You've been at this for thirty seconds! What did you do?"

"I, Stan, beat you," he chortled, and went back to the basketball game.

Don't get me wrong. I was thrilled that the dishes were all done. But this was kind of creepy!

So the next day after dinner, I didn't go hide in the basement. I stuck around to see how Stan could do forty-five minutes of cleanup in thirty seconds.

I was walking into the kitchen with an armload

of dessert plates. And then *poof!*

They disappeared.

"What the—"

And there was Stan, standing in the middle of our spotless kitchen, grinning at me. "I, Stan, win again."

I threw open the cupboard and gawked. There were the plates that had vanished from my hands. Five seconds ago they had been smeared with chocolate cake. Now they were washed, dried, and stacked.

I pointed at Stan. **"You've got helpers, right? A bunch of guys hiding in the pantry?"**

Even while I was saying it, I knew it was stupid. A hundred people couldn't do the dishes that fast. And they definitely couldn't make my armload of plates go *poof!*

On Friday night, I had to stick to Stan like glue. I followed him into the kitchen. I followed him out of the kitchen. I even followed him to the bathroom. When he emerged, munching on a tissue, there I was.

"Do you require something of me, Devin?" he asked innocently.

"I'm not letting you out of my sight for one second!" I snarled. "Even if it kills me, I'm going to see how you do those dishes so fast!"

He seemed surprised. "But Devin, the dishes have already been done."

"*What?*" I sprinted back to the kitchen. Another perfect job. "Oh, no! Not again!"

When did he do all that work? I watched every move he made! I didn't take my eyes off the guy. The one time I looked away was when he stuck his finger up his nose. Who could blame me? Nose picking is not a spectator sport!

It dawned on me like a sunrise. It was the nose! Stan always said he wasn't picking it.

> It's NOT whether you win or lose. It's how you pick that counts!

What if he was telling the truth? Maybe he was doing something else—something that only *looked* like picking.

After all, noses were meant for smelling, breathing, and blowing. They were there to perch your glasses on. Nobody said anything about doing the dishes!

There was only one explanation for all this: my exchange buddy had a magic nose!

Chapter 6

NOT YOUR AVERAGE, RUN·OF·THE·MILL SCHNOZ

"Good night, Devin," called my mother. "Good night, Stan. Sleep well."

I got into bed. But sleep wasn't even part of the plan. How could I sleep, with that nose only a few feet away in the other bed?

As usual, Stan was out like a light the second his head hit the pillow. You could tell by his microwave-oven snoring. I jumped out of bed, tiptoed over, and peered down at my exchange buddy. Just as I suspected! The power hum was coming right from his magic nose!

I took out my mini-flashlight and shone the beam at Stan's schnoz. It looked like a pretty regular nose to me. I had to get a look inside. But how?

Then it came to me. My mom had one of those mirrors—the kind that magnifies everything. I ran for the bathroom.

Oh, no! Roscoe was taking one of his famous five-hour showers! I could hear him soaping and whistling.

If you interrupt my brother in the shower, you automatically start World War Three. But I needed that mirror. I decided to take a chance.

I eased the bathroom door open.

Squeak!

Behind the shower curtain, the whistling stopped. "Who's there?" Roscoe demanded.

I snatched the mirror up from the vanity and made a break for it. The door shut with a too-loud snap.

"That better not be you, Devin!" came a growl from inside.

In the hall, I watched as the mirror unfogged. My own face appeared, giant-size. Perfect. This would be as good as a microscope right up Stan's nostrils.

I ran back into my room. My swan dive into bed would have won me an Olympic medal.

Angry footsteps started down the hall. I shoved the mirror under my pillow and started to work on my I've-been-asleep-for-hours look.

The door opened a crack. "Devin?" came a whisper.

I kept my mouth shut. Stan snored on.

"Did you just barge in on me?"

But a world-class faker is impossible to catch. I faked sleep so well that I even dozed off for real. The next thing I knew, Roscoe was gone, and it was after two in the morning.

Silently, I crept out of bed. It was time to learn the secret of my exchange buddy's magic schnoz.

I crouched over Stan and carefully rested the mirror on his upper lip. Then I shone my mini-flashlight into his nostrils, and peered down at the glass.

My heart nearly leaped out my throat. Now, I'm not a nose expert. But you don't have to be a genius to realize that **this was not your average, run-of-the-mill schnoz.** The inside of Stan's nose was all shiny, silver and chrome. There were hundreds of tiny buttons, switches, dials, and blinking colored lights.

No wonder Stan snored a power hum. I was amazed he didn't have to plug himself into the wall like a toaster! This nose wasn't magic at all! It was—

"A machine!" I blurted.

"A computer," corrected an all-too-familiar munchkin voice.

Chapter 7
INTERSTELLAR DWEEBS

Oh, no! Stan was awake!

"I can explain everything," I babbled. "I was . . . uh . . . *jealous* because you've got such a great nose. And you know how you're always picking it? Well, I just wanted to see what was so *good* in there—"

Stan didn't say a word. He just lay there with his eyes crossed.

That always happened when my exchange buddy looked into a mirror. It was like he was hypnotized.

"What kind of guy has a computer up his nose?" I mumbled to myself.

"All Pants have nasal processors," Stan replied, still cross-eyed.

"Yeah, right," I snorted. "You expect me to believe there's a whole town outside Chicago where everybody has a computer in his schnoz? **I mean, I've heard of laptops, but *nosetops?***"

"Pan isn't a town," he told me. "It's a planet."

"Aw, come on, Stan! Quit fooling around—"

All at once, his nose began to twitch. A high-pitched beeping sound came out of his nostrils. I checked Mom's mirror. The blinking lights were going crazy, flashing like a nervous Christmas tree. Switches flipped. Dials whizzed like tiny pinwheels. A miniature satellite dish wheeled around and around. What was going on in there?

A superpowered light shone through the curtains. I dropped the mirror and ran to the window. Our backyard was as bright as a summer afternoon!

Suddenly, a large gleaming object descended out of the sky. It was shaped like a giant stop sign—flat with eight sides. It was the color of aluminum foil covered in the same kind of blinking lights that were up Stan's nose. A flashing neon pipe on the top puffed a shower of sparks.

You couldn't spend a whole year in Mr. Slomin's class without recognizing what this was.

"A UFO!" I rasped, terrified. I threw myself
to the floor and scrambled under the bed. Okay,
it wasn't very cool. But there was no rule of
coolness about how to act when a spaceship is
landing in your backyard.

That's when I saw Stan's feet. He was getting up!

"Hide!" I whispered urgently.

A hand reached down and picked the mirror up off the floor. The bare feet began to walk away.

"Stan! Come back!" I hissed. "There's a UFO out there! A real UFO!"

I heard the door close. Desperately, I tried to picture the pamphlet from the National Student Exchange Program. It said you had to house and feed your buddy and take him to school with you. There was nothing about rescuing him from space invaders.

I shook my head to clear it. What was I thinking? Dweeb or not, Stan was my buddy. I had to look out for him—no matter what he had up his nose.

I crept out from under the bed, got up on my knees, and peered over the windowsill. The spaceship's lights were dim. It was parked in our yard, right in Dad's prize flower garden.

A tiny black dot appeared in the wall of the craft. It grew larger until it had become a big round door. A staircase descended, and a red carpet unfurled to the petunia bed. Two aliens strolled down and stood at the foot of the steps, waiting.

At least, I *thought* they were aliens. They looked totally human. To be honest, they looked kind of like Stan, only older—the same crew cuts, white shirts, and ties knotted so tight that they stuck out in front.

In a flash, I understood everything. It was like all the pieces of a puzzle had been put together at the same instant. Mr. Slomin's UFO at the airport! It was Stan! I didn't have to save Stan from aliens because Stan was an alien, too!

It was all true! Pan really *was* a planet, not a small town outside Chicago!

Even though I was scared, I was kind of disappointed, too. I always figured aliens would be real cool-looking. You know, silvery blue skin, huge black eyes, antennae, funky laser guns, stuff like that; I never expected interstellar dweebs.

A NErd is a NErd is a NErd.

Stan rushed across the lawn.

"Greetings from Pan, Agent Mflxnys," said one of the aliens. "May the Crease be with you."

Stan was out there talking to—*a pair of Pants!*

Chapter 8

A NOSE PICKERS' CONVENTION

"Welcome Zgrbnys the Extremely Wise, and Gthrmnys the Utterly Clever," I heard my buddy announce. "How are things on Pan?"

"Oh, just the same old belt loops and cuffs," said Zgrbnys with a shrug.

"The annual Suspender Festival has begun in the Panhandle," put in Gthrmnys. "The Grand Pant himself threw out the first button this year. But enough about home. How have you progressed in your mission?"

"I, Stan, am masquerading as a student in an exchange program," Stan told him. "No one suspects my true identity. I fit right in."

"Oh, sure!" I muttered sarcastically. I could hardly tell him apart from all the other munchkin-sounding, paper-eating, nose-picking dweebs.

"'Stan'?" repeated Gthrmnys in confusion. "What is the meaning of this strange word?"

"It's the name I'm called at my Earthling elementary school," my buddy explained.

The two aliens doubled over with knee-slapping laughter.

"'Stan'!" guffawed Zgrbnys. "Where do Earthlings come up with such ridiculous names?"

"That other one from your last report was even more absurd," chuckled Gthrmnys. "Devin! What kind of a Neptunian Ice Worm would be named Devin?"

I couldn't believe I was being made fun of by a couple of nerds whose names sounded like stomach gurgles. But you can't waste too much time being insulted when your yard is full of aliens.

I had a little trouble eavesdropping on their conversation. The three Pants spoke clearly enough. The problem was they kept picking their noses, so their voices were muffled. It looked like a nose pickers' convention out there!

Life sure can pitch you a lot of curves. One minute you're a normal kid; the next, **you're spying on nose pickers from outer space!**

"I, Stan, have discovered a remarkable Earth device." He handed them my mother's makeup mirror.

I stared. These guys had spaceships, and a *mirror* was a big deal to them?

"It's a truth enforcer," Stan went on. "It's impossible to lie while looking into it."

To demonstrate, he held the mirror in front of their faces. Two sets of alien eyes crossed.

Zgrbnys announced, "I'm much smarter than Gthrmnys."

"Zgrbnys is a moron compared to me," declared Gthrmnys.

Stan took the mirror away, and the two aliens glared at each other resentfully.

Finally, Zgrbnys said, "We must study this baffling object in our laboratory on Pan." Absently, he tossed Mom's mirror over his shoulder. It was about to shatter against the metal of the ship, when a mechanical hand shot out and caught it in midair. Just as suddenly, the mirror was whisked in through the door and out of view.

"What else have you learned about this planet, Agent Mflxnys?" asked Gthrmnys.

"It's very difficult for us Pants to understand Earthlings," Stan told him. "Their main interest seems to be something called 'being cool.' They even have rules about it."

"I had no idea the climate was so important to them," mused Zgrbnys, picking away thoughtfully.

"However, I, Stan,
have used my Pan-Tran
translator to talk with an
Earth-dog named Fun-
gus," Stan went on. "He is
a much more sensible life form."

Well, what do you know! Stan wasn't just
barking back at Fungus! He could speak *Dog*.

"What forms of entertainment are popular on
Earth?" prompted Gthrmnys.

"Scratching, chasing cats, and drinking out of
the toilet," Stan replied. "Also, there is some-

thing called a fire hydrant. It is so deeply re-spected that every time you pass one, you must salute it by raising a leg."

"I love native ceremonies," said Zgrbnys approvingly.

"According to Fungus, Earthlings love to bury things," Stan continued. "Especially bones, which are an Earth delicacy."

"How do they taste?" Gthrmnys inquired.

"Not very tender," Stan admitted. "I, Stan, much prefer the flavor of the paper on Earth. It has a nice texture, delicately spiced with ink. The chefs at Sears serve a catalog that is an absolute feast. You must try it."

"Next time," promised Zgrbnys. "Right now, we have an urgent meeting with Agent Shkprnys on Mercury."

Even from my second-story window, I could see my exchange buddy turn pale. "Shkprnys, the One and Only? On Mercury?"

"Don't worry," Gthrmnys assured him. "If your work here goes well, tens of thousands of Pants will be dining on Sears catalogs very, very soon."

What?! Did that mean what I thought it did?

There was only one explanation for so many aliens on Earth. **An invasion! And it was coming *very, very soon!***

After some farewell nose picking, the visitors got back in their ship. First the carpet disappeared. Then the stairs. The big round door shrank and shrank until it was a tiny dot that winked out of existence.

Stan stood there waving as the spacecraft lifted itself off Dad's petunias. It rose up above my window and banked over on its side. Then it hovered for a moment, and zoomed into the night, whizzing around like a balloon with a leak in it. At last, it disappeared.

I didn't move a muscle. I knelt there, frozen, until I heard the back door, and then footsteps in the upstairs hallway. I dove under the covers and faked sleep while Stan let himself into our room.

He got into bed. Almost immediately, I heard the microwave-oven hum of his nose computer.

I opened one eye and peered over at my exchange buddy. Who would have thought that this harmless-looking, nerdy guy was a spy for an invading army? Pretty soon, we Earthlings could be up to our waists in Pants—and not the kind you wear, either.

I set my jaw. I had to stop it. But what could a kid do? Call the police and say, "I'm only nine, but I happen to know the whole planet is about to be attacked by nose pickers from outer space"? They'd throw me in the nuthouse.

I couldn't even tell my parents. I'd just get in trouble for making up stories. It would be that much harder to save the world if I got grounded.

No, I had to do this alone. Stan may have been a highly advanced alien from the other side of the galaxy, but he was still a dweeb. ☛ **Rule 24:** A cool person always has an advantage over a dweeb. I just had to find his weakness.

But what? He had spaceships and technology. He could do just about anything with his nose; I could smell with mine, and that was pretty much it.

What weaknesses did a guy like that have?

The answer would have to come from Stan himself. And I knew the perfect way to squeeze it out of him.

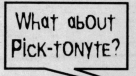

What about PiCK-TONYTE?

Chapter 9

THE CONSTELLATION OF THE BIG ZIPPER

"Has anybody seen my magnifying mirror?" Mom asked at breakfast the next morning.

I started choking on my Froot Loops. The last I heard, that mirror was on its way to the planet Mercury.

Dad reached over and slapped me on the back.

Roscoe's eyes narrowed. "It was Devin!" he accused. "He was snooping around the bathroom last night while I was in the shower! I'll bet he took it!"

"I did not," I defended myself. It was sort of true. I brought it to my room. But it was Zgrbnys and Gthrmnys who "took" it.

I glanced over at Stan to see if he would rat me out. But the dweeb was barking something at Fungus. He was probably telling him what happened to the mirror, because the two of them shared a pretty good laugh about something.

Mom was annoyed. "Well, please keep an eye out for it," she told us. "It's a very good one. I don't want it to get broken. I'm sure it's just lying around somewhere."

My heart sank. It was lying around somewhere, all right. **Somewhere around the solar system.**

I took Stan to school the back way. My plan was to sneak in before the bell, so I didn't want to run into anyone we knew.

I opened the custodian's entrance, and ushered Stan in ahead of me.

"Where are we going?" he asked.

"I want to show you something cool."

He looked blank. "But I, Stan, am quite comfortable with the temperature."

What a dweeb! I had to remind myself that this was a dangerous alien. The future of the whole world could depend on how I handled him.

I led him to the art room, and peered inside.

Perfect! No teachers in sight. I pulled Stan in after me. Instantly, his eyes crossed.

You see, the art room has a whole wall of mirrors. Mirrors are truth enforcers for Pants. Stan said so himself.

I turned to my exchange buddy. "All right, Mr. Alien, the jig is up! I know everything about you and your nasal processor, and your home planet, and your fellow nose-picking invaders! You're not even a kid, are you? You're 147 years old, just like you said!"

"Incorrect," Stan replied. "My exact age is 146 years, 8 months, 27 days, 12 hours and 16.2 minutes."

Jackpot! He was spilling his guts! "Okay, now you're going to tell me all about Pan."

The crossed eyes blinked. "Pan is a medium-sized planet in the constellation of the Big Zipper. It is roughly eighty-five thousand light-years from Earth."

"Who were those two guys in the backyard last night?" I continued.

"Professional thinkers," said Stan. "On Pan, only our cleverest people are allowed to join the Smarty-Pants."

"You're kidding!" I blurted. **"Smarty-Pants?"**

"The Smarty-Pants can think in six dimensions," he informed me. "They can answer a question even before it's asked; they can program any VCR in the galaxy. They know the meaning of life, the capital of the Crab Nebula, and why manhole covers are round. Their IQs are so large that even *they* can't count that high. They are the most important citizens of Pan, except for the Grand Pant himself, and his assistants, the Under-Pants."

What *was* this, a comedy routine? Smarty-Pants, Under-Pants, the Big Zipper—

"I suppose there's a T-shirt planet somewhere," I said sarcastically. **"In the constellation of the Short Sleeve."**

Stan's eyes never uncrossed. "I know of no such place."

I had to quit fooling around. This could be a matter of life and death. Earth was in danger.

"When is the invasion going to start?" I demanded.

He looked blank. "What invasion?"

"Don't try to deny it!" I pushed him right up to the mirror. His eyes got so crossed I thought they'd roll down his cheeks.

"But Pan is a peaceful planet," he told me.

"We don't even have an army."

"That's just what a spy would say," I accused. "Right, *Agent* Mflxnys?"

"I, Stan, am not that kind of agent," he insisted.

"Oh, yeah? What kind of agent are you, then?"

"A travel agent," he announced.

I was thunderstruck. "A *travel agent*? But— that's impossible! I heard those Smarty-Pants guys talking about your people swarming all over Earth!"

"Yes," Stan agreed. "Tourists. We Pants are the greatest tourists in the galaxy. We work two weeks per year and go on vacation for the other fifty. I, Stan, am in charge of all the test tourists here on Earth."

"What are test tourists?" I asked suspiciously.

"Pants like me," he explained. "They pose as humans. But they're really doing research to see if Earth can become Pan's newest vacation resort. I, Stan, use my nasal processor to beam our findings to the Smarty-Pants. The Smarty-Pants report to the Under-Pants, who make a

presentation to the Grand Pant himself. It's all very top drawer."

I let my breath out in a long sigh of relief. "Oh, phew! I was freaking out! I thought we were going to have a whole nose-picking army attacking us from spaceships!" I was so happy I actually hugged him. I know Rule 8 says: ☞ No hugging, but I was pretty emotional. "I don't care if you're an alien. I'm just glad Earth isn't in danger."

"There *is* one small problem," Stan admitted. "After scouring a hundred and fourteen planets in fifty-three star systems, the Smarty-Pants

have narrowed the choices down to two final-
ists—Earth and Mercury."

"Mercury?" I repeated. "Who'd want to go
there?"

"I, Stan, agree. It's not the humidity. It's the
heat. But the travel agent on Mercury is—" He
gulped. "Shkprnys, the One and Only."

I frowned. "Who's Shkprnys?"

"Only the greatest agent in the history of the
Pan-Pan Travel Bureau," Stan said in awed respect. "It was his idea to build the Red Spot
Amusement Park on Jupiter. He made meteor
surfing the fastest growing sport in the galaxy.
He was the one who told the owner of the Little
Dipper, **'We could use another
of those, but next time make
it *big*.'** "

"Well, if he's so good at his job," I reasoned,
"he's bound to see that Earth is the better
planet."

Stan shook his head. "A long time ago, when
Shkprnys was a Training Pant, he was sent on a
mission to Earth. Wouldn't you know it? He got
very itchy poison ivy. His ship ran out of

calamine lotion near Halley's Comet, and he scratched for seventy thousand light-years. He's had a grudge against Earth ever since."

I shrugged. "So we lose. Let Mercury have all the tourists. Who needs the extra traffic, anyway?"

"You don't understand," Stan insisted. "Mercury has a spectacular view of the rings of Saturn. But there's something in the way."

"What?" I asked.

"Earth. So it would have to be moved, of course."

I was shocked. *"Moved?* Where?"

"Somewhere out past the orbit of Pluto," admitted Stan.

"Past *Pluto*?" I cried. "But—that's too far from the Sun! We'll all freeze!"

"The Pan-Pan Travel Bureau realizes this would condemn Earth to a frosty future." It was Stan's turn to shrug. "But we Pants take vacationing very seriously, and a view is a view, and—" He looked horribly distressed. "I, Stan, am most sincerely sorry, Devin."

Before I could react, there was a commotion

outside in the hall.

"Let me through!" shouted someone.

I went to the door—and nearly got trampled.

"Stand aside in the name of planetary defense!" the voice bellowed right in my ear.

It was Mr. Slomin!

Chapter 10
DOING SOMETHING COOL

The teacher was red-faced and wild-eyed—the way he always looked when he was on a UFO hunt. UFOs! Aliens! Who ever thought Mr. Slomin would turn out to be right about that stuff?

He must have sprinted all the way from his car, because he was huffing and puffing.

"I've got proof!" he wheezed, waving a roll of film. "Proof that aliens visit Earth! Last night I took pictures of a UFO landing right near your house, Devin! Did you see anything?"

"No," I replied quickly.

"Yes," said Stan.

I totally forgot that we were still in front of the mirror. Stan *had* to tell the truth. He had no choice!

He started to spill the beans. "Your 'UFO' is a space cruiser of the first fleet of his most tailored majesty, the Grand—"

I slapped my hand over his mouth. If Mr. Slomin found out about Stan, he might turn him in to the Air Force. Remember what happened to E. T.? And Stan was the travel agent in charge of Earth! Without him—*whoosh!* Out past Pluto.

I pushed him out of the art room hard enough to put him through the hallway wall. His eyes uncrossed as he slid down to the floor, dazed.

Mr. Slomin rushed into the photography darkroom. "I've got to develop this film right away!" He slammed the door shut behind him.

This was all I needed—pictures of Stan and his two weirdo friends, standing by their spaceship

with their fingers up their noses. It would be on the the front page of every newspaper in the world!

* EXTRA! EXTRA! *
READ ALL ABOUT IT:
Aliens pick their noses, too!

I had to destroy that film! I counted to three, took a deep breath, and yanked the door open.

"*Aaaaaaaaaaaah!!*"

There was Mr. Slomin, with the film stretched out like a ribbon in front of him. Even in the dim light, I could see his face changing color—first to red, then to purple.

"It's *ruined!*" he howled. "The only proof the UFO Society ever had! Devin, don't you know film gets spoiled if you expose it to light?"

"Sorry," I mumbled.

"You're on detention for this!" he roared. "A *month* of detentions! No, a *year*!"

"But Mr. Slomin," came a voice from the hall, "I, Stan, am the one to blame."

"What?" Mr. Slomin stormed out of the dark-room and turned burning eyes on my exchange buddy. "Explain yourself!"

"I, Stan, made Devin ruin your film," Stan told the teacher. "I—dared him to open the door."

I couldn't believe it! Stan was trying to get me off the hook!

Taking the rap to help a friend—that was . . . that was . . .

Why, that was Rule 17!

S t a n   M f l x n y s ,   nose-pick-ing   paper-eating,   alien-dweeb travel   agent,   was   doing   some-thing *cool!*

Chapter 11

I WILL NOT RUIN ANY MORE PICTURES OF UFOS

Mr. Slomin developed his film anyway, but the results were—hooray!—very bad. There were no pictures. Only a long strip of blank negatives remained from his night of UFO-spotting.

He was a one-man thunderstorm, lightning bolts and all.

"You're *both* on double-detention!" he roared at us. "Now, get to class! The bell's about to ring!"

As we hurried through the halls, I whispered, "Thanks—"

"*Silence!*" thundered Mr. Slomin.

All day, Stan and I sat side by side under our teacher's furious glare.

Didn't it figure? For the first time, I really

wanted to talk to Stan. There was so much I needed to say. But if Mr. Slomin heard even the slightest little peep coming from either of us today, we were both dead meat.

Even at recess, I didn't get a chance to speak with the guy—not with all the nose-picking jokes and half the class dancing around singing, **"I, Stan, Stan the Man, Stan from Pan, the Panty Man!"**
One thing was different this time. I sure wasn't going to let those jerks get away with making fun of *my* exchange buddy.

"Hey, shut up!" I snapped. "Leave him alone!"

At lunch, when Stan ate his cardboard chocolate milk container, Calista tried to make a big deal about it.

"Ooh, gross! Look, everybody! That's totally disgusting!"

I fixed her. "Poor Stan," I whispered. "He suffers from a rare vitamin deficiency. That's why he eats paper. Because he needs more vitamin P."

I made her feel so guilty she was almost in tears. She even gave him her lunch bag for dessert.

"Take out your writing journals," announced Mr. Slomin when we got back to class. "Today's topic is UFOs."

Calista raised her hand. "Mr. Slomin, the newspaper said that there are *no* UFOs. The sighting at the airport last week was all a big mistake."

"Then why did the same spaceship come back last night?" challenged the teacher.

"Really?" breathed Wanda.

"I have proof—" The teacher glared at Stan and me. "I mean, I *had* proof. The government doesn't want us to know that alien races visit us. At my last UFO Society meeting, we figured out that the first spacecraft got close enough to the airport to drop a package into the baggage system."

A package named Stan! Uh-oh. Those UFO Society guys were pretty sharp. I had to throw Mr. Slomin off the scent!

I opened my journal and wrote: *There are plenty of "flying objects" at the airport, and none of them are unidentified. They're called planes.*

That was no good. Mr. Slomin would get mad and flunk me!

Suddenly, a loud whisper came from Tanner. **"Steam shovel!"**

Steam shovel was Class 4C's new code word. It meant that Stan was "picking" his nose again. The joke was that his finger was like the digging arm of a big power shovel. Of course, I knew it wasn't *real* picking. What was Stan up to?

I looked down. My journal entry was erasing itself like the ink was being lifted clear off the paper! Then, to my amazement, a full-page essay appeared. It was even in my handwriting!

It was Stan! He knew I was getting myself in trouble, and he was using his nose computer to save me from Mr. Slomin. But with the teacher watching us like a hawk, I couldn't even say thanks.

What a day! When it was finally 3:30, we still had our double detention to live through. Mr. Slomin made us write two hundred lines each: *I will not ruin any more pictures of UFOs.* Worst of all, he sat there staring at us the whole time. So Stan couldn't even use his nose computer to do the work for us.

At last, when the hour was over, we scram-

bled out of the school like we were being released from prison. We ran all the way home. On
the porch, I leaned on Stan as the two of us
caught our breath.

"Thanks for saving me in journal-writing," I
panted. "It was a really cool thing to do."

"Cool?" Stan was confused. "My nasal
processor has indicated normal temperatures all
day."

"Listen, Stan," I explained patiently. "I don't mean cool like *cold*. I mean cool like *hip—happening—sweet—awesome*!"

Up went the steam shovel finger again. Stan seemed even more bewildered. "My computer does not recognize these words the way you are using them." He frowned. "How can I, Stan, be a travel agent on Earth if I barely understand the place myself?"

"I'll tell you everything you need to know," I assured him. "But you've got to promise that you won't let them move us out past Pluto! I can barely stand the winter in *this* orbit! I hate shoveling snow!"

"I, Stan, will do my best," Stan said sincerely. "But I don't stand a chance against Shkprnys, the One and Only. Why would the Grand Pant listen to me instead of a travel agent who could fill a Roach Motel in hyperspace? Shkprnys is a legend, and I—" He shrugged. "—I, Stan, am just a kid."

"Just a kid?" I echoed. "I thought you were 147 years old."

"That *is* a kid," he told me. "On Pan, the voting age is 250. Shkprnys is well over five hundred."

"I'll tell you what," I offered, ushering him in through the door. "Tonight I'll put all my rules of coolness on flash cards. When I get through with you, you'll be Pan's number one Earth expert. Then the Grand Pant will have to pay attention to you."

He seemed worried. "Being cool is extremely complicated. Even the Smarty-Pants don't understand it. And they know why manhole covers are round."

"Don't sweat it," I said. "I wrote the book on coolness. If anyone can help you, I can."

"Stan, is that you?" called Roscoe from the den. "I taped yesterday's Bulls game. Come on, let's watch it!"

Stan looked at me. "Would this be a cool thing to do?"

I nodded. "Very cool."

We plopped ourselves down on the couch beside Roscoe. Chicago had a 29–27 lead early in the second quarter.

Michael Jordan was handling the ball. Suddenly, he blew past the defense, leaped high in the air, and executed an unbelievable reverse slam dunk—I gawked—*all with his finger up his nose!*

I wheeled to face Stan. "*Michael Jordan* is an *alien*?" I whispered incredulously.

He shrugged. "You didn't think a mere Earthling could jam like that, did you?"

Chapter 12

DUMMY PANTS

Maybe it was the idea that Michael Jordan was one of the test tourists, and Stan was his boss. But I started to have a lot more respect for my exchange buddy.

We made a pretty good team. I gave him great things about Earth to tell the Smarty-Pants. And he used his nose computer to help me with chores around the house.

You know how fast Stan took care of the dishes? Well, his nasal processor could make a bed in half that time. Cleaning my room took less than a second. With the flick of that steam shovel finger, all our stuff would be back in its place. The carpet would even be vacuumed.

I'VE gOt tO gEt ME ONE OF thOSE.

"This is better than maid service," I chortled, checking out our perfect closet. "Hey, what happened to your Michael Jordan shirt?"

"Oh, McInlys needed it back," he replied. "There was a laundry strike at the United Center. All his jerseys were sweaty, and mine was the only clean one on Earth."

That weekend, Mom put me in charge of cleaning out the garage.

"You'd better start warming up your schnoz," I advised. "Our garage is a disaster area, no lie."

He just smiled sweetly and stuck his finger up his nose. Three seconds later, he was done.

"Not possible!" I exclaimed. "Cleaning that garage takes two days! We've got lawn chairs, and gardening stuff, and sports equipment, and old shoes, and tools! And it all has to be hosed down! And then put back!"

"The task is complete," Stan assured me.

So I took his word for it. We went back to work on his report to the Smarty-Pants.

About an hour later, Mom appeared in the doorway. She was bug-eyed. "Devin, I don't know what to say."

My first thought was that Stan's nasal processor had trashed the garage.

"I—I didn't do it!" I blurted.

She threw her arms around me and kissed my
cheek. "Of course you did it. I've never seen the
garage looking better!"

"Uh—Stan helped," I managed.

She hugged him, too. "I can't believe how
much work you did. All that cleaning, putting up

those new shelves for the paint cans—and how did you ever untangle that snarl of hoses? Your father and I have been trying for years!"

"It went fast," I told her with a wink at Stan.

"You didn't happen to see my makeup mirror out there, did you?" she asked, shaking her head. "It's still missing."

"Sorry, Mom," I mumbled. And when she was gone, I turned to my exchange buddy. "Hey, when are those Smarty-Pants guys coming back with Mom's mirror?"

Stan shuffled uncomfortably. "There's been a little accident."

"They broke it?" I asked.

"No," he assured me, "it's in one piece. But that piece was ejected out the trash chute of their ship." He looked sheepish. "It disappeared down the black hole of Cygnus X-1."

"What?" I was horrified. "I thought they were supposed to be Smarty-Pants! **They sound like a couple of Dummy Pants to me!**"

"It could happen to anybody," Stan defended his fellow Pants. "Black holes are hard to spot in deep space. They're very dark."

"But that's an expensive mirror," I complained. "Can't they fly into the black hole and get it?"

"Oh, no," Stan said seriously. "Nothing can escape the pull of a black hole. Not even light. If they fly in, they could never fly out. They'd be sucked down."

"Would they die?" I asked.

Stan shrugged. "Nobody knows. No one has ever flown into a black hole. One theory is that the black hole spits you out somewhere. But it could be anywhere in the universe. You might end up a hundred billion light-years away in a distant galaxy. Even the Smarty-Pants aren't sure."

Oh, great. Mom always wanted to travel. Well, she was stuck at home, but her mirror sure was getting the grand tour. "At least they didn't break it," I mumbled.

Suddenly, Stan sprang to his feet and put his finger up his nose.

I eyed him suspiciously. "Listen, Stan. I'm taking your word for it that the nose picking is for official business. If you're sneaking in a few extra picks—"

"This is urgent!" he interrupted me. "My nasal

processor has intercepted a message to the Smarty-Pants. It's Shkprnys's latest report on Mercury."

"What does it say?" I asked.

Stan ran to the computer on my desk. He yanked out the printer cable and stuck the loose end up his nose. The operating lights went crazy, blinking brighter and faster than ever before.

"Ugh," I grimaced. "You expect me to use that after it's been up your schnoz?"

A single page printed. I stared at the message from another world.

Chapter 13

MESSAGE FROM MERCURY

✴✴✴ PANT-O-GRAM ✴✴✴

TO: *Smarty-Pants Main Thinking Center*
FROM: *Shkprnys, the One and Only*

*Forsooth, Mercury hath great warmth
to sun thy buns . . .*

I looked up from the paper. "What language is this?"

"Oh, it's English," Stan chuckled. "Remember, Shkprnys left Earth four hundred years ago. That's how people talked back then."

I snorted. "Who does he think he is? Shakespeare?"

"Yes," Stan replied.

"*What?!*"

He looked at me earnestly. "You didn't think a mere Earthling could write like that, did you?"

"Shakespeare? *William* Shakespeare? But he's dead! He died hundreds of years ago!"

Stan shook his head. "Shakespeare didn't die. He just got poison ivy. That's the only reason he left Earth."

I was bug-eyed. "Are you telling me that **Romeo and Juliet was written by a travel agent?"**

"Well, he wasn't a travel agent yet," Stan explained. "He was still a Training Pant. Kind of like kindergarten here on Earth. It was fine for Shkprnys to scribble his little plays back then. But it's no career for an adult."

"So to get the Grand Pant to pick Earth over Mercury," I said slowly, "we're going to have to write a better paper than *Shakespeare*?"

"I, Stan, told you it was a long shot."

"Man, we'd better get busy!" I turned back to the report we'd been working on.

Great Tourist Attractions of Earth

DEVIN'S LIST

- video games
- Disney World
- comic books
- the Grand Canyon
- MTV
- Hawaii
- waterskiing

STAN'S LIST

- dog humor
- mirrors
- traffic jams
- going to the dentist
- delicious paper
- homework
- allergies

I stared at him. "You expect to beat Shakespeare with *this*? People *hate* traffic jams and homework! And what's so great about allergies?"

"Smarty-Pants scientists have eliminated dust and mold and ragweed," Stan explained.

"So there are no allergies on Pan."

"That's good," I began. "Isn't it?"

"For us Pants, sneezing is the most wonderfully entertaining activity there is," he informed me. "There's no feeling quite like a nostril-busting blast of wind shooting through a supercomputer. Every single one of your trillion gigabytes tingles." He turned tragic. "At least, that's what I've heard. The last Pant to sneeze was Nfrgnys the Snuffler way back in 1745."

Maybe it was all this allergy talk, but a little dust got up my nose. "A-*choo!*"

"That looked like fun," said Stan wistfully.

"Maybe it's better when you have a computer up there," I admitted.

"I, Stan, believe that Pants will flock to Earth for a chance to be allergic again."

"You mean," I said incredulously, "that you expect people to travel eighty-five thousand light-years just to sneeze?"

Stan looked annoyed. "I, Stan, invite you to come up with something better."

It takes all kinds to make a galaxy . . .

"Everything on my list is better than sneezing," I argued. "Like waterskiing. What could be more exciting than zooming across the lake behind a speedboat? Wiping out, and swimming to shore—"

"Swimming?" Stan put his finger up his nose. "My nasal processor does not recognize this word."

I was horrified. "You mean you can't swim?"

The steam shovel finger probed a little deeper. "My computer has searched every book in every library on Pan," Stan reported. "At no time on record has any Pant performed this 'swimming.'"

"But we've got fourth-grade field day coming up on Monday!" I cried. "The swimming race is the most important event!"

"Perhaps I, Stan, should not participate in field day."

"Oh, you're participating," I assured him. "All *three* of us are."

The fried-egg eyes looked confused. "All three of us?"

"Right," I told him. **"You, me, and your magic nose!"**

Chapter 14
ZAP!

"What perfect weather for field day!" exclaimed Mr. Slomin. "Blue skies with just a hint of winter around the corner!"

Soccer Sam was showing Tanner how to keep a ball in the air using only his knees and chest. I have to admit Tanner was getting pretty good.

"Hey, Devin, look at this!" he called to me. "That field day trophy is as good as ours!"

"I don't know about that," I said slyly. "You're up against some pretty tough teams."

"Like who?" challenged Sam.

"Like—" I smiled sweetly, "—me and Stan."

Tanner laughed so hard that he lost control of the ball. "You and *Stan*? You guys don't have a prayer—not unless nose picking is a new event this year!"

I just kept on smiling. And guess who turned out to be our opponents for the very first event? Tanner and Sam.

It was two-on-two soccer. Tanner and I were the goalies.

Sam stole the ball and danced around Stan. My teammate offered about as much defense as a mailbox. He just stood there while Sam took a booming kick.

And then Stan put his finger up his nose.

It happened so fast you could barely see it. The ball hurtled toward the open side of the net. Suddenly, Stan zipped out in front of it, and— *pow!*—he headed the ball so hard that it took off like a rocket. It flew clear across the field. Tanner dove for it, but he had no chance. 1–0.

"What a play!" cried Mr. Slomin. "Stan, how did you do that?"

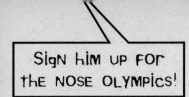

Sign him up for the Nose Olympics!

"He, Stan, has been practic-
ing," I supplied smugly.

Stan scored four more goals, and we skunked
them 5–0. Stan also starred in the volleyball
game, the egg-and-spoon race, the beanbag toss,
the obstacle course, and the pogo-stick competition. He won all the track-and-field events by a
nose—if you know what I mean.

I was his partner in the three-legged race. He went so fast that I felt like I was being pulled alongside a speeding car.

By the time Mr. Slomin led us over to the high school's indoor pool, we had won every single event. Only the swimming relay stood between us and the field day championship.

While we were changing into bathing suits, I noticed Stan was looking really pale. I gave him a friendly nudge. "Don't worry if you're not such a terrific swimmer."

"That's not it," he said nervously. "I, Stan, have intercepted another message from Shakespeare. He has completed Mercury's official tourist slogan. We have to respond with a slogan for Earth!"

"Not now!" I insisted, tying a string to the earpieces of his glasses. I plopped them back on his nose and marched him out to the pool. "We're in first place by a mile. We would have to finish dead last in this race to lose the trophy."

He gaped. "You mean swimming happens in *there*?" he asked, pointing. "In *water*?"

"You go first, and I'm next," I coached. "Just—you know—follow your nose."

"On your marks," announced Mr. Slomin. "Get set—"

"But Devin," he whined, "I, Stan, cannot—"

The teacher blew his whistle. "Go!"

The other kids dove in. Stan didn't budge.

"Go!" I hissed.

"But—"

What could I do? I reached out and shoved him over the side.

Stan belly flopped into the pool like a
thousand-pound bag of cement. His head went
under, and he breathed in a huge snootful of
water.

ZAP!

A lightning bolt shot out of his nose. When he
came up again, his nostrils were shooting sparks.
Smoke puffed out of his ears.

"Your schnoz!" I shouted. "Use your schnoz!"

He reached in with a finger. Nothing happened.

"Keep trying!" I yowled.

But Stan was already sinking to the bottom of the pool in a shower of frothy bubbles. I had to jump in there and rescue him.

When I finally hauled him out, he smelled like burning machinery. His ears smoldered.

Wanda won the first lap, with Cody hot on her heels. Their buddies, Calista and Joey, dove in.

Remember how we'd have to finish dead last to lose the trophy? Well, scratch that. Not finishing at all gets you disqualified. **Almost drowning gets you laughed at.**

Calista hit the finish line amid a roar of cheers.

I'll bet I was smoking worse than Stan when Mr. Slomin added up the field day final results.

"First place, Calista and Wanda; second place, Tanner and Sam; third place, Joey and Cody . . ."

It went on for a pretty long time, but he finally got to us. "Last place, Devin and Stan. Too bad, fellows. You were winning until the very end."

I turned on my exchange buddy. "What happened?"

He pulled up his glasses which were over his mouth. The fried-egg eyes looked haunted. "My nasal processor must never come in contact with H_2O!"

Uh-oh. "You mean—"

He nodded miserably. "I, Stan," he announced in a watery munchkin voice, "have short-circuited my nose."

Chapter 15

THE PANIC BUTTON

I cleaned my room the old-fashioned way that afternoon. It was torture. I had to pick up every single comic book, chess piece, Magic Marker, and every dollar of Monopoly money *myself*!

You never appreciate what you have until it's gone.

"Try your nose again," I said to Stan.

He reached up there, but it was no use. He may as well have been picking it for real.

CrY ME a riVer.

"Nothing," he mourned. "I, Stan, have shorted out the central processing control. We Pants call it the Panic Button."

"Well, this stinks," I mumbled. "So much for maid service."

"It's more serious than that, Devin," Stan said in agitation. "The Smarty-Pants received Shakespeare's slogan at three o'clock. It was a smash hit."

"That good, huh?"

He nodded. "*'To tan or not to tan. That is the question on Mercury.'*"

I frowned. "What's so great about that?"

"It's brilliant!" cried Stan. "Half of Mercury is always facing the sun. The other half is always in the dark. So, depending on whether or not you want a tan, that's the side of the planet you go to."

"That's the best Shakespeare can do?" I asked.

"It's much better than the old slogan," Stan informed me. "*'Come to Mercury. It's like a sauna out here.'*"

"This is the best news I've heard all day," I promised Stan. "Shakespeare's slogan stinks. I'll bet we can come up with something about Earth that blows away *'To tan or not to tan.'*"

Stan looked distressed. "But how could I, Stan, send our slogan to Pan? My nasal processor won't work without a new Panic Button. That's the only way to get a message home."

I shrugged. "Can't the Smarty-Pants fix it?"

"The Smarty-Pants can fix anything, of course," he said. "But Zgrbnys and Gthrmnys might not come here for another month. Now that Mercury's slogan is in, the clock starts ticking. I, Stan, have exactly one week and one hour to respond. Otherwise Mercury gets chosen automatically. And that means—"

I finished the sentence. "*Whoosh!* Out past Pluto." I thought fast. "Hey, what about some of the other Pants living on Earth? You know, the test tourists, like Michael Jordan. Couldn't he get you a new part?"

He shook his head. "The Panic Button is advanced Smarty-Pants technology. Most ordinary Pants wouldn't have it. And their nasal processors wouldn't be strong enough to communicate with Pan directly. Except—" He looked thoughtful. "There is one test tourist in California who used to be a Smarty-Pant. He quit to join the artistic union—the Tights and Tutus."

"This guy isn't another five-hundred-year-old playwright, is he?" I said suspiciously. "Or is he just in the NBA?"

"Neither," said Stan. "His name is Lnrdnys. But here on Earth he's known as Leonardo DiCaprio."

"Leonardo DiCaprio?" I echoed. **"The *movie star?*"**

Stan shrugged. "You didn't think a mere Earthling could act like that, did you?"

I grabbed Stan's arm. "Let's go call him."

"We communicate by nose," he informed me.

> SO, why didN'T hE USE his NOSE COMPUTEr TO UNSiNK ThE TiTANiC?

"I, Stan, do not have his phone number. We'll have to reach him by mail."

"By mail?" I was horrified. "Are you crazy? Movie stars get a million letters a day! What makes you think he'll read ours?"

"He reads them all," said Stan.

"How do you know?"

"Lnrdnys has a very large appetite," he explained. "He's a growing boy of only 120. He

CHOMP!

eats all his fan mail—but he reads it first."

He took a piece of paper out of my desk and nibbled at the corner. "Mmm. Tasty."

"Don't eat Leonardo DiCaprio's letter," I said sternly. "We want to put him in a good mood. Hey, if he and Michael Jordan are both Pants, how come they're cool-looking, and you and those Smarty-Pants guys dress like meganerds?"

"Lnrdnys and Mchlnys have been on Earth too long," Stan explained as he wrote. "When you run out of high-fashion white shirts and polka-dot ties, you have to settle for Earth clothes."

I peered over Stan's shoulder at the paper.

Dear Lnrdnys the Ravenously Hungry,

I am off-line. Please send me one replacement Panic Button. Extremely urgent!

Yours truly,
Agent Mflxnys (Stan)
Pan-Pan Travel Bureau

PS: Loved you in _Titanic_.
PPS: May the Crease be with you!

"Hey, Stan," I asked while he addressed the envelope, "what's this Crease you Pants are always talking about?"

"There's a Crease in the fabric of the universe," he explained. "An endless amount of energy flows through it. That's where we Pants get the power for our spaceships, our nasal processors, and everything on Pan."

Fungus came along with us to the mailbox. The two of them were barking the whole way. I felt kind of left out.

"What's he saying?" I asked.

"Fungus is a big Leonardo DiCaprio fan," Stan translated.

"Yeah, well, so is Lindsay," I warned. "Don't tell her you know the guy, or we'll never hear the end of it."

Stan opened the mailbox and dropped the letter inside. Suddenly, he covered his face. "A-*choo!*"

When he took away his hands, he was grinning from ear to ear. "That was fantastic! I, Stan, have experienced sneezation!"

"Gesundheit," I said sarcastically.

"Do you suppose that I, Stan, might be allergic to something?"

"You're probably just getting a cold," I replied. "You know, from your dunk in the pool today."

"A cold? A *cold?*" I'd never seen anybody so happy. "Allergies, perhaps, but I never dreamed I would be lucky enough to catch a cold!"

He practically danced all the way home. Fun-

gus and I had to run to keep up with him. When we rounded the corner, we found the whole family standing outside. They were gathered around the big tree in our front yard. It was lying flat on the grass beside a gigantic hole in the lawn.

"What happened to the tree?" I asked.

Dad shook his head, bewildered. "I can't explain it! One minute it was standing there. Then it just . . . popped out, roots and all!"

Lindsay was crying. "But what would make a whole tree jump out of the ground?"

We could only exchange baffled looks.

Chapter 16

A FLYING ROLL OF
TOILET PAPER

With the letter on its way to Leonardo Di-Caprio, we set to work on a tourist slogan for Earth. When the new Panic Button arrived, and Stan could fix his nose, we had to be ready with something at least as good as *"To tan or not to tan."*

Every day after school, we held a brainstorming session. Every night, before falling asleep, we tossed ideas around. But by Saturday morning, all we had was:

<u>DEVIN'S LIST</u>
- *Earth: It's A World of Fun*
- *Mmm, Mmm, Earth*

- Go, Big Blue
- Mercury Bites

STAN'S LIST
- Come to the 847th Cleanest
  Planet in the Galaxy
- Pigeon Capital of the Cosmos
- Free Oxygen

"It's no use," said my exchange buddy. "I, Stan, have writer's block."

"Me, too," I admitted. "Man, I'll bet Shakespeare never gets writer's block."

"That's why he's 'The One and Only,'" Stan sighed. "While I, Stan, have no title. I'm just—Mflxnys. Mflxnys the—" He shook his head. "Nothing."

But I wasn't going to lie down and die like Stan. It wasn't *his* planet that was heading for the deep freeze. I practically dragged him to the bus stop. How does an alien travel agent learn about Earth? From an *Earth* travel agent!

The local transit pulled up, and its doors folded open. Stan and I got in line behind the

other passengers. They each paid their fare.
Then it was Stan's turn. He stuck his nose into the coin box and snorted.

TaLK abOUt dirTY MONEY!

I thought the driver was going to have a heart attack. "That's disgusting! What are you—a pig?"

Quickly, I paid for both of us and hustled Stan to an empty seat. He was really sorry for doing

such a dumb thing. "That was my mistake. I, Stan, should have remembered that my nasal processor is on the fritz."

"You're not thinking," I said crossly. "On Earth we pay with our money, not our noses."

"We tried money on Pan, but it was a disaster," he explained. "Pants can't resist paper. People ate their life savings. Lnrdnys devoured almost fifty-thousand pantaloons and had to go to the hospital with severe indigestion. He barely had enough cash left to pay his doctor bill. So now checking, credit cards, even mutual funds are in our computers, hooked into the planetary bank, the Pocket." He looked sad. "When my Panic Button shorted out, my accounts all reset to zero."

He lifted a Kleenex to his face. I thought he was going to cry, but instead—

"A-choo!"

This was the fifth day of his cold, and he was loving every minute of it. He refused to take any medicine. He wouldn't even eat chicken soup. My mother thought his appetite was suffering, but I knew the real reason. He didn't want to get better. For him, "sneezation" was a barrel of laughs.

Suddenly, the driver slammed on the brakes. "What the—" A telephone pole had fallen across the road, blocking our lane. The bus screeched to a halt two inches in front of it.

I looked out the window as we drove around it. "The wind?" I said dubiously.

But nothing could take Stan's mind off the joy of sneezing. He grinned all the way downtown.

The driver was still mad at Stan when we got off. "Hey, kid. From now on, keep your nose to yourself."

"A-*choo!*" Stan replied with a wave of apology.

There was a commotion on the street. Something was wrong with the fountain in front of Clearview Travel. Instead of water, a thick pink liquid was bubbling out of the spout.

A little kid stuck his face in the middle of it and took a taste. "It's milk shake!" he cried in delight. "Strawberry milk shake!"

"Fascinating," commented Stan. "Milk shakes occur in nature, like oil gushers and hot springs."

"No, they don't!" I snapped, shoving him

ahead of me through the revolving door into the
travel agency. "A lot of weird stuff has been happening, but it's not normal. Now pay attention.
We're here to get slogan ideas."

I picked up a handful of vacation brochures
and fanned them like playing cards under his
nose. "Check this out: Paradise Island, Bahamas.
White sand, blue water, sun, surf—"

I could see Stan wasn't very impressed.

"Water, Devin. We Pants have to avoid it. The Pan-Pan Travel Bureau wouldn't be too pleased with spaceship-loads of dissatisfied customers, with their Panic Buttons fried, and their savings reset to zero."

"Well, how about this, then?" I persisted. "Snowboarding in the Canadian Rockies. What a vacation!"

"Humdrum," Stan yawned. "We're looking for scenery, atmosphere, wildlife."

The manager came over. "Can I help you boys find something?"

"Oh, yes, please," said Stan. "Do you know of any place dark and damp with plenty of insects?"

The man gave him a strained smile. "How about my basement?"

"What he means," I explained quickly, "is we're looking for somewhere—you know—bad."

I could see that he wanted to throw us out. So I added, "It's for a school project." Adults will do almost anything if they think they're helping education.

So he dug up an ancient cobweb-covered file marked UNUSUAL DESTINATIONS. The top folder was entitled SIBERIA WINTER CARNIVAL.

I didn't get to see much more because a puff of dust from the old papers went up Stan's nose.

"*A-choo!*"

There were screams from the washroom at the back of the office. The door burst open, and out ran a terrified lady. **She was being chased by a flying roll of toilet paper.** It caught up with her near the water cooler, wrapped her from head to toe like a mummy, and then took off after the manager.

In that instant, everything became clear. I wheeled to face my exchange buddy. "It's *you*!" I rasped.

"Me?" snuffled Stan.

"Every time you sneeze, something crazy happens! Remember? You sneezed at the mailbox right before our tree popped out! *And* when the pole fell over! *And* when the fountain started spitting up milk shake!"

Stan considered this. "It *is* logical. My nasal processor is powered by the Crease. But because my nose has a short circuit, huge amounts of loose energy are released by each sneeze."

"What can we do to stop it?" I hissed.

Stan looked noble. "I, Stan, must immediately cease sneezation—a-*choo*!"

The whole office tilted over on its side. Big desks and computers went crashing into the wall that was now the floor. The carpet flapped, releasing a blizzard of dust.

"Hold your breath!" I yowled at Stan.

But he'd already inhaled a cloud of the stuff. "A-*choo!* A-*choo!* A-*choo!* A-*choo!* . . ."

Now the furniture was airborne. A cement truck drove through the front window and rear-ended a filing cabinet. Milk shake from the fountain oozed in through the broken glass, soaking the papers that lay everywhere. Plane tickets and schedules turned to mush.

☛ **Rule 31:** Always get out of there before anybody has a chance to figure out it's all your fault.

I grabbed Stan by the arm, and we started climbing toward the revolving door.

Chapter 17

SOMETHING WEIRD
IS GOING ON

Every Monday at three, Mr. Slomin taught Current Events. Each student got a copy of the *Clearview Post*. I took one look at the headline and almost swallowed my tongue.

SOMETHING WEIRD IS GOING ON!

Scientists still can't explain what turned Clearview Travel into a demolition derby last Saturday. But even stranger things have been happening around town since then.

What could make a seventy-foot dandelion grow in front of City Hall in a single night? Did the water tower really tap-dance on its support beams? How come the Clearview Copper Mine is producing goat cheese? What changed all the toilet seats at police headquarters into rosebushes? No one really knows. . . .

"We're dead!" I whispered to Stan. "If anybody finds out that *your nose* is the cause of it all, they'll throw us in jail! Or worse, they'll make us clean it up! How'd you like to be sent over to Clearview Travel with a broom?"

Even Stan had come to realize that sneezing wasn't such a great thing after all. "This is no time for jokes, Devin. It's exactly one week since Shakespeare submitted his dazzling slogan, '*To tan or not to tan.*' There's only one hour left before—"

"*Whoosh,*" I finished glumly. "Out past Pluto."

"We have no slogan," Stan went on. "And even if we did, we have no way to communicate with the Smarty-Pants."

"Where's Leonardo DiCaprio with our new Panic Button?" I demanded.

"I, Stan, hope he didn't eat my letter before reading it."

I was horrified. "Could that happen?"

"If he was having an extra-hungry day," Stan admitted.

Well, that was reassuring. I was ten times more worried now.

"Quiet, everyone," ordered Mr. Slomin. "I want to finish Current Events before it's time to go home. Now, who would like to comment on the article?"

Wanda raised her hand. "I think it's scary."

"But kind of funny, too," added Joey. "You know, the part where the chief of police had to go to the hospital to get the thorns pulled out."

A lot of kids laughed, but not Stan or me.

"It's not funny *or* scary," the teacher told us. "It's *suspicious*. It's no accident that these strange events are happening right after two UFO sightings. This is the work of aliens—*Stan!*"

I almost jumped out of my skin. **Did Mr. Slomin *know?***

"Stan, I gave you those tissues for your cold," the teacher said crossly. "Stop eating them."

"Sorry, Mr. Slomin." But as soon as Stan took the tissue away from his face, he sneezed.

The venetian blinds on our windows clattered up and down three times.

Nervous laughter buzzed through the room. Mr. Slomin frowned.

"A-*choo!*" Stan sneezed again.

The teacher's heavy desk launched itself up off the floor, flipped over, and slammed down again.

Mr. Slomin jumped back like he'd been burned. He goggled at the upside-down wreckage of his desk. Papers fluttered around it like butterflies. No one was laughing now.

I had to stop this before Mr. Slomin put two

and two together. I made a flying, nostril-pinching leap at Stan, but I was too late.

"A-choo!"

The front chalkboard melted into a thick gray liquid that oozed down the wall onto Mr. Slomin's shoes.

"Yikes!" Our teacher leaped out of the gooey puddle. You could still read the words *Current Events* in the mushy slop on his loafers.

"What's going on?" Calista quavered.

"Wait a minute." Mr. Slomin looked from Stan, to the puddle, and back to Stan again. "Every time *you* sneeze—"

Oh, no! Mr. Slomin had figured it out. The jig was up.

I felt my eyes well up with tears. Yeah, I know ☛ **Rule 2:** No crybabies. But even my rules of coolness didn't count anymore. The Air Force would take Stan away. Then we'd miss the deadline for sure! And poor Earth would be out past Pluto faster than you could shiver.

It was the end! There was no way out of this mess!

And then the bell rang.

Chapter 18

NOTHING COULD SAVE
US NOW

Stan and I headed for the door like we'd been shot out of a cannon.

"Hey!" called Mr. Slomin. "Come back here, you two!"

But a brick wall wouldn't have stopped us. We hurdled a couple of kindergarten kids and zoomed out the school yard gate.

I don't think all the power in the Crease could have gotten us home any faster. Sweating and gasping, we clattered up the front steps onto the porch.

"Safe!" Stan breathed.

"Not yet!" I wheezed. "Mr. Slomin's going to come after us!" My mind whirled. "You have to hide, and I'll say you took the bus back to Chicago!"

"Pan," he reminded me.

"Oh, whatever! Pan!"

The door opened, and my mom peeked out. "Hi, boys. Stan, you'll never guess what came for you in the mail today. You got something from—of all people—Leonardo DiCaprio! Did you write him a fan letter?"

I was hit by such a wave of relief that I almost fainted right there on the spot. Leonardo DiCaprio had come through with a new Panic Button! And we still had twenty minutes to come up with a slogan!

Mom handed Stan the envelope. "Now promise you'll share it with us at dinner." And she went back inside.

A bloodcurdling scream cut the air. ***"Leee-ooo!"***

Onto the scene galloped my sister. She was followed by the seven other members of the Leonardo DiCaprio Fan Club, Clearview Chapter.

Lindsay snatched the letter right out of Stan's

hand. "It's true!" she shrieked. "This is *his* hand-writing! Leo touched this envelope! In person!"

"Give that back!" I snapped. "That's Stan's mail!"

But those eight girls were screaming so loud that I couldn't even hear myself.

I leaped forward and blocked the stairs. "Forget it, Lindsay! Give me that letter!"

And my sister—an innocent little first-grader—stomped on my foot so hard that I saw stars.

"**Yeow!**"

While I was hopping up and down in pain, all eight of them shoved right by me. They ran to the side yard and climbed the rope ladder to the tree house that was the fan club's headquarters. Lindsay pulled the ladder up after them.

Stan shook his head. "Lnrdnys has a startling effect on Earthling females. How odd. On Pan, he's considered an ugly duckling."

"Well, this is just great!" I exploded, dragging Stan over to the tree. I circled the thick trunk like a stalking panther. "If they open that letter, they'll probably lose the Panic Button! And

we've got no way to get up there and stop them!"

"Wait!" said my exchange buddy tensely. All at once, he began to bark.

"Aw, come on!" I urged. "In fifteen minutes, we turn into a planet of Popsicles! This is no time to call the dog!"

But Stan continued to yelp and growl. And when Fungus bounded up from the backyard, he and Stan talked things over.

"What is it?" I demanded.

Good old Fungus— He grows on you.

"Neither of us can get into that tree house," my exchange buddy explained. "But Fungus can. I, Stan, have just made him a deputy agent of the Pan-Pan Travel Bureau. He'll get the letter for us."

"You're a genius!" I crowed. "You should have been a Smarty-Pant! You're a lot brighter than those two clowns who dropped Mom's mirror down a black hole!"

The fried-egg eyes turned tragic. "Alas, I, Stan, flunked out of Smarty-Pants University. I never figured out why manhole covers are round."

The plan was simple. Fungus jumped into my arms. Then Stan braced himself at the foot of the tree. I clambered up his back and sat on his shoulders. From there it was an easy reach. I raised Fungus over my head to the platform of the tree house. He climbed aboard, barking and wagging.

I heard Lindsay's friend Brittany exclaim, "Fungus! What a clever dog! You can climb trees!"

There was a lot of shuffling on the plywood floor as all the girls gathered around to pet Fungus.

"All right," said Lindsay. "This is the moment we've been waiting for. Let's open Leo's letter."

It all happened so fast that I'm amazed we weren't killed. I hoisted myself up a little and peered into the tree house. I was just in time to see Fungus snatch the letter right out of Lindsay's grasp.

"Fungus!"

Sixteen frantic hands made a grab for the dog. The letter clamped in his jaws, Fungus scrambled across the floor and took a flying leap into my arms. He tipped me, and I tipped Stan. The three of us—attached like one very tall person—toppled over backward.

"*Oof!*" We hit the ground like a ton of bricks. Fungus spat the letter into my hand and high-tailed it to his doghouse. Who ever said dogs are dumb animals?

The rope ladder came down off the tree house and smacked me right in the face. Lindsay led her crew over the side.

"Attack!" she roared.

Stan and I staggered to our feet and started running. Just as we approached the house, a car came speeding up to the curb. The door flew open, and out burst Mr. Slomin.

"Stop right there, Stan Mflxnys! I want a word with you!"

"Aw, no!" I howled.

What a way for this to end! We beat the clock! We had the Panic Button in our hands! It wasn't fair. We were so close. . . .

But nothing could save us now!

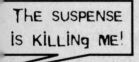

THE SUSPENSE IS KILLING ME!

Chapter 19

WHAT A SMALL UNIVERSE

As Mr. Slomin marched up to us, a little square window opened in the sky. A shiny object came hurtling straight down, whistling through the air.

Bonk!

It struck Mr. Slomin right on the top of the head. Our teacher took two wobbly steps and crumpled to the grass, unconscious.

I goggled at the item that had dropped out of nowhere.

"Mom's makeup mirror!" I exclaimed.

"Fascinating," said Stan. "The black hole of Cygnus X-1 lets out right over your house. What a small universe!"

"Ooooh!" groaned Mr. Slomin.

"He's starting to wake up!" I hissed. "Quick! Get that thing in your nose!"

Stan ripped open the letter, and there it was. I couldn't believe it! This Panic Button—this wondrous piece of technology—looked like half a grain of uncooked rice.

Stan handed me the letter. I barely dared to breathe while his steam shovel finger installed the replacement part.

There was a click, and the whir of a microwave oven.

How many nights had I lain awake, cursing that annoying noise? Now it was the most beautiful music in the world.

My exchange buddy beamed. "I, Stan, am back on-line."

"Quick!" I urged. "A slogan—"

And then the eight members of the Leonardo DiCaprio fan club caught up with the person who had their letter—me.

I won't try to sugarcoat it. They beat the daylights out of me. I know it's not very cool to get creamed by first-graders. But when you're outnumbered eight to one, at least you have an excuse.

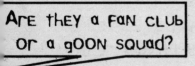
ArE thEY a FaN CLUb Or a gOON SQUad?

"I give up!" I managed. "I surrender! Take the letter!"

Lindsay snatched the paper out of my hand. The other seven gathered around to hear the words of their idol.

"What does it say?" begged Brittany.

My sister began to read:

Dear Stan,
Take this and shove it up your nose.

Sincerely,
Leonardo DiCaprio

There was a shocked silence among the girls.

"Shove it up your nose?" Brittany repeated. "Why would Leo write such a mean letter?"

"This calls for an emergency fan club meeting," decided Lindsay. "Back to the tree house, everyone."

I looked at my watch. Three minutes to Pluto!

At that moment, Mr. Slomin woke up. He got to his feet and fixed Stan with blazing eyes.

"All right, Stan," he growled. "I'm wise to you.

The weird things happening around town are connected to your sneezing. Tell me what you know about the UFO sightings."

"Your suspicions are correct, Mr. Slomin," Stan began. "I, Stan, am—"

I stared at my buddy in horror. His eyes were crossed! We'd left the makeup mirror lying on the grass. Now it was glinting in his face! I dove on it and flipped it over.

"—a simple exchange student from Pan," he finished, eyes straight again.

"Oh, right. Pan," sneered Mr. Slomin. "I've looked in the atlas. There is no Pan outside Chicago. There's no Pan in any state. Now we're going to try a little experiment."

From his jacket pocket, he pulled out a pepper mill and ground it all over Stan's nose.

"A-*choo!*" sneezed my exchange buddy.

Mr. Slomin ducked like he was waiting for the lawn furniture to rise up and fly.

Nothing happened. Now that the nose computer was fixed, Stan's sneezes were completely harmless.

Mr. Slomin tried a little more pepper.

"A-*choo*! A-*choo*!"

Still nothing.

"Maybe you imagined it all," I suggested to our teacher.

Mr. Slomin was furious. He threw down his pepper mill in disgust and shook his finger at Stan. "I've got my eye on you, Mflxnys. You know more about this than you're saying." And he got into his car and squealed away, yelling threats about calling the Air Force.

I checked my watch again. My eyes almost popped out of my head. "Thirty seconds!" I howled. "Quick! Call the Smarty-Pants!"

"But we have no slogan," Stan protested.

"Call anyway! Fake it! Stall!"

Stan put his finger up his nose and made the transmission.

"This is Agent Mflxnys on Earth. I, Stan, have been off-line until this very moment. Do you read me?"

I held my breath. Seconds felt like hours. Finally, Stan flashed me thumbs-up. He had made contact.

All at once, he turned pale. "Earth's slogan? Yes, of course it's ready. The slogan is—uh—the slogan is—" He looked at me helplessly.

I don't know what made me do it. It was like my brain shut down, and my body snapped into action. I picked up the pepper mill and ground a black cloud of the stuff right in Stan's face.

"—the slogan is—a-c *h o o* !"

And then I heard a funny sound. It took me a moment to realize it was coming out of Stan's nose. It was—I strained to listen—cheering! Applause! Shouts of "Bravo!"

Unbelievable! These were voices from eighty-five thousand light-years away, on Pan!

"Yes, you can believe your ears," Stan said to them. "That was sneezation. It's just one of the fabulous vacation activities on Earth. That's my slogan, 'a-*choo.*' I, Stan, defy Shkprnys to do any better."

I looked at my watch and allowed myself to start breathing again. We beat the deadline by two seconds!

"We made it, right?" I squeaked. "We're not getting whooshed past Pluto?"

Stan was weak with relief. "The Smarty-Pants have agreed to do extra study on both planets before a decision is made on the new tourist spot. Earth is still in the running!"

"Hah!" I celebrated. "In your face, Shakespeare! Your brilliant slogan lost to a sneeze!"

"I've got to file an official report immediately," Stan announced.

And there, right on my front lawn, he dug his finger further up his nose than ever before. It was a steam shovel job big enough to uncover an underground city. He was working the controls of his nasal processor so fast and so hard that I could see his arm muscles bulging through his white dress shirt.

"Stan, not here!" I rasped. "The whole neighborhood can see you! Wait till we get inside!"

Stan dropped his hand guiltily. "I'm sorry," he said in his saddest munchkin voice. "After all your flash cards and all your help, I, Stan, have once again acted like a dweeb. No wonder I have no title. I can't do anything right." He was so dejected that he couldn't even look me in the eye. "I'm an embarrassment to you, Devin. I, Stan, will never become cool."

It was the very first moment I realized that I wouldn't trade Stan for a hundred Codys and Wandas and Sams. The luckiest day of my life was the day he came rolling down that baggage chute!

I clamped a hand on his skinny shoulder. "I just made up a new rule of coolness, and this is the

I FEEL warm and FUZZY aLL OVEr.

most important one of all: ☛ **Saving the planet automatically cancels out every dweeby thing you've ever done.** So you are cool. You want a title? From now on, you are Mflxnys, the Totally Cool."

He got all misty-eyed. "Devin—you honor me! I feel like a child of eighty again! To sneeze and be cool, both in the same week! I, Stan, am so excited I could go to the dentist!"

Okay, so I lied about Stan being cool. But there was no better exchange buddy—not in eighty-five thousand light-years!

PLANET of the NOSE PICKERS

CONTENTS

Chapter 1
MY FRIEND THE ALIEN

✳ DEVIN HUNTER'S RULES OF COOLNESS ✳

☛ <u>Rule 47:</u> When you live with an alien, you've got to be willing to make a few changes in your life.

Take me, for instance. I used to think that a nerdy little guy with a squeaky munchkin voice and thick glasses that make his eyes look like fried eggs was a dweeb. It goes to show how wrong you can be. That "dweeb" just might be a 147-year-old alien from the planet Pan, like my exchange buddy, Stan Mflxnys.

Everybody else in my fourth-grade class got to host a buddy from another part of the country. I got to host one from another part of the *galaxy*. Cody was from Texas, and Wanda was

1

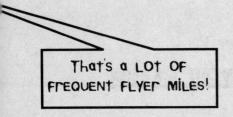

That's a LOT OF FREQUENT FLYER MILES!

from California. Those places are pretty far, sure. But Pan is eighty-five thousand light-years away. Top that.

I've never been there, but I'm pretty sure it must be the most nutso place in the universe. For starters, people from Pan are called Pants. They come from the constellation of the Big Zipper. Their president is known as the Grand Pant. His assistants are the Under-Pants. I know it sounds like a comedy routine, but it's all true! I signed up for an exchange buddy, and I got Stan from Pan. My life hasn't been the same since.

I even had to change my Rules of Coolness notebook. Talk about messy! There's stuff crossed out everywhere. For example, Rule 41 started out No nose picking. I had to rewrite it to say No nose picking unless you're operating the special minicomputer that all Pants have up their schnozzes.

So when I said, "Stan, quit picking your nose!" I didn't mean that there was any actual picking going on. But there he sat, with his finger buried up to the second knuckle. And on the other side of

the den, our piano was *playing itself*! Nasal processors can do that. They can do almost anything.

"Pants are not nose pickers," Stan replied, highly insulted. "I, Stan, am using my nasal processor to send ion pulses to the keys of your musical instrument."

"Well, those ion pulses are tone-deaf," I complained. "That's not music. It's torture."

"Really?" Stan was surprised. "That song is number one on the WPAN hit parade—'Wide Waling Chords' by the Fly Boys."

"It sounds like 'Old McDonald Had a Farm' mixed with a police siren," I growled. "Cut it out. I'm trying to watch TV."

"You're not watching TV," Stan accused. "You're just flipping channels. Why are we wasting time? Our social studies project is due on Friday, and we haven't even started it yet."

I shrugged. "Use your schnoz to do it." That was the best part of having Stan as an exchange buddy. With one pick of his nose, he could do the dishes, cut the grass, clean our room, or even write a ten-page essay for school, all in a split second. It was heaven. I hadn't done any homework or chores since the day the guy got here. Except for the week his nose broke down. That had almost been a total disaster.

"I'll bet your nasal processor can whip us up an A-plus social studies project," I added, through a wide, lazy yawn.

"But it can't," Stan said seriously. "The project has to be on the greatest achievements of the human race. My nasal processor can only get information about *Pan*. It knows very little Earth history."

4

"You mean—" I was shocked. "You mean, we're going to have to—*work*?"

The fried-egg eyes examined me closely. "Fascinating! I, Stan, have just realized something about earthling behavior. When I use my nasal processor to do all your work for you, I'm not doing you a favor."

"Yes, you are!" I howled. "A *huge* favor! Please don't stop!"

Stan shook his head. "By not working, you forget *how* to work. You become a sofa turnip."

"You mean a couch potato? No way!" But while I was saying it, I looked down at myself

lying there amidst the cushions. Candy bar wrappers and soda cans were strewn all around me. A half-eaten bag of Doritos was perched on my chest. Past it, I could just make out the beginning of my soon-to-be potbelly peeking out from the bottom of my shirt. **"Oh, no! I'm a couch potato!** I'm going to flunk social studies!"

COUCH POTATOES ARE MY FAVORITE VEGETABLE.

"We can't let that happen," said Stan gravely. "If either of us gets a failing grade in a school assignment, I, Stan, will have to quit the National Student Exchange Program."

That was a big problem. As nerdy as Stan was, the whole future of Earth depended on him. Stan was a travel agent, which is a really big job on Pan. Pants are the greatest tourists in the universe. They work two weeks per year, and go on vacation for the other fifty. Stan's goal was to make Earth Pan's newest vacation spot.

I held my head. "If you have to leave, you won't be able to push for Earth. So the Grand Pant will probably pick—"

"Mercury!" we chorused in agony.

Oh, no! Mercury was the other finalist for resort planet. But Earth was blocking Mercury's spectacular view of the rings of Saturn. If Mercury got picked, Earth would have to be moved—all the way out past the orbit of Pluto. **We'd freeze!**

What a mess! The decision on the new tourist planet could come any minute. Stan had his test tourists working overtime. He was sending tons of reports home to Pan about how great Earth is. How could he stop all that for something as dumb as social studies? But if we got an F on that project, he'd have to leave anyway. Either way, Earth was the big loser.

What could we do?

SOCIAL STUDIES CAN BE hazardOUS TO YOUr PLANET.

Chapter 2

THE UFO NUT

School was our best hope. If we could get an extension for a week or so, maybe we could save Earth by Friday, and still have the weekend to throw together a project. We had to try.

First thing in the morning, Mr. Slomin asked for progress reports on our projects. Hands shot up in our crowded classroom. Remember, we had twenty-three regular students plus fourteen exchange buddies.

Mr. Slomin picked Calista and her exchange buddy, Wanda.

"We're doing a diorama of the invention of the surfboard," announced Wanda, the Californian.

"Nice idea," the teacher approved, writing it down. "Joey and Cody, how about you?"

Cody, the visiting Texan, stood up. "Our project is about oil drilling. We're doing a diorama, too."

"Pssst!" hissed Tanner Phelps, poking me in the back. "What are you guys going to do a diorama of? The invention of nose picking?"

☛ **Rule 20:** If you don't have a good comeback, keep your mouth shut.

I gave him a dirty look, but no answer. I couldn't tell anybody that Stan wasn't really picking his nose! How would I explain what he actually *was* doing? I was the only one who knew Stan was an alien. To the rest of the kids, he was the geek in the white dress shirt and polka-dot tie. They made fun of him because he ate paper.

I'll admit it—I was the first one to point out what a weirdo Stan was. But on Pan, paper is a delicacy. They don't even have money anymore because people were snacking on their life savings. Anyway, I think it's mean to laugh at a guy because his idea of a tasty treat is *The Clearview Post*, or the paper plate instead of the sandwich. After all, everybody's different.

"Naturally, we study the *human* race because it's the only race we know," Mr. Slomin was saying. "Of course, there are many other species in the galaxy. We haven't met them yet, but we know they exist. They come in the many UFOs that visit Earth."

Everybody groaned. Mr. Slomin was a real pain in the neck about unidentified flying objects. He was even president of the Clearview UFO Society. Those guys spend every night staring into telescopes, scanning the skies for spaceships. Of course, the rest of the class was groaning because they thought Mr. Slomin was crazy. Stan and I were groaning because we knew Mr. Slomin was *right*. He had come very close to catching us one time when Stan had visitors from Pan. Even now he never looked at us without a frown of suspicion.

Mr. Slomin took note of the last few project ideas. "That's everybody except"—he consulted his list—"Devin and Stan. What are you two doing for your assignment?"

I leaped to my feet. "Oh, a diorama. Definitely."

"A diorama of what?" the teacher asked.

I was struck dumb.

"We're still working on the diorama part," Stan supplied. "When that's finished, we'll work on the 'of what' part."

Mr. Slomin glared at us. "What's that supposed to mean?"

"It means we need more time," I jumped in. "A week . . . okay, how about four days? No? Well, then, give us the extra weekend, and we'll have it ready on Monday."

Mr. Slomin slapped his desk so hard that it made a sound like a pistol shot. "No extensions," he said firmly. "I can see that you two haven't even chosen your topic!"

But later, when everyone was doing a math quiz, the teacher sidled up to us and whispered, "On second thought, I might consider giving you

the extra weekend—*if* you'll tell me what you know about the UFOs that have been sighted around Clearview lately."

"We have no idea about that," I said quickly.

He scowled. "In that case, I expect your project first thing Friday morning. **If it's one second late, you'll both receive the F's you deserve!**"

"Aw, twill!" mumbled Stan under his breath. And I knew he was really upset, because *twill* is a very bad word on Pan.

But we weren't dead yet. If we couldn't get an extension from Mr. Slomin, we had to get one from the Pan-Pan Travel Bureau.

"How do we do that?" I asked on the way home.

"It's kind of a long shot," Stan admitted. "First I, Stan, have to get approval from Agent Shkprnys on Mercury. Both travel agents must agree to the extension."

As if it wasn't bad enough that Earth was facing a trip to the deep freeze out past Pluto, Mercury's travel agent was the real kicker. Shkprnys was the greatest agent in the history of the Pan-Pan Travel Bureau. I could see Stan shaking in his boots every time he said the guy's name. Shkprnys was the agent who had the idea to open a seafood restaurant in the Crab Nebula; the Red Spot Amusement Park on Jupiter was his baby; he even spearheaded the plan to line up eighteen black holes for the best golf course in the Milky Way. The guy was a travel superstar, and a national hero on Pan.

If Earth got picked instead of Mercury, it would be the first time Shkprnys ever lost. So the odds were already stacked against us.

I opened our front door, and ushered Stan in ahead of me. "I wish there was some way I could listen in on you two guys," I said anxiously. "Remember, I'm the one whose planet is going to get frosted."

Stan looked thoughtful. "There is one possibility—" He put his finger in his nose. "Calling Agent Shkprnys. Come in, please. This is Agent Mflxnys on Earth." Then he went over to our television set, detached the cable, and shoved the end up his other nostril. Instantly, the set clicked on.

13

I WANT MY NTV:
ALL NOSE,
ALL THE TIME.

At first there was a test pattern that said PLEASE STANDETH BY. And then the picture cleared to reveal a pale, round-faced man with long hair and a small, trimmed pointy beard. Around his neck he wore a stiff white ruffle.

He said, "Forsooth, Agent Mflxnys. What dost thou want?"

I already knew who the guy really was, but it was still a shock to see him and hear the way he talked. **Shkprnys was Shakespeare—** *William Shakespeare*, the famous writer from four hundred years ago!

It was a long, crazy story. Shakespeare wasn't human; he wasn't even Shakespeare; he was an alien named Shkprnys. He lived on Earth and wrote his plays all those years ago when he was a Training Pant. But Pants can live to be a thousand. So Shakespeare—the *real* Shakespeare!—was alive and well, and working for Mercury.

"May the Crease be with you, Agent Shkprnys," said Stan respectfully. "I, Stan, have called to request a delay in the decision about the new vacation planet."

"Forsooth!" exclaimed Shakespeare, who said

that a lot. "What is thy reason for this delay?"

"It's an Earth custom," explained Stan, "known as a social studies project."

Shakespeare smiled sweetly. "Thy words have touched my heart. Thou shalt have all the time thou needest. Forsooth, I shall myself maketh the arrangements with the Pan-Pan Travel Bureau. The Grand Pant is a personal friend of mine."

Stan glowed. "Agent Shkprnys, you're as wonderful as everyone says you are. I, Stan, have never known an opponent this fair."

"We are rivals, yea, verily," replied Shkprnys smoothly. "But this is a friendly competition. May the best planet win, forsooth." The screen faded to black, and the words THE ENDE appeared.

Stan broke the connection by pulling the cable out of his nose.

"Seems like a pretty nice guy," I commented. "Are you sure we can trust him?"

Stan was offended. "*Trust* him?! Devin, that's Shkprnys the One and Only! He wrote the words 'To thine own self be true'! What could be more honest than that?"

"Just checking," I said soothingly.

☛ **Rule 37:** Never insult another guy's hero.

Chapter 3

WHO CRASHED THE FLYING SAUCER?

That night I enjoyed the first decent sleep I'd had in days. Earth wasn't exactly safe yet. But at least I knew we weren't going to wake up frozen in a block of ice out past Pluto, where the sun looks as bright as a ten-watt bulb. Good old Shakespeare. He was starting to be my hero, too.

I'M TOUCHED.

Stan and I had even gotten started on our social studies project. My dad had given us a big wooden crate, and we'd painted it and everything. It was drying overnight in the backyard. All we had to do was figure out what to stick in it. We wouldn't get an A-plus, but at least we wouldn't flunk.

So we were sleeping away—I'd finally learned to tune out Stan's snoring. (Because of his nose computer, he made a noise like the hum of a microwave oven.) Then, all of a sudden,

CRASH!!!

Instantly awake and alert, we both jumped up and ran to the window. There was our diorama box, busted into a million pieces. And those million pieces were on fire. Above the flames, like a frying pan on a gas stove, was perched a space-ship.

I glared at Stan.

He looked sheepish. "It's one of ours. A Button-Fly 501 Space Cruiser."

I knew that already. I'd seen a ship from Pan. I recognized the shape—shallow and eight-sided, like a giant stop sign. The door started as a tiny dot, then grew and grew. A staircase descended, and a red carpet unrolled across the lawn.

Out stepped two Pants I had seen before. They were dressed exactly like Stan, with the same white dress shirts, and black polka-dot ties that were on so tight they stuck out in front. Their names were Zgrbnys the Extremely Wise and Gthrmnys the Utterly Clever. They were members of the most respected class on Pan—professional thinkers known as the Smarty-Pants.

It's pretty hard for us earthlings to get a sense of just how intelligent these guys have to be. Compared to them, **Einstein was a hamster.** The Smarty-Pants can think in six dimensions. Their IQs are so large that even they can't count that high. They can read the entire dictionary in five minutes, and remember most of the words.

They know the secret of happiness, the infinity times table, and even why manhole covers are round. It's unbelievably hard to become a Smarty-Pant. Stan used to be in Smarty-Pants University, but he got kicked out because he flubbed the question about the manhole covers.

Careful not to wake up my family, Stan and I crept downstairs and let ourselves out into the yard. I kind of hung back, but Stan stepped forward for the formal greeting.

"Welcome, Zgrbnys and Gthrmnys. May the Crease be with you."

Zgrbnys looked disgusted. "The Crease should have been with Gthrmnys when he was piloting through the Great Magellanic Cloud! **My nine-hundred-year-old grandmother flies better than that!**"

Gthrmnys flushed bright red. "The sun got in my eyes!"

"The sun was forty light-years away!" snapped Zgrbnys. "We were in the blackness of space!"

"The black got in my eyes!" Gthrmnys insisted.

"What happened?" Stan asked anxiously.

"We sideswiped an asteroid," said Zgrbnys sourly. "It was all his fault."

"Was not!"

"Was so!"

INTErStELLar road ragE.

Stan regarded the small dent in the silver side of the craft. "That doesn't look too bad. Your nasal processors could fix it in no time."

"But what about the scratch?" demanded Zgrbnys furiously. "Nasal processors can fix a dent, but they can't match paint!"

"If we go back to Pan with a scratch on our ship," complained Gthrmnys, "people might think we did something—dumb!"

Stan was horrified. "No one could ever think that about a Smarty-Pant!"

I stepped forward. "Why don't you go to Larson's Hardware Store?"

Zgrbnys looked at me like I was a very pesky insect. "Quiet, earthling. Your primitive brain cannot begin to understand our situation."

I shrugged. "What's to understand? You had an accident, and now you're too embarrassed to own up. That's why you need Larson's. They're great at matching paint."

"This earthling is wise," observed Gthrmnys.

Stan introduced me. "This is my friend Devin Hunter. You won't meet a smarter earthling. He wrote the Rules of Coolness that I put in my last report."

"Yes, I read these rules," sneered Zgrbnys. "They are wrong. They would have no effect whatsoever on the temperature, which, I should point out, is cool enough."

I took my exchange buddy aside. "Listen,

Stan, are you sure these guys are real Smarty-Pants? They don't seem that bright to me."

But Stan's fried-egg eyes were practically whirling with excitement. "Don't you see, Devin? This is a big chance for us! If we can help Zgrbnys and Gthrmnys with their problem, they'll put in a good word for Earth with the Grand Pant!"

"But how do we pull that off?" I demanded. "My folks are going to notice a spaceship standing in the backyard, you know! Not to mention two six-foot dweebs arguing about who crashed the flying saucer! We'll never come up with a cover story for all that!"

Stan looked at me like I was crazy. "Devin, we have two of the greatest minds in the galaxy here to help us." He turned to the Smarty-Pants. "Please use your natural super-genius to devise a believable story for Devin's family."

"Nothing could be simpler," said Zgrbnys smugly. "We'll say that the ship is a giant silver octagonal mushroom that has sprung up out of the ground overnight."

Of course! Why didn't I think of that?

23

"And we," added Gthrmnys with enthusiasm, "are inspectors from the *Guinness Book of World Records*, in charge of their mushroom department."

I looked at Stan, but he was completely convinced. I guess when you live 147 years hearing about how brilliant Smarty-Pants are, it's pretty hard to believe that they could be a couple of knuckleheads like this pair.

"All right," I said. "Here's what we're going to do. . . ."

Chapter 4

UNCLE ZACK AND UNCLE GUS

When I heard the scream, I knew Mom had discovered the Smarty-Pants in the guest room.

I leaped out of bed and went tearing down the hall. "Don't worry, Mom!"

She was pointing at the doorway. "But there are two strange men in there!"

"They're not strange," I assured her. **"Well, okay, maybe they're a little strange.** But they're Stan's uncles. They pulled an all-nighter on the bus from—Chicago. I didn't want to wake you, so I set them up in the guest room."

She looked only slightly relieved. "Oh. They're—quite welcome, of course. Uh—just how long are they planning to stay?"

"Only a couple of days," I assured her. "They're helping us with our social studies project. It's a big surprise, so could you please tell Lindsay and Roscoe and Dad to stay away from the garage?"

That's where we'd hidden the spaceship. And just in case someone peeked in the window, we had it draped with a New York Yankees tarpaulin that Zgrbnys and Gthrmnys happened to have in the cargo bay.

I sweated all through breakfast. The whole family was there, meeting Uncle Zack and Uncle Gus. I mean, we couldn't very well call them by their real names, could we?

Wouldn't you know it—those so-called geniuses couldn't remember which one was supposed to be Zack, and which one was supposed to be Gus.

"So," said my father, pouring out more coffee, "what do you fellows do for a living?"

"They're in the intelligence business," supplied Stan.

"They're *spies*?" blurted my older brother, Roscoe.

"Of course not," said Zgrbnys. "We're geniuses."

Mom smiled. "But what actual job do you do?"

"Thinking, mostly," put in Gthrmnys. "But there's also a lot of pondering, ruminating, cogitating, and envisioning."

And dictionary swallowing.

"We sometimes put in two-hour days," added Zgrbnys.

"Oh," nodded Dad. "Consultants."

Roscoe stared at the sports section of the morning paper. "Hey, this is weird. Someone stole the giant tarp that covers the infield at Yankee Stadium. And get this—the groundskeeper insists he saw a UFO fly away with it."

"I wonder what happened to it," mused Mom.

"Well, it's not in the garage, that's for sure," announced Gthrmnys.

I choked. Orange juice really stings when you snort it out your nose.

Gthrmnys popped his napkin into his mouth and chewed happily. Then he stuck his hand in the maple syrup, came up with a gooey, dripping glob, and washed his face with it.

"Ooooh!" exclaimed my kid sister, Lindsay.

"That's **gross!**"

But Dad was laughing. "Gus, you're a riot! You really know how to entertain the kids."

"Thank you," chorused both Smarty-Pants.

Gthrmnys got annoyed. "I'm Gus!"

"No, *I'm* Gus!"

Fungus, our cocker spaniel, jumped up onto the table, and started to lick "Uncle Gus's" sweet sticky face. Fungus barked.

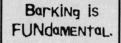
Barking is FUNdaMENTaL.

Gthrmnys barked back.

Lindsay clapped her hands with delight. "You talk to dogs, too, just like Stan!"

I held my head. I'd forgotten that the nasal processors have Pan-Tran translators that can speak Dog. Oh, man, it just couldn't get any worse than this!

The doorbell rang. Mom went to answer it.

"Oh, hello, Mr. Slomin. What brings you here so early in the morning? Do you need to speak with Devin and Stan?"

I knew Mr. Slomin was there in the kitchen without even turning around. I could feel his eyes burning into the back of my neck.

"I'm not here as a teacher," Mr. Slomin said sternly. "This is official business of the UFO Society. One of our members spotted a spacecraft landing in this area last night. Did anyone here notice anything?"

"We were all asleep," said my father. "Maybe Stan's uncles saw something. They got in pretty late."

"Our specialty is thinking, not observing," put in Gthrmnys.

"Uncles?" Mr. Slomin looked closely at Zgrbnys and Gthrmnys. "Yes, I see the family resemblance. Well, Mr. and Mrs. Hunter, I'll get to the point. There is something very suspicious in your garage. It's covered by a New York Yankees tarpaulin—exactly the kind that was stolen by a UFO last night. Please unlock the garage at once."

"Oh," chuckled my dad. "You're talking about the boys' social studies project. They're very excited about it. We all promised to stay away so as not to spoil their surprise."

"The mushroom story would have been much more believable," Zgrbnys muttered to Stan.

I had a sickening feeling that school was going to be torture today.

Sure enough, Mr. Slomin was like a bloodhound. He kept saying things like, "You boys look pretty tired. Were you up in the middle of the night, maybe?" and "Where would you get a Yankees tarpaulin? They don't sell them in stores."

"This is agony!" I whispered to Stan at recess.

Stan nodded. "We were fortunate that your parents wouldn't let him in the garage."

I groaned. "You know what the worst part is? Those two so-called geniuses are all alone in our house! Who knows what kind of trouble they're getting into right now?"

Stan was horrified. "Devin, how can you say that? They're *Smarty-Pants*! They know why manhole covers are round! Whatever they do, I, Stan, am sure it will be exactly the right thing!"

I practically shook all the way home. I'm not sure what I expected to see—maybe a pile of rubble where our house once stood. And two interstellar dweebs with their fingers up their noses, telling me it was really a mushroom that looked exactly like a busted-up house!

We came to our block and rounded the corner. The house was still there, thank goodness. But Zgrbnys and Gthrmnys were nowhere to be found.

Chapter 5

NOSE PICKERS ON TV

"Oh, no!" I moaned. "Those two idiots are on the loose in Clearview!"

"Devin!" Stan was really angry with me. "What's the matter with you? They're not 'on the loose.' They used their super-intelligence to decide exactly the best place to be, and they went there."

We checked the garage. Under the tarp, the spaceship was completely repaired, including the touch-up paint.

"They're ready to go!" I wailed. **"Why aren't they gone?"**

"Have a little faith," Stan scolded me. "They know best. Knowing is their business. Look at Fungus. He isn't worried."

That's because Fungus is a *dog*. If he has a

bowl of kibble, and the toilet seat is up, what does he have to worry about?

Lindsay came home. Roscoe came home. Mom and Dad came home. No Smarty-Pants.

"Where are Zack and Gus?" asked Dad, stowing his briefcase.

"Out," I said faintly.

My mom started rattling around in the kitchen. "Should we hold supper for them?"

Stan leaned over to my ear and whispered, "The Sears catalog is unharmed, but the Yellow Pages are chewed through to the L's."

"I think they ate already," I called to Mom.

By seven o'clock, I was really starting to panic. I know Rule 3 says **Never panic**. But I was ready to phone all the jails to see if the cops had arrested any nose pickers.

NEVEr FiNgErPriNt a NOSE PiCKEr.

"Devin! Stan! Come quick!" called my mother from the den. "*Jeopardy!*'s on."

"Not now," I yelled back.

"But the show is on tour this week. Tonight they're broadcasting from *Clearview*! We can't miss it."

So we joined the rest of the family in the den. It's not often that a dinky town like Clearview gets to host a big-time TV show like *Jeopardy!* When we got there, Alex Trebek was introducing the evening's contestants.

"Please welcome a retired schoolteacher from Hicksville, New York, Miss Zelda Gluck. And two consultants, both from Pan, Illinois, Gus Gthrmnys and Zack Zgrbnys."

I wheezed so hard that I must have sucked in half the air in the room. Our two Smarty-Pants were standing right there with Alex Trebek on national TV!

> IS ALEX TREBEK
> AN ALIEN, TOO?
> NO, JUST A CANADIAN.

"Stan, look!" exclaimed Roscoe. "It's your uncles! Why didn't they tell us they were going to be on *Jeopardy!*?"

Because they *weren't* going to be on *Jeopardy!* Not until they used their nose computers, I'll bet, to get on the contestant list!

Stan was practically glowing. "Devin!" he whispered. "This is the best possible thing that could have happened!"

"Just peachy!" I groaned sarcastically.

"No, really," he insisted. "If the Smarty-Pants have a good time here on Earth, they'll pass that along in their report to the Grand Pant. And what could be more fun for Smarty-Pants than showing off how smart they are?"

"They've already shown *us* how smart they are," I murmured tragically.

"Yes, but now they'll get to show an entire planet!"

"Hey, look, Stan," piped up Lindsay. ***"Your uncles are picking their noses on TV!"***

I couldn't take it another second. "We've got to get down to that studio!"

We raced out. I jumped on my bike and hauled Stan up onto the handlebars. Then I pedaled like mad for downtown and the TV studio that was broadcasting *Jeopardy!*

The place was packed, but Stan used his nasal processor to get us front row seats.

The show was almost over. And I have to say that the "uncles" were doing really well. They were tied with 38,700 dollars each. Miss Gluck was in third place with three dollars.

"Wow!" I whispered to Stan. "I've never seen anybody run up so much money on *Jeopardy!* before."

He was smug. "There's never been any Smarty-Pants on *Jeopardy!* before."

"Well, this is the most exciting duel we've had in a long time!" enthused Alex Trebek. "Gus and Zack have not made a single mistake between them. That's something to bear in mind as our contestants think of their secret wagers for Final Jeopardy!"

"I don't have to make a secret wager," announced Gthrmnys. "I will, of course, bet everything."

"I, too, bet everything," said Gthrmnys stoutly.

The studio audience gave them a big cheer.

The two Smarty-Pants stuck their fingers in their noses in intense concentration.

The category was Trivia. Alex Trebek read out the final answer. The three contestants had to come up with the question.

" 'This is the reason manhole covers are round.' "

I thought Stan was going to launch himself up through the ceiling of the studio. "They know this!" he chortled gleefully. "All Smarty-Pants know this! It's the number one fact at Smarty-Pants University!"

"So how come they're not writing?" I asked.

It was true. Zgrbnys and Gthrmnys stood frozen with their fingers up their noses. They looked like a couple of nose-picking statues. The music played; the time ran out.

Miss Gluck had no answer.

"What was your wager?" asked Alex Trebek. "Ah, two dollars. That leaves you with a total of one dollar. Now we move on to the two gentlemen from Illinois. Will this be a tiebreaker? Will it be the biggest payoff in *Jeopardy!* history? Let's see what you've written."

The screens in front of Zgrbnys and Gthrmnys lit up. They were both blank.

Stan was thunderstruck. "But they *know* this!"

Alex Trebek looked grave. "Oooh, I'm sorry, fellows. Since you bet everything, your winnings are reset to zero. Miss Gluck, you are our new *Jeopardy!* champion, with a grand total of one dollar! Congratulations!"

The audience didn't clap. They didn't even move. No one had ever seen so much money wiped out in the wink of an eye.

"But why didn't they answer?" Stan barely whispered.

The last thing that was broadcast on TV was Zgrbnys and Gthrmnys trying to strangle each other.

Then the network cut to a commercial.

What is this, Jerry Springer?

Chapter 6

ALL ABOARD FOR OUTER SPACE

It's a good thing Stan and I were there to help Alex Trebek break up the fight. What a great guy! Brave, too. He didn't even complain when Zgrbnys gave him a fat lip. He said it didn't hurt much, and makeup could take care of it for tomorrow's show. Then he bundled all four of us, and my bike, into a *Jeopardy!* van, and had us driven home.

Out on the front porch, Stan turned his fried-egg eyes on his fellow Pants. "I, Stan, know why you didn't answer that last question."

Zgrbnys looked embarrassed. "You do?"

Stan nodded. "Manhole covers are classified information, right? You can't give the secret away to non-Smarty-Pants!"

I laughed in all three of their faces. "I've flunked enough tests to be able to recognize someone who doesn't have a clue what the answer is. And when Alex Trebek asked about manhole covers, you two were as blank as a TV screen with the cable out. You guys have *no idea* why manhole covers are round, do you?"

Zgrbnys turned on Gthrmnys. "Why didn't you tell me you didn't know?"

"Why didn't *you* tell me *you* didn't know?"

"But didn't you have to know it to pass the

Smarty-Pants Aptitude Test?" asked Stan.

"It wasn't on the test," Zgrbnys admitted, shamefaced.

"No one ever asked me, either," confirmed Gthrmnys, with a heavy sigh. "And now we'll be kicked out of the Smarty-Pants Union."

That gave me an idea. "Who's going to know except me and Stan? We'll make you a deal. We won't tell anybody about the manhole covers thing if you promise to put in a *very* good word for Earth to the Grand Pant."

They looked bewildered. "What for?"

"So we'll get picked for vacation planet," I explained, exasperated. "The big decision is coming up, you know."

"But that decision has already been made," said Zgrbnys. **"Earth lost."**

"Not possible!" gasped Stan. "I, Stan, made an agreement with Agent Shkprnys on Mercury—"

"Agent Shkprnys isn't on Mercury," said Gthrmnys. "He's been back on Pan for days, shaking hands and kissing babies. He told the Pan-Pan Travel Bureau that you quit, and that's why the reports stopped coming."

"Twill!" cried Stan. "Shkprnys tricked us!"

"Watch your language!" snapped Zgrbnys. "You don't say the 'T' word in front of Smarty-Pants!"

I admit it; I went nuts. "Oh, no! It's really happening! We're going out past Pluto! And I wouldn't let Mom buy me any long johns because they broke ☞ **Rule 43: long johns look like thermal ballet tights!** It's over! It's over—"

"Not yet," Stan interrupted grimly. "I, Stan, am going to Pan to tell Earth's side of the story. And you, Devin, are coming with me."

I stared at him. "Are you nuts? Dad wouldn't even sign the permission slip for the overnight at Scout camp! You think he's not going to notice if I travel to another planet eighty-five thousand light-years away?"

Zgrbnys butted in. "Your limited intelligence cannot understand space travel. It takes only a few hours to fly to Pan. But here on Earth, sixty years go by."

"Sixty years?!" I howled.

"But coming home," Gthrmnys took up the explanation, "you *lose* sixty years, and arrive

only a few seconds after you left. Your family will never know you have been gone. See how simple it is?"

My head was spinning. Okay, I was going to Pan. I had no choice. I owed that much to my family and my fellow earthlings.

Please, please, *please* let Earth be here when I get back!

Make sure you return your library books before you go.

Chapter 7

A FLOATING MUSHROOM

"All right, I'll go," I announced. "But we've got to figure out a way to get the spaceship out of the garage and take off without my parents noticing."

Stan shrugged. "That should be no problem at all. We've got two of the keenest minds in the galaxy to help us out."

"Of course!" exclaimed Zgrbnys. "We will reprogram our nasal processors to fill your house with several thousand crickets. They will chirp so loudly that it will cover up the sound of the spaceship."

That didn't sound too good to me. "And how do we get rid of the crickets afterward?"

That kind of plan really bugs people.

Gthrmnys dismissed this with a wave of his

46

hand. "Since we will be gone, that will be your family's problem."

"No crickets," I said firmly. "Stan and I are going to go in there and play the TV loud. Just beep Stan's nose computer when you've got the ship ready. I'll get you the garage door opener." I ran to the car, which was parked on the street. I snatched the clip-on remote control from the sun shade and handed it to Zgrbnys.

"I will need several hours to analyze this high technology," the Smarty-Pant told me.

I was disgusted. "There's only one button! Even you guys couldn't mess it up!"

Then came the toughest job of the night— walking into the den like everything was normal.

"Stan," said my mother, "are your uncles all right? We saw what happened on *Jeopardy!*"

"Oh, they're fine, Mrs. Hunter."

"Did they kill each other?" piped up Lindsay.

Through the window I could see the garage door opening. I leaned over and bumped up the TV volume a couple of notches.

"Devin, that's a little loud," my father complained.

"Sorry, Dad, can't hear you." I raised the sound even higher.

Roscoe jumped in. "How come Devin's allowed to blast the TV, but I get in trouble if I turn up my stereo?"

I caught a brief glimpse of the spaceship backing out of the garage, hovering a foot above the driveway. I punched the volume up to maximum.

"Devin!" screeched my mother. "Have you lost your mind?"

I looked at Stan, but he shook his head. No signal yet from the Smarty-Pants.

And then, over the blaring of the TV, I could just make out an all-too-familiar voice:

"Stop in the name of planetary

GUESS WhO?

defense!"

My heart leaped up into my throat. It was Mr. Slomin! And this time he had a bona fide UFO in his sights!

"I—I—I gotta check the twist-ties on the garbage!" I grabbed Stan, and we bolted out of the house like we'd been shot from a cannon.

Outside, a horrifying sight met my eyes. The ship hung there, its round door open wide.

Gthrmnys was halfway up the staircase, caught in the beam of Mr. Slomin's flashlight.

"Back away from that spacecraft!" bellowed our teacher.

Gthrmnys tossed him a haughty look. "What spacecraft?"

It was stupid, but you had to admire the guy's nerve.

"It's not a ship!" called Zgrbnys from inside. "It's a large floating mushroom—"

Before he could finish, things got a little wild. Gthrmnys tried to make it into the ship, but Mr. Slomin ran up, grabbed him by the foot, and hung on.

"Let me go, you primitive life-form!" cried Gthrmnys.

With a wild bark, Fungus erupted out of his doghouse, and fastened his teeth on Mr. Slomin's ankle.

"Yeo w!"

The teacher let go, and Gthrmnys rushed aboard.

Stan squeezed my arm. "Devin—the door!"

I looked. The black circle was growing smaller. "Run!" I bellowed.

Stan raced up the stairs and hurled himself inside. "Hurry!" he urged me.

I was hot on his heels, screaming all the way. I felt the carpet and stairway start to fold up under me. I launched myself like a torpedo through the rapidly shrinking door. *Wham!* I hit the floor of the cabin hard, and scrambled back to my feet. "Safe!" I cried, weak with relief.

And then, a split second before the opening spiraled shut, Mr. Slomin squeezed through. Fungus was still clamped heroically onto his leg. The door became a dot, and then winked out of existence.

"Stop!" I hollered. "Our teacher's on board!"

But by the time the words were out of my mouth, our house was a tiny speck, and we were higher up than I'd ever been before, even on an airplane.

That's when I noticed the garage door opener clipped to Gthrmnys's shirt pocket. I snatched it away and snapped it onto my belt. I had to get this back to Mom and Dad.

But first it was going to take a little ride. We all were.

Chapter 8

ALIEN ABDUCTION

"*Alien abduction!*" bellowed Mr. Slomin. "*Alien abduction! HELP!*"

"You haven't been abducted, earthling," called Zgrbnys from the controls. "You jumped on board."

Mr. Slomin turned blazing eyes on Stan. "I was right! There *have* been UFOs in Clearview! And *you* have been cooperating with the aliens!"

"Incorrect, Mr. Slomin," Stan explained. "I, Stan, *am* an alien. I am Agent Mflxnys of the Pan-Pan Travel Bureau, under command of His Most Tailored Majesty, the Grand Pant."

He'd show you his business card, but he ate it.

The teacher turned to me. "How could *you* go along with all this, Devin? Don't you have any loyalty to your planet?"

52

I was so upset that I couldn't even get my mouth to work. Here I was, a kid who'd never even been to sleepaway camp, heading for the other side of the galaxy just to save Earth. And my own teacher was calling me a traitor!

"It's not what you think—" I began.

But Mr. Slomin had shifted his attention to the Smarty-Pants at the controls.

"As President of the UFO Society, it is my duty to warn you that you're making a big mistake! We may not have fancy ships like this, but **when it comes to kicking butt, Earth is the best there is!** If you don't take me back this minute and surrender yourselves to our authorities, Earth is going to send a fleet to wipe up the galaxy with you guys!"

Zgrbnys and Gthrmnys started laughing so hard I was afraid they were going to crash the ship.

"Oh!" Zgrbnys gasped. "That's rich! That Pan might have something to fear from a Q-class planet like Earth!"

"And their fleet!" giggled Gthrmnys. "Why, the fastest rocket on Earth would take over a

billion years to get halfway to Pan! Ooooh, we're so scared!"

I thought Mr. Slomin was going to blow a gasket. "Who are you calling Q-class? Class A, all the way! That's our motto! Earth is no pushover! We have *nuclear power*!"

That made the Smarty-Pants laugh harder. And even Stan, who had much better manners, couldn't hold back a chuckle or two.

"I'm so sorry," he apologized. "I, Stan, don't mean to be rude. **But on Pan, we use nuclear power for our popcorn poppers and toilet flushers.** Our main source of energy is the Crease."

The Crease is a wrinkle in the fabric of space, whatever that means. Stan says there's unlimited energy coming from it. Yeah, I know, he could be making it up. But you kind of had to believe it. There we were, after all, streaking across the sky.

Suddenly, the ship dipped and swerved, knocking us all off our feet. I fell into Stan, and the two of us tripped over Fungus. Mr. Slomin's feet slipped out from under him, and he landed flat on his back and whacked his head on the shiny silver floor. He lay there, out cold and snoring.

"It might get a little bumpy back there as we land," came a very late warning from pilot Zgrbnys.

I was amazed. "Are we at Pan already?"

"No," said Gthrmnys. "St. Louis."

"*St. Louis!?*" Maybe the Crease wasn't such hot stuff after all.

"We have to pick up another passenger," Stan explained. "One of my test tourists needs a ride home." The test tourists were Pants like Stan. They posed as humans while doing vacation research on Earth.

I looked away from the window because it was making me dizzy. One second, we were miles above Earth. The next, we were touching down in a dark backyard somewhere in St. Louis, Missouri.

The door opened, and the staircase and red carpet descended.

"Welcome, Mgwrnys the Swinger," Stan greeted his employee.

I gawked. Standing right in the doorway was none other than Mark McGwire of the St. Louis Cardinals, the home run king!

"Stan!" I gasped. "Mark McGwire is an alien?"

Stan shrugged. "You didn't think a mere earthling could hit like that, did you?"

HE WON THE HOME
RUN TITLE BY A NOSE!

Chapter 9

LEFT TURN AT THE GLOBULAR CLUSTER

Zoom! We were off again. I could tell that this time we were going a lot farther than St. Louis. When I looked back out the window, Earth was just a tiny blue marble against a starry sky that stretched on forever.

Suddenly, I felt a lump in my throat the size of an apple. Sure, I knew I was breaking ☞ **Rule 12: Homesickness is for losers.** But my whole family was back on Earth, and everybody I knew. If something went wrong on this trip, I would never see them again. Mom, Dad, Lindsay, Roscoe—well, to be honest, half a galaxy seemed like a pretty good barrier between Roscoe and me. But he *was* my brother, and I would probably miss him.

DOES ANYONE HEAR VIOLIN MUSIC?

Stan must have noticed my long face. He came and sat down beside me, placing a comforting hand on my shoulder. "Don't worry, Devin. I know eighty-five thousand light-years seems like a long way. But for us at the Pan-Pan Travel Bureau, it's like a Weekend Getaway Special. I, Stan, know Pants who'll journey forty thousand light-years just to have dinner at a restaurant with really good napkins. You're thinking about this like an earthling. Try to take the Pant view."

I brightened a little. If there was one good thing to come from this terrible mess, with Earth being in such danger and all, it was my friendship with Stan Mflxnys. He wasn't cool; but as dweebs went, he was the best.

Near the cargo hatch, Fungus and Mark McGwire were deep in conversation. It sounded like the dog pound back there. You never heard so much barking.

I nudged Stan. "What are they talking about?"

"Oh," Stan said airily. "Fungus noticed a little kink in Mgwrnys's swing last season. He's giving him a few pointers."

I goggled. My dog, who begs for table scraps and drinks out of the toilet, was coaching the great Mark McGwire! What a galaxy!

"Hey, Stan," I whispered. "Are you sure those two Smarty-Pants are safe enough drivers? They're staring at their ties instead of, you know, the road."

Stan looked surprised. "Of course they are. How can a pilot navigate without his tie?"

I was mystified. "Polka dots tell you where to go?"

"They're not polka dots," he explained. "They're star maps. We Pants can find our way home from anywhere. Of course, when you enter a new sector, you have to change ties."

According to the ties, our flight plan took us out of the solar system, past the Big Dipper, with a left turn at Globular Cluster M11, and straight on to the red giant star, Ama.

"And that's close to Pan?" I asked.

"Oh, no," Stan said seriously. "In fact, Ama is even farther from Pan than Earth."

I was confused. "You mean we're flying in the wrong direction?"

Stan shook his head. "You see, Ama is right next to the entrance to hyperspace. In hyperspace, we can pick up a shortcut all the way to Pan on the other side of the galaxy. We Pants call it the Pan-Ama Canal."

Our spaceship gave a sickening lurch.

I nearly jumped out of my skin. "What was that?"

Pilot Zgrbnys had the answer. "Hyperspace! Tighten your suspenders and hang on to your belt loops!"

"That's an old saying on Pan," Stan whispered to me.

Hyperspace was kind of scary. There are no stars, so it's completely black in there, except for your own running lights. And you're moving so fast you can hear it. It sounds like "Flight of the Bumblebee" at a hundred times normal speed, being played by a mosquito on a tiny kazoo. We were vibrating so much that Fungus started to howl, and Mr. Slomin woke up. And then, suddenly, it all stopped, and we were out.

I ran to the window. There it was—the constellation of the Big Zipper. It really *was* a zipper—hundreds of stars lined up in pairs. And at the very top—

"Devin, look!" cried Stan joyfully. "It's Pan!"

"Well, we made it," declared Zgrbnys as we began to descend. "A brilliant job of piloting by me."

"You never could have done it without my expert navigation," put in Gthrmnys.

"Big deal!" snorted his partner. **"You can read a tie."**

As we broke through the clouds, I could

see that the land was kind of a khaki color.

"This region is called the Panhandle," my exchange buddy explained. "I, Stan, grew up here."

We set down with a soft bump. A recorded voice announced, *"Welcome to Pan Intergalactic Spaceport, located in the beautiful twin cities of Levi-Strauss. This greeting is brought to you by the planet Mercury—Pan's newest resort, a barren, scorched wasteland, handpicked by Agent Shkprnys himself. Leave your coat at home, and bring your gas mask, because the air on Mercury is one-hundred-percent poisonous. Gaze up at the breathtaking rings of Saturn, with no other planet blocking your perfect view. Remember: to tan or not to tan—that is the question on Mercury."*

I turned horrified eyes to Stan. "You mean they've moved Earth *already*?"

"It's just a commercial," Stan soothed. "Shkprnys is famous for advertising a place before it opens. We still have time to reach the Grand Pant. Okay, take off your shoes."

"Why?" I asked.

Stan looked at me like I had a cabbage for a

head. "You don't want to track dirt on the carpet, do you?"

I frowned. "What carpet? We're *outside*."

"Outside is where the carpet is," Stan explained.

I peered through the window. That khaki

color—it was fuzzy shag carpeting!

"You mean you've carpeted—"

"The whole planet," finished Stan.

"What for?"

MY MOM did the same thing with our living room.

"It's a long story," Stan admitted. "A few hundred years ago, the Smarty-Pants were experimenting with a combination intelligence booster and root beer. They constructed the galaxy's first trillion-gallon soda-pop can. Wouldn't you know it? There was an earthquake, and the can got shaken up."

I clued in. "Don't tell me they opened it."

He nodded sadly. "It sprayed the whole planet. Even today, the polar ice caps are covered in frozen root beer. And when the grass started dying, the Grand Pant had no choice but to carpet everything. But the Designer Jeans picked such a light color that it was getting filthy all the time. Do you know how much it costs to steam-clean three hundred billion square feet of carpet?"

"I guess a lot."

"Over fifty million Pantaloons," Stan informed me. "And that's with a coupon. The Pocket, our planetary treasury, was going broke. The Grand Pant had to outlaw shoes to avoid a depression."

I stepped out of my sneakers and kicked them under my chair. A whole planet where shoes are illegal, thanks to the genius Smarty-Pants. Didn't it figure?

Outside the ship, Stan stuck his nose in a slot marked INSPECTION STATION—SNORT HERE. I had to register my garage door opener as an alien device. Fungus had to do the same with his dog collar. So did Mark McGwire with his baseball bat.

"Where's Mr. Slomin?" I asked Stan.

Before he could answer, a booming voice thundered, "You people will rue the day you kidnapped the president of the UFO Society!"

I pointed to a glass cubicle. "It's coming from in there!"

"That's the office of the Under-Pant in charge of visitors!" Stan exclaimed.

I threw open the door. There stood our teacher, red-faced and yelling at an important-looking Pant behind a tall desk.

"Earth will make you pay for this!" roared Mr. Slomin. "We invented the space shuttle and peel-and-stick postage stamps. We'll figure out a way to get even with you!"

The Under-Pant was laughing so hard that he could barely keep from falling off his chair. "Earth?" he croaked. "Do you spell that with a

WELCOME TO Urth.

U?" Finally, he managed to get his trembling finger up to his nasal processor. "Ah, here it is. Earth—an extremely distant and unimportant planet, known for its high-quality traffic jams and allergies, and a race of extremely intelligent dogs who know great knock-knock jokes. Class: Q."

I could almost see smoke shooting out of our teacher's ears. "We're *not* Q-class!!" he roared. "Earth is Class A, all the way!" He bolted out of the office and raced down the hall.

Chapter 10
PANTS·PORTATION

"**M**r. Slomin!" I cried. "Come back!"

I grabbed Stan and the two of us shot down the corridor after our teacher. We rounded the corner just in time to see him burst out of the spaceport building and into the street.

"After him!" I cried.

Stan and I galloped through the exit. Instantly, I bounced off some guy and got knocked flying. It's a good thing they carpeted the whole planet or I probably would have brained myself.

I tried to get up. It was impossible. Dozens of people stepped over me, knocking me down again. Pants brushed by to the left and right. This place was *packed*! And everybody was dressed in white shirts and polka-dot ties. Their fingers bobbed in and out of their noses.

> JUST LIKE the MaLL at ChristMas.

I was in Nose Picker Land!

The kids in my class who were so grossed out by Stan—Calista, Tanner, and the others—they'd *croak* if they saw Pan! They wouldn't know who to make fun of first.

A hand reached down and pulled me up. It was Stan.

Desperately, I scanned the sea of Pants around us. "Where's Mr. Slomin? Where did all these aliens come from?"

He looked cross. "Devin, you're on Pan now. *We're* not aliens. *You* are."

I wracked my brain. "Fungus! He can track anything!" I put two fingers in my mouth and whistled. Good old Fungus came running. But when I sent him out into the crowd, he got into a conversation with the first Pant he ran into.

"Not that guy!" I cried. "Find Mr. Slomin! Aww—"

"All those years on Earth he's had nobody to talk to," Stan reminded me. "He's probably saved up a lot to say."

I had one last chance. I took a deep breath and bellowed, "Stop that earthling!!"

Instantly, two sets of arms grabbed me from behind.

"Consider yourself stopped," came the voice of Zgrbnys over my left shoulder. "Thanks to brilliant quick thinking by me."

"Excuse me," countered Gthrmnys over my right, "*I* stopped him first."

"No, *I* stopped him first."

"Not *me*!" I howled. "The *other* earthling! Mr. Slomin!"

Zgrbnys glared at me. "Smarty-Pants execute instructions exactly and perfectly. If you want someone to read your mind, call the Seersuckers."

"They give away free lollipops," added Gthrmnys, as the two walked off in a huff.

"It's too late now," I moaned. "We'll never find Mr. Slomin in this crazy crowd. Oh, man, we broke Rule 4!"

"Rule 4?" questioned Stan.

"Always stay on your teacher's good side," I explained miserably. "You know, joke around with him, volunteer for school plays and stuff. And— oh, yeah—don't get him lost on a strange planet!" I looked around frantically. "Aw, man, now Fungus is gone, too! This place is nuts! Why is everybody so frantic?"

Stan shrugged. "Remember, we Pants have only two weeks in the office to store up fifty weeks of vacation time. We have to work incredibly hard. See? There are Suit Pants rushing to meetings; Short Pants on their way to school. Look—" He pointed. "There are the Fire Pants battling a blaze with their Panty-Hose. Everybody is busy on Pan."

REgULAr or CONTrOL-TOP?

"What about those guys?" I asked. Several young Pants sat right in the middle of the carpeted street. "They don't look busy to me. I think half of them are asleep."

"Oh, those are the Slacks," Stan explained. "They're the laziest citizens of Pan. They've turned off their nasal processors and gone back to a simpler way of life. They relax all day, eating the many loitering tickets the Police Pants give them."

My head was spinning. I had to calm down. It's easy to start thinking of Pan as a big joke because of Under-Pants, Panty-Hoses, the Big Zipper, and junk like that. But there was nothing funny about Earth's future being on the line.

I thought back to my Rules of Coolness.

☛ **Rule 15:** When you've got a million things to do, focus on the most important one.

Sure, we had to find Fungus and Mr. Slomin. But a fat lot of good that would do us if we couldn't save Earth. That had to be Job One.

"How do we get in to see the Grand Pant?" I asked Stan.

"We have to go to the Planetary Bureau," Stan

explained. "That's where the government is."

"Okay," I said. "Where's your car?"

"Car?" Stan repeated. "There are no motor vehicles on Pan."

I frowned. "Then how are you supposed to get anywhere?"

"In a Jumper." Stan led me down an alley away from the crowd. My eyes fell on a small, velvet-covered sofa right next to a sign that said PANTS-PORTATION.

I took a seat beside Stan on the couch. "This is pretty cool," I told him. "On Earth you have to stand while waiting for the bus. When does the Jumper come?"

"It's already here," Stan replied.

I looked around. "No, it isn't. There's nothing here but this cou—"

Suddenly, our sofa launched itself straight up. With a soft whistling sound, it soared a thousand feet in the air. The speed was dizzying. I felt like my stomach was down around my socks.

I'm amazed I didn't throw up.

Chapter 11
#1 THE BELTWAY

"*Aaaaaaaaaah!!*" I shrieked.

"Sorry," said my exchange buddy. "I, Stan, should have remembered that Earth furniture is the nonflying kind."

"Don't they have seat belts on these things?" I rasped. If I fell off this couch, there wouldn't be enough left of me to send home in a test tube!

"Destination?" came a voice from the armrest.

"Planetary Bureau," said Stan.

And we hurtled forward at ninety miles an hour. My stomach shifted from my socks to the back of my throat.

I had to admit the view was pretty nice—pink sky, orange mountains, yellow lakes, red canyons.

73

I pointed. "Hey, look! You've got the Goodyear Blimp on Pan!"

"Not exactly," replied Stan, tight-lipped.

As we passed by the big balloon, I was able to read the sign on the side: VISIT BEAUTIFUL MERCURY.

"Shakespeare!" I muttered under my breath.

From high up, I could see dozens of that cheater's billboards all over Levi-Strauss. COME TO MERCURY—IT'S LIKE A SAUNA OUT HERE; MERCURY—NUMBER ONE UNDER THE SUN; LET YOUR BLOOD BOIL ON MERCURY. Wherever we went, an annoying jingle played over and over:

> *A hot rock with a cool view,*
> *Mercury's the place for you.*

And then we were dropping out of the pink sky—a thousand feet straight down. I recontacted my stomach on the way.

Just when it seemed like we were about to be smashed into a million pieces, our Jumper slowed down and we got off the couch and stepped into the carpeted street.

I was so dizzy that I fell on my face three times before my head finally cleared.

We were right in front of a huge building: #1 The Beltway. Carved in the stone wall was E PANTIBUS ZIP'EM.

"'Out of many Pants, one Big Zipper,'" Stan translated. "That's the motto of our planet."

I felt a little shiver. If Earth was going to be saved, it would be right here. This was the place, and now was the moment.

It's a big deal to get an appointment with the Grand Pant. You have to fill out a lot of forms. Stan came back from the clerk with a wheelbarrow full of paper.

"You've got to be kidding," I grumbled. "Mr. Slomin doesn't give this much homework in a year."

"Don't be such a sofa turnip," Stan chided. "Okay, here's question one: What is your shoe size?"

I blew my stack. "Shoe size? What do they need to know *that* for? You don't even *wear* shoes on Pan!"

"Devin, this is for the Grand Pant!" Stan exclaimed. "Do you think it would be easy to get in to see a president or a prime minister on Earth?"

"Oh, all right," I groaned. "Size six."

"I, Stan, am a size four. Question two: Why are manhole covers round? That's a trick question. Only the Smarty-Pants, the Under-Pants, and the Grand Pant himself know that."

"What about Zgrbnys and Gthrmnys?" I challenged. "They blanked on it on *Jeopardy!*"

Stan ignored me. "Question three: Do you suffer from bad breath, jock itch, hangnails, or athlete's foot?"

What about dandruff?

Heart sinking, I dug deep into the wheelbarrow and pulled out the very bottom sheet.

Question 400: In your own words, explain everything that's happened in your entire life. (You may write on the back if you need more space.)

After three very long hours, we pushed our wheelbarrow to the office of the Under-Pant in charge of forms.

This guy was huge. I mean, we've got some

pretty husky people on Earth, but the Under-Pant in charge of forms was like a water bed in a white dress shirt and polka-dot tie.

"Now, that's what I call an Extra-Large Pant," I whispered to Stan.

The Under-Pant stuck his head in our wheelbarrow and took an enormous bite out of the paper stack.

HE NEEdS TO gO ON a diET—aLL TracinG PaPEr.

"*No-o-o-o-o-o!*" I sprang forward to save our work.

But the guy must have been part vacuum cleaner, too. He just kept stuffing his face. By the time I finally managed to pull the wheelbarrow away, it was empty.

I was enraged. "Why did you eat all our forms?"

He rolled his eyes at me. "What did you expect me to do—read them?"

"Yeah!"

He was shocked. "But I'd starve! Besides, if I read the forms, I'd have to let people in to see the Grand Pant."

"But isn't that the whole point of your job?" asked Stan.

"Oh, no," the Under-Pant said seriously. "My job is to keep people away from the Grand Pant. He never sees anybody. He's far too important."

"But this is an emergency!" Stan pleaded. "A whole planet's future is at stake."

"Oh, all right," sighed the Under-Pant. He stuck a pudgy finger up his nose. Come back at four-thirty—"

"Hooray!" I cheered.

"On May sixth," the water bed went on.

"May sixth?!"

"In the year 2168," the Under-Pant finished.

There was a polite knock at the door.

"Forsooth," came a voice. "Might I poppeth in to see His Most Tailored Majesty?"

The big Under-Pant leaped to his feet. "Sir! May the Crease be with you! What an honor! Go right in!"

"Wait a minute!" I exploded. "How come *he* doesn't have to wait till 2168?"

Then I got a look at the guy in the doorway. Round face, clipped beard, all that forsooth stuff. The newcomer was none other than *Shakespeare!*

I instantly thought of about ten new Rules of

Coolness just by looking at him. Stuff like: **Don't wear leotards**, and **Pointy slippers are for elves**. This guy put the double *E* in "dweeb."

I grabbed that sneak by his white ruffled collar. "You dirty rotten low-down back-stabbing crook—"

He addressed Stan. "Greetings, Agent Mflxnys. And this young knave must be Devin Hunter." Playfully, he reached over and poked at the garage-door opener on my belt. He laughed. "Thy device remindeth me of Earth. It looketh pretty, but it doeth nothing."

Stan spoke up. "Agent Shkprnys, you promised Earth an extension. Yet you traveled to Pan and closed the deal for Mercury. I, Stan, don't understand."

Shakespeare shrugged. "I remembereth not any extension."

"Liar, liar, pants on fire!" I shouted. "You double-crosser! What about 'To thine own self be true'?"

That rotten Shakespeare laughed right in my face. "To mine own self I was true, earthling. Thine own self is thy problem." And he waltzed straight through the door and in to see the Grand Pant.

I grabbed Stan and tried to follow, but the Under Pant in charge of forms blocked our way. We bounced off that water bed stomach like a couple of Ping-Pong balls.

"Aw, come on!" I wailed. "You let Shakespeare through!"

"Shkprnys is a legend," the Under-Pant explained.

"Devin is considered a legend on Earth," Stan wheedled.

"Yeah . . . I . . . won a lot of merit badges in Cub Scouts!" I blustered.

"How can you two compare yourselves to Shkprnys the One and Only?" the Under-Pant said scornfully. "You're barely out of kindergarten."

"Kindergarten?" I cried. "Stan is 147 years old!"

"Exactly," the Under-Pant said smugly. "On Pan, kindergarten lasts until you turn ninety. You don't get out of diapers before your twenty-first birthday."

Boy, was I mad. I'm not usually a mean person. But if I didn't blow off steam, my head was going to explode. I narrowed my eyes and said the cruelest thing I could think of to a big-shot Pant. **"You're so dumb that I'll bet you don't even know why manhole covers are round!"**

Stan shot me a horrified look, but I didn't care. If my planet was going out past Pluto, I had more important problems than insulting a water bed.

All at once, the Under-Pant threw his huge head into his chubby arms and started *sobbing*!

"I'm ruined!" he howled. "It was only a matter of time before people found out!"

I guess Pants take their manhole covers pretty seriously.

Chapter 12
FILET OF PHONE BOOK

Stan was shocked. "You don't know, *either*?"

"You can't threaten me!" the big Under-Pant blubbered. "Go ahead! Tell the whole planet! I still won't let you in to see the Grand Pant!"

He outweighed us by a couple of tons. What could we do? We got out of there.

When we were back on the crowded Beltway, I turned to Stan. "Now what?"

His fried-egg eyes looked tragic. "Only the Grand Pant has the power to change the decision to pick Mercury. I, Stan, am sorry, Devin."

I was horrified. "You mean there's no chance for Earth?"

At that moment, a small wooden stick came sailing through the air and hit me right in the chest.

"Woof!" came a gruff voice.

Through the crowd barreled a burly figure in a St. Louis Cardinals baseball uniform. He ran right up to us and snatched the stick off the carpet. It was Mark McGwire.

"Mgwrnys!" exclaimed Stan. "What are you doing?"

"Staying in shape in the off-season," replied the home run king. "My new trainer suggested fetching sticks."

"What new trainer?" I asked suspiciously.

"Your dog, Fungus," he explained. "He had a lot of great exercises for me. Too bad there aren't any fire hydrants here on Pan.

Baseball is going to the dogs.

Hey, how come you guys look so upset?"

Sadly, Stan told him about Shakespeare's double-crossing. "And now we can't get an appointment to see the Grand Pant. We can't even get a message to him."

The great slugger shrugged. "*I* can."

"How?" I asked.

McGwire reached into his duffel bag and took out his bat and a baseball. He handed the ball to Stan. "Got a pen?"

Stan wrote:

Your Most Tailored Majesty,

Agent Shkprnys cheated! Earth is still in the running for resort planet. I promise to explain everything tomorrow.

Your faithful travel agent on Earth,

Agent Mflxnys

P.S. Urgent!

I still didn't get it. "But how are you going to send this ball to the Grand Pant?"

"His Most Tailored Majesty lives in the penthouse of the Planetary Bureau," McGwire explained. He drew back his bat and tossed the ball up in front of him.

POW!

On Earth it would have been a seventhousand-foot home run. The ball took off like a rocket. It soared high up the side of the building until I lost it in the pink sky. And then—

CRASH!!!

Stan went white to the ears. "You broke the Grand Pant's window!"

Quickly, the home run king packed his bat away. "If anybody asks," he mumbled, "I never left Earth." And he shouldered his duffel and disappeared into the crowd.

"Don't worry," I told Stan. "I broke Roscoe's window once. It wasn't too expensive."

He looked nervous. "But the Grand Pant's window was a gift from the legendary frosted glassmakers of the Milky Way."

PEOPLE WhO LiVE iN gLass hOUSES ShOULdN'T gET ELECTED GRaND PaNT.

"Oh—well, baseball players make a lot of money." I changed the subject. "Come on, let's look for Fungus and Mr. Slomin, okay?"

"Soon," promised my exchange buddy. "Right now, I, Stan, require food."

All at once, I realized I was starving, too. We hadn't eaten anything since dinner before the Smarty-Pants went on *Jeopardy!* It seemed like a year ago.

"Okay, let's eat." I frowned. "Do they have Burger King on Pan?"

Stan put his finger up his nose. "We're in luck, Devin! Can you believe that we're here during the two weeks my mother isn't on vacation? She's a fantastic cook."

So we grabbed another Jumper—a love seat with flowery throw cushions. We flew to Stan's house in the Capri District. This time I only fell down once after we landed. I was kind of proud of myself for that.

Stan stuck his nose in the lock at 28 Inseam Avenue. There was a click, and the door swung wide.

"Mom?"

Their reunion was pretty emotional. On Earth it would have broken a few of my Rules of Coolness. But when you get to be 147, I guess you've earned the right to dweeb it up a little when you see your mom after a long trip.

Finally, the mushy stuff was over, and I got my first good look at Mrs. Mflxnys. I did a double take.

"Stan!" I blurted. **"Your mother looks exactly like the Mona Lisa!"**

"She *is* the Mona Lisa," Stan said seriously.

"What?!"

"I mean she was the model for the 'Mona Lisa,'" Stan amended. "She was on Earth as a Training Pant even before Shakespeare."

"But how did you get to be the Mona Lisa?" I asked Stan's mom. "Did you win a contest?"

Mrs. Mflxnys laughed. "I was stationed in a country called Italy. One day, a very nice man named Leonardo da Vinci asked if he could paint my portrait, and—" She gave me a half smile. "And it came out quite well."

"Quite well?" I cried. "Every kid on Earth has to learn about that picture for art class! It's the most famous painting of all time!"

"Devin," Stan chuckled. "the 'Mona Lisa' is a very nice try for an earthling artist. But naturally, one of the Painter Pants could do a much better job with his nasal processor."

I had to agree that nasal processors were pretty handy gadgets. That gave me an idea. "Hey, Stan, while we're on Pan, do you think *I* could get a nose computer? I mean, eighty-five thousand light-years is a long way. I wouldn't want to leave without a souvenir."

Stan looked bewildered. "Where would you put a nasal processor?"

I shrugged. "Up my schnoz, same as you."

"That's impossible," Stan told me. "An earthling's head is filled with brains, so there's no room for anything else."

"Don't Pants have brains?" I asked.

"Of course. Two of them," said Stan. "They're behind our knees."

CɑLL thE OrthOPEdist. I NEEd brɑiN surgEry.

"Let's have dinner," suggested Mrs. Mflxnys.

Hooray! Boy, was I famished. "I could eat a horse!" I promised Stan.

He didn't get the joke. "Why would you ingest a large equestrian mammal?"

But when we got to the kitchen, I realized the joke was on me. Heaping plates of food covered the table. It was all paper.

"What *is* this?" I heaved.

"A meal fit for a king-sized Pant!" crowed Stan. "Filet of phone book with fountain-pen ink gravy. Stir-fried newsprint with cardboard florets. And for dessert, Dictionary Delight with confetti sprinkles and white-out sauce on the side."

I gagged.

Chapter 13

TWELVE THOUSAND NEW E·MAILS

Let's just say that I didn't eat a really big dinner. Paper isn't my idea of a tasty treat. Mostly, I just pushed the stuff around my plate to make it look smaller. I'm kind of an expert at that from liver night at my own house.

But for Stan, it was his first home cooking since he'd left for Earth. He was like a starving shark. Even after Mrs. Mflxnys had gone to bed, he sat at the table, attacking his fourth helping of Dictionary Delight.

What a sweet tooth.

I was worried. "You know, Stan, even if we do get in to see the Grand Pant tomorrow, why should he believe us? We can't prove Shakespeare cheated."

"We'll just have to show him that Earth is the superior planet," Stan mumbled, his mouth full of paper shreds. "If only we had done our social studies project! Then we'd have lots of terrific things to say about Earth and the human race."

"We need Mr. Slomin," I said earnestly. "He's a social studies expert. Maybe we should check the newspapers to see if there's a story about a nut-job earthling running around town."

"Devin," Stan chided me, "we could never have newspapers on Pan. They'd be eaten before anyone could even read the headlines. We get our

news from a vast computer web of information."

"You mean the Internet?" I asked.

He chuckled. "On Pan, we use the Internet to pass notes in preschool. I, Stan, am talking about the Overall. It's the network of every single nasal processor on Pan."

He stuck his finger up his nose. "Access the Overall." He frowned. "Uh-oh. I, Stan, have twelve thousand new E-mails to read. That's what I get for traveling to the other side of the galaxy."

"Never mind that," I said sternly. "Is there anything about an earthling on the loose? And maybe an Earth dog? If I go home without Fungus, I may as well not go home."

"Hmmm." Stan frowned. "All the chat rooms are clogged up with stories about a hilarious new street comedian. They've nicknamed him the Clown Pant."

"Have you ever heard of this guy?" I asked.

"He just started appearing today," Stan replied, twisting his finger as he worked his nose computer. "He shows up somewhere and does a routine that has everyone rolling on the carpet. Then he disappears just as suddenly. No one even knows his real name. Wait a minute—I'm getting a message."

He ran over and plugged his nose into a socket. There was a flicker, and then the entire wall turned into a giant TV screen.

The picture was fuzzy at first, but the figure of a man slowly started to come into focus.

"Mr. Slomin?" I asked the giant-sized image that was blurring all around us.

The picture became clearer. My heart sank. It wasn't our teacher. In fact, it was the last guy in the universe I wanted to see just then.

Chapter 14
DOUBLE·CROSSETHED!

My most *un*favorite Pant—Shakespeare.

"O Agent Mflxnys, Agent Mflxnys, wherefore art thou, Agent Mflxnys?"

Stan stepped out into the middle of the room. "Here I am, Agent Shkprnys."

"Forsooth! May the Crease be with thee!"

"May a runaway asteroid make a crease in your ugly face," I muttered under my breath. I'm not the forgiving type.

Even Stan was pretty fed up with Shakespeare by this time. "I, Stan, realize that you are a Pant whose belt loops would be hard to fill. But we're very upset at how you tricked us."

"I knoweth this," said Shakespeare sadly from the wall. "Methinks I feel like a cad. I shall maketh this contest fair again."

"How?" asked Stan.

"Forsooth," he replied, "the Grand Pant is a personal friend. On the morrow, when the clock striketh noon, come to the Planetary Bureau, and I shall gettest thee a meeting with His Most Tailored Majesty."

Stan glowed with happiness. "Oh, Agent Shkprnys, I, Stan, am sorry I ever doubted you. You truly are the One and Only! Thank you so much!"

"Mentioneth it not," said Shakespeare. "Until the morrow then. Forsooth!"

He faded out, and THE ENDE appeared on the wall.

"I don't trust him," I declared. "Not after he bamboozled us like that."

"Relax," Stan insisted. "He said he was sorry."

I was still nervous. Rule 32 says: If a guy burns you once, don't give him a chance to do it again.

But we had to go along with Shakespeare's plan. After all, what choice did we have?

We stayed up half the night searching the Overall for Fungus and Mr. Slomin. We found nothing. What lousy luck that this Clown Pant guy showed up at exactly the same time we did! Nobody wanted to talk about anything else.

In the morning, we said good-bye to Mrs. Mflxnys.

Farewell, Mona!

"I'm so glad you boys found me at home," she told us. "I leave for another vacation today. I've got the most exciting trip planned. I'm going to Mercury."

"Mercury?" we chorused.

"It was discovered by Shkprnys himself," she gushed. "I can't wait to see the rings of Saturn!"

"Aw, Mom," Stan whined. "Why did you have to pick *there*? Can't you go back to the Horsehead Nebula for the annual Naysayers Convention? Or what about the Ring Nebula? It's very shiny this time of year."

She gave him that famous Mona Lisa half smile. "It's too late. I've already snorted my ticket."

"Well, all right," Stan told her. "But I, Stan, wouldn't count on that view of Saturn. **There just might be a big blue planet in the way!**"

On the jump back to town on a leather sofa bed, I was really nervous. I didn't trust

Shakespeare as far as I could throw him. I was pretty sure he wasn't going to show up.

But as our Jumper set us down in front of the Planetary Bureau, there he was, ruffled collar, leotard and all. He was waving at us and calling something. What was he saying?

"Forsooth! There they are! The vile knaves who broketh the Grand Pant's window! **Arresteth them!**"

Police Pants were running at us from all directions. Before I knew it, we were both in handcuffs.

"I'm a cuffed Pant," Stan said in disbelief.

I was so mad I could hardly see straight. "I'll get you for this," I seethed at Shakespeare.

He laughed in my face. "I quaketh with fear, earthling. Forsooth, a planetary tug-ship is already in the Pan-Ama Canal on its way to taketh Earth out past Pluto. When the clock striketh three, thy planet shall be a large blue Popsicle."

I stuck out my jaw. "I read *Romeo and Juliet*," I growled. "It really, really stank."

Chapter 15

TWO HUNDRED YEARS IN PRISON

"Well, I can't believe it's come to this," I said miserably. "We're in jail."

"We Pants call it the Planetary Holster," Stan informed me.

"Holster, hoosegow, slammer." I moaned. "It's still jail."

I turned blazing eyes on Stan. "Why can't Police Pants take fingerprints like everybody else?"

"Nose-printing is a far more efficient way to keep track of criminals on Pan," Stan explained.

I scrubbed at the black ink on my nose. "It's pretty embarrassing, you know!" Until you have to bend over and press your

What happens if you get a NOSE job?

schnoz on an ink pad, you don't know what it is to feel like an idiot.

A Pan jail isn't very much like an Earth prison. There are no bars and no cells. It seems like you could just make a break for it. But the prison uniform is a wide metal belt. If you try to escape, you get sucked back by a giant magnet in the rear of the holding cell.

"We'll get out of here," Stan promised. "We have to if we're going to save Earth."

"What's the point of saving Earth?" I grumbled. **"When my parents find out I was in jail, it'll be the end of the world anyway."**

"All right, you menaces to society!" called the sergeant. "Lunch!"

A metal tray came clattering across the cement floor.

Our only fellow prisoner, an old Pant named Quxfthnys, took a bite and gagged. "Blecch! This is cruel and unusual punishment! How do they expect us to eat this garbage?"

He slid the tray over to Stan, who made a face. "It's inhuman. It's un-Pant, even."

I peered over Stan's shoulder. My eyes nearly

popped out of my head. A mountain of chili nachos towered over a piping hot pepperoni and double-cheese pizza. French fries and onion rings surrounded three hamburgers with the works. For dessert there was a giant gooey chocolate cake. And best of all, not a piece of paper in sight.

I'm not embarrassed to say I ate like a pig.

Stan was horrified. "Devin, how can you think about food at a time like this?"

I'M GETTING HUNGRY JUST READING IT!

"I'm starving," I defended myself between mouthfuls. "Remember, I can't just dump out a filing cabinet and chow down like you."

"It's almost two o'clock! The tug-ship is barely an hour away from Earth!" He snatched up the metal tray, sending onion rings flying.

"Hey!" I snapped. "I wasn't finished yet!"

My exchange buddy dumped out the rest of lunch and banged the tray on the floor. "Sergeant!" he yelled. "When do we get our bail hearing?"

"Pipe down in there!" the sergeant ordered. "We have to wait for the Under-Pant in charge of forms to come over and eat your paperwork."

"But we've got to get to the Planetary Bureau!" Stan protested. "It's urgent!"

"You should have thought of that before breaking the Grand Pant's window!" the sergeant shot right back.

"You broke the Grand Pant's window?" asked Quxfthnys. "Wow! I'm a small-time crook compared with you. I'm only here for wearing shoes on a public carpet."

Miserably, we sat there in the slammer, watching Earth's final hour tick away. Two-

fifteen. Two-thirty. I wondered if I'd ever see my house again. And if I did, would it be frozen into a block of ice on a dark, frostbitten planet?

"All right!" barked the sergeant. "Mflxnys and Hunter. You're charged with destroying the personal property of the Grand Pant. This crime carries a penalty of two hundred years in prison."

My giant lunch lurched in my stomach. *"Two hundred years?!"*

Stan raised his hand. "Uh, sir? Could my friend possibly get an earthling discount? Humans don't live two hundred years."

> IF YOU CAN'T DO THE TIME, DON'T DO THE CRIME.

"That's no excuse!" snapped the sergeant. "Fruit flies only live two weeks, but we just sentenced one to ten years for buzzing around the Grand Pant's watermelon. Now—how do you plead?"

"Not guilty!" I squeaked. "It was Mark McGwire!"

That broke Rule 9: Never rat out your friends. I'll make it up to you, Mr. McGwire. I'll let my dog turn you into a *star*.

"Let's see what you say after a few hours of interrogation," he snarled.

Interrogation! I didn't like the sound of that. Were we going to be tortured? Beside me, Stan was starting to sweat.

The sergeant reached for me, and I almost jumped out of my skin. But he was only unlocking my metal belt. "All right, Earthling," he growled, "*promise* you won't try to escape."

I frowned. Promise? "Oh, sure," I said. "I promise."

"I promise, too," added Stan readily.

And he freed us. I was amazed. If Earth ran its jails this way, they'd be empty.

As the sergeant marched us through the halls of the Holster, I whispered to Stan. "Get ready to make a run for it!"

Stan was appalled. "But, Devin! We *promised*!"

"And he believed us," I chortled. "What a chump!"

"But a Pant's word of honor is even more important than his nose!" Stan protested.

"Earth is more important than anything!" I hissed. I looked around. "This place is crawling

with Police Pants. How can we create a diversion?"

At that very moment, one of the younger
cops pointed out the window. "Hey, look, everybody! It's the Clown Pant!"

Pandemonium broke loose. People were cheering and patting each other on the back. Then
every single Police Pant in the building stampeded
straight out the front door.

Quxfthnys was hot on their heels. "Come on,

guys!" he called to us. "It's the Clown Pant! He's the funniest Pant in the universe!" He joined the rush, but two feet from the exit, his metal prison belt got too far from the giant magnet. With a *zap*, he was yanked back to the cell like a dog who has run out of leash. "Twill!" he exclaimed dejectedly.

Stan started to follow the Police Pants into the crowd of onlookers that had formed around the famous comedian.

I grabbed his arm. "What are you, nuts? Let's get out of here!"

"But it's the Clown Pant!" he cried.

I was furious. "I don't care if it's the whole circus! *Run!*"

"Devin, *look!*"

He got an arm around my shoulders and wheeled me about. I gawked. I goggled. I almost died.

It was the Clown Pant, all right. He stood at the center of a huge cheering crowd of adoring fans. Was he a jovial entertainer with a million-dollar smile? No way! He wasn't even a Pant!

He was Mr. Slomin!

REALLY?

Chapter 16

A WEREWOLVES CONVENTION

I couldn't believe my eyes. *Mr. Slomin?!*

"How could Mr. Slomin be a comedian?" I asked in amazement. "He isn't funny! He never even smiles—not unless he's giving somebody six months of detentions."

Then the famous and celebrated Clown Pant began his comedy routine.

"A terrible revenge is coming!" declared Mr. Slomin, his face bright red. "It's coming from the planet Earth!"

The crowd roared with laughter.

"What's so hilarious about that?" I asked Stan.

Stan looked apologetic. "Well, I, Stan, love Earth, but it *is* Q-class, and—no offense—couldn't fight its way out of its own atmosphere."

I was still too shocked to be insulted.

Mr. Slomin was just getting warmed up. "Right now the armies of all the great nations are combining into an invasion force!"

The laughter swelled like someone had bumped up the volume. A loud guffaw escaped Stan. He tried to cover it up as a cough.

"I'm sorry." He chuckled. "But no planet has *armies* anymore. **That's so second millennium.**"

"One of these days," promised Mr. Slomin, waving his arms like a wild man, "your skies will darken with our stealth bombers, AWACs, smart bombs, and cruise missiles!"

Well, that must have been the most hilarious joke of all. Those Pants hurled themselves down on the rug and howled. It sounded like a werewolves convention during a full moon. Even Stan couldn't hold back a pretty big laugh.

"Let me guess," I said sarcastically. "Cruise missiles are out of style, too?"

Duh.

"No, we still use them," he gasped, wiping the tears from his eyes. "To deliver Chinese menus! Oh, this is so funny!"

"Well, the show's over," I said firmly. "We've got to get Mr. Slomin to the Planetary Bureau. He's the only guy who can tell the Grand Pant all the great things about Earth."

As Mr. Slomin's hysterical audience rolled around on the carpet, we tiptoed through the crowd. I accidentally kicked one guy in the head, but he was laughing so hard, I don't think he even noticed.

ALL the WORLd LOVES a CLOWN.

"Cruise missiles!" he wheezed. "What are they going to attack us with? Chop suey?"

"Hold the noodles on mine!" wailed a lady next to him.

Mr. Slomin was still raving. "We'll show you who's a Q-class planet! We're class A, all the way! We're gonna—"

"Mr. Slomin!" I called. "Over here!"

"Devin!" Our teacher pulled me aside. "It's going to be easy for Earth to fight these aliens. They're morons. All they do is laugh. What a bunch of saps."

Poor Mr. Slomin. He honestly thought that Earth was going to war because Pan had kidnapped the president of the Clearview UFO Society.

"There's a better way!" I pleaded. "We're going to take you to a man called the Grand Pant. Can you tell him everything that's great about Earth and the human race?"

"Of course. I'm a social studies teacher." He dropped his voice to a whisper. "But is it wise to give them too much information about Earth? They could use it against us in the war."

"What war?" Stan asked in confusion. "How could Earth ever attack Pan? Earth doesn't even know that Pan exists; it has no way to reach Pan; and the odds of Earth defeating Pan are six trillion trillion to one. That would be harder than winning all fifty of your state lotteries and being stung to death by bees on the same day."

"You're just trying to scare Earth out of kicking your butts!" Mr. Slomin told Stan.

"If you can convince the Grand Pant how great Earth is," I insisted, "Earth will be in no danger from anything." I turned to the crowd. "Okay, folks, the show's over!" I announced.

"Go home and eat some Kleenex or something."

We got a standing ovation as we made our escape down the carpeted street, dragging Mr. Slomin along with us. I looked at my watch. Two-forty-five! **The tug-ship would be at Earth in only *fifteen minutes!***

"But, Devin," Stan protested as we ran, "how are we going to get in to see the Grand Pant? We don't have an appointment, remember?"

"We'll get in," I promised through clenched teeth. "Trust me."

At the Planetary Bureau, we strode right past the suckers filling out tons of paperwork. We stormed straight into the office of the Under-Pant in charge of forms.

The extra-large Pant leaped up and blocked the door when he saw us. "You again?" he sneered.

I had never felt so determined. I was an irresistible force of nature, like a tornado. "Out of my way, Jumbo!" I roared. "We're going in there, and nothing's going to stop us!"

"Hah!" The big Pant's many chins vibrated
with the booming of his voice. "What makes you
think you're important enough to get a meeting
with the Grand Pant?"

"Not *me!*" I exclaimed, putting an arm around
Mr. Slomin's shoulders. "Don't you know who
this is? Stand aside, Water Bed, and make way
for the one and only Clown Pant!"

Chapter 17

THE GREAT MILLENNIAL VAULT

"The Clown Pant?" The Under-Pant in charge of forms straightened his back and snapped a military salute which ended with his middle finger up his nose. A fifteen-foot-high door opened and he bellowed. "Sire, the fabulous and incomparable Clown Pant has come to perform for you!"

Stan was blown away. "This is it, Devin!" he hissed, pointing inside. "The Hanger!"

I frowned. "Why do they call it the Hanger?"

"It's where all the most important Pants hang out," Stan explained with awe and respect.

If you took a giant movie theater and covered every seat and every wall with gleaming gold leaf, then you'd have something that looked like the Hanger. The place was packed with Pants—

an ocean of white dress shirts and polka-dot ties. We were fixed in the stare of a thousand fried-egg eyes.

"Look," Stan whispered. "It's the Cabinet of Under-Pants, next to the Smarty-Pants Council of Wisdom. On the left, those are the Pedal Pushers and the Sweat Pants. Together, they're in charge of physical fitness for the whole planet. Now look to your right. Those are the Bell Bottoms, who sound the alarm in times of crisis. The Baggy Pants handle garbage disposal and carpet cleaning. The Parachute Pants forecast the weather for the Cargo Pants, who make sure all shipments and packages get where they're going. The Ski Pants control the polar regions. Beside the Press Gallery, where the Pressed Pants do their reporting, you'll see the Designer Jeans. They all have the same name, Devin. If you go to their office and call out, 'Hey, Jean,' every single one of them will come running. And there at the front"—his voice quivered with emotion—"is His Most Tailored Majesty, the Grand Pant."

That's ENOUgh PaNTS tO OPEN a TaiLor shOP!

I gawked in amazement. Not at the

115

Grand Pant. I mean, if you've seen one dweeb in a polka-dot tie, you've seen them all. But there, right at the great man's side, sat Fungus!

"Fungus!" I snapped. "Bad dog! I've been worried sick about you!"

The Grand Pant leaned over and barked something at Fungus.

"He's asking if Fungus is your owner," translated Stan.

"I'm *his* owner!" I snapped. "Dogs don't own people; people own dogs."

The Grand Pant frowned. "Hmmm. I thought dogs were in charge on Earth, followed by parakeets, mongooses, caterpillars, moss, and *then* humans."

"It's definitely humans, sire," Stan supplied. "But dogs come in second as man's best friend."

"As well they should," agreed the Grand Pant. "Why, Fungus knows knock-knock jokes that haven't even made it to this part of the galaxy yet." He turned to Mr. Slomin. "But I understand *you* are the master when it comes to jokes, Clown Pant. They say you can make a Pant laugh himself out of his pleats. Entertain us with your vast humor."

"This is it, Mr. Slomin," I urged. "Do it. Tell him how awesome Earth is."

It was just like social studies class. Mr. Slomin talked about the Pyramids, the Great Wall of China, the cathedrals of Europe, and the towering skyscrapers of today. He told the Grand Pant about the "can do" human spirit, from the invention of the wheel to Marco Polo and Columbus and the great voyages of discovery.

DID hE MENTION tHE INVENTION OF cHEap JOKES?

He was fantastic! He may have been a UFO freak and the weirdest teacher in school, but today he was my hero. I looked at the Grand Pant. *Nobody* could send us out past Pluto after a speech like this!

The leader of Pan gave a huge yawn. "This guy isn't funny. I haven't laughed once." He stood up. "Guards, remove these earthlings from the Hanger."

Oh, *no*! I checked my watch and freaked out. It was 2:55! The planetary tug would be at Earth in *five minutes*! All was lost! And my family, my town—everything I knew—was headed for the deep freeze!

A Police Pant grabbed me from behind. I shook myself free. I had never been so mad in my entire life. The future of a whole planet was at stake, but did the Grand Pant care? No! He sealed our fate with no more concern than he would give to clipping his toenails!

Well, I just started screaming insults at the guy. "You're a bum! Your mother wears army boots! I hate your guts! You stink! You're so stupid that—that—"

And suddenly, I remembered. Here on Pan, what was the worst thing you could say to somebody? If you really want to hurt a guy, you say, *"You don't even know why manhole covers are round!"*

I have never heard so many gasps of horror all at the same time. The floor shook as the entire government of Pan leaped to its feet in outrage. I thought Stan was going to disintegrate.

The Police Pant grabbed me again. "How dare you disrespect His Most Tailored Majesty?"

The outrage on the face of the Grand Pant melted away to reveal a look of deep sadness. "The earthling is right," he admitted after a moment. "I *don't* know why manhole covers are round."

Shock greeted this announcement. Half the government fainted into the arms of the other half. Fingers shot up noses as the Pressed Pants transmitted this breaking news to their bosses.

"What's more," the Grand Pant went on, "*nobody* knows. The secret has been locked away for centuries in the Great Millennial Vault."

All eyes turned to the corner of the Hanger. There stood a faintly glowing safe the size of a washing machine. It was surrounded by a short wooden fence marked PANTS AT WORK.

Stan found his voice at last. "Forgive me, sire, but I, Stan, have been off the planet. Wasn't the Great Millennial Vault supposed to be opened at the coming of the year 2000?"

The Grand Pant nodded. "Yes, but it's stuck,"

he replied. "And the Smarty-Pants aren't clever enough to get it open. Inside lies the answer to the question that has baffled our people for two thousand years."

I went ballistic. "Are you crazy?! **Are you double-crazy?!** Five billion earthlings are going to freeze in two minutes and you people are worried about stupid manhole covers?!"

I admit it. I went nuts. I pulled the garage-door opener off my belt and flung it with all my might at the Grand Pant.

It bounced off his royal nose and landed on the floor. He staggered slightly, and his Most Tailored Toe stepped right on the button.

There was a *bloop*! like a car alarm and—I stared—

With a loud creaking sound, the door of the Great Millennial Vault swung open!

Chapter 18

WHY MANHOLE COVERS ARE ROUND

I couldn't believe it. Pants were thousands of years ahead of us, and yet none of them could crack that vault. But my plain old earthling garage-door remote control just so happened to work on exactly the right frequency! There stood the Great Millennial Vault, door wide open.

Jaws dropped in amazement. Fingers fell out of noses. Man, you could have heard a pin drop in the Hanger at that moment!

The Grand Pant reached into the vault and pulled out a small scroll. He unrolled it and read it. When he looked at me, there were tears in his eyes.

"The smartest of the Smarty-Pants were unable to open that vault," he said emotionally. "What is this miraculous device that has accomplished it so easily?"

"It was invented by an earthling!" I cried. **"Who's about to be frozen in"**—I looked at my watch and almost swallowed my tongue—**"five seconds!!"**

The Grand Pant put his finger up to his nasal processor. "This is a direct order from the First Nose. I am calling the tug-ship back from Earth."

I felt the greatest relief I've ever known. Now I understood what "in the nick of time" meant.

The Grand Pant smiled at me. "Any society that

Or, in the pick of time.

can create such a marvel must never be tampered with. Who knows what they might invent next? Maybe even bread that's already sliced when you buy it at the store."

A delighted *"Ooooh!"* rippled through the crowd.

"Sire!" Stan breathed. "Are you saying that—"

The Grand Pant nodded. "Earth will be Pan's newest vacation resort!"

"Na-a-a-a-ay!!" came an anguished cry.

Down the aisle of the Hanger sprinted Shakespeare. He ran in short, awkward steps, probably because his leotard was too tight.

I couldn't resist gloating a little. "What's the matter, Shakey? Having a rough day? Maybe you rented a blimp and a few thousand billboards all for nothing?"

That big cheater's face was bright red under his pointed beard. "Thy Most Tailored Majesty," he pleaded with his leader. "Forsooth, how canst thou rippeth me off this way?"

The Grand Pant shrugged. "Sorry, Shkprnys. I never did like Mercury. That place has no atmosphere."

And then William Shakespeare had a good old-fashioned temper tantrum, just like any two-year-old on Earth.

"Forsooth!" he wailed, throwing himself to the floor and pounding it with balled-up fists. "No fair! Thou art all a bunch of twill-heads! **This stinketh big-time!** *Now is the winter of our discontent!*"

I WANT MY VACATION PLANET!

The Grand Pant looked displeased. "This is

not the behavior I expect from the greatest travel agent in history."

But Shakespeare was out of control. "Thou art foul knaves who are not worthy of my talents! May thy next vacation be on a runaway asteroid bound for a dark nebula with cheesy hotels and recycled paper!"

"Take him away," the Grand Pant ordered the guards. "It's time for me to speak to all Pant-kind."

While Shakespeare was dragged out kicking

and screaming, the Pants in the Hanger put their fingers up their noses.

"It's the Emergency Coverall Broadcast System," Stan explained around his hand. "Throughout the galaxy, every single Pant has turned on his nasal processor to hear this."

In other words, it was the largest mass nose-pick of all time. **The Galactic Gross-out.**

"Citizens of Pan," the Grand Pant announced, "two thousand years ago, an important secret was lost to us. Today that secret was regained, thanks to a young earthling. Let me share this great truth with all of you. From now on, everyone from the wisest Smarty-Pants to the tiniest Diaper Pants will know the reason manhole covers are round. It's because a round manhole cover can never fall into the hole. No matter which way you turn it, it always fits perfectly."

What?!! Hundreds of Pants and at least one human (me) looked blank. No matter which way you turn it . . . ?

And then the teacher in Mr. Slomin finally came out.

"It's simple geometry," he explained, like he

126

was standing in front of class 4C, and not on the other side of the galaxy. "A square one could be tilted straight up, turned on a slant, and dropped inside. And it's true of every other shape—except a perfect circle. That's why manhole covers are always made round."

I got all excited for that?

A "Big deal!" died on my lips. All those Pants were clapping. And cheering. Some of them were standing on their chairs, screaming with excitement.

"Brilliant! Simply brilliant!" remarked the Grand Pant. "I declare a planetwide holiday. Let's all go on vacation!"

"The Pan-Pan Travel Bureau can start work on some long-weekend getaway specials," Stan added breathlessly.

That's when I must have overloaded. Chalk it up to being a gazillion miles from home. Or maybe it was Earth's close brush with the deep freeze. Whatever the reason, these aliens were driving me crazy. Weren't there any *important* things to think about?

"What's the matter with you people?" I

howled. "You've got spaceships, and nose computers, and the power of the Crease! But what do you waste your lives on? *Manhole covers*, for crying out loud! I mean, who cares? That would be like the president of the United States spending all his time worrying about why the handrail of an escalator always moves just a little bit faster than the part you stand on!"

Dead silence fell in the Hanger. The Grand Pant looked at me with keen interest. "That's true, young earthling," he said with a frown. "The handrail always *does* seem to go faster."

"That's not what I meant—" I began.

But the leader of Pan was lost in thought. "It's a mystery. An enigma. A conundrum. There must be an explanation. But what?"

"This is even more fascinating than manhole covers," said Stan in wonder.

"Smarty-Pants, put your best thinkers on the job," commanded the Grand Pant. "Top-drawer priority. I need the answer as fast as possible, maybe sooner."

"You'll have it within one hundred seventy-five years," guaranteed the head Smarty-Pant.

"And don't lock it in a vault this time!" the Grand Pant said peevishly.

Yeah, I know. They were totally missing the point. But when you're dealing with aliens, you can't always expect them to think the way you do.

That led me to a new rule of coolness, maybe the most important one of all:

☞ **<u>Rule 99:</u>** *It takes all kinds to make a galaxy.*

Chapter 19

CLASS A, ALL THE WAY

Hyperspace wasn't nearly as scary on the trip back to Earth. In fact, it was kind of fun—like a roller coaster that could go five hundred million miles per second. I'd like to see Space Mountain do that!

Of course, the main reason I enjoyed the trip home was because I was in a good mood. Everybody was. Stan and I were thrilled by the billboard we saw at the entrance to the Pan-Ama Canal:

VISIT EARTH
CLASS A, ALL THE WAY
WEEKEND PACKAGES AVAILABLE
3 DAYS/2 NITES—ONLY 350 PANTALOONS
(Gravity Not Included)
SNORT 1-800-BIG-BLUE

Mark McGwire was happy because Fungus had given him a brand-new off-season workout. Fungus was wagging his tail from two days of nonstop conversation. And Zgrbnys and Gthrmnys were content because they now understood why manhole covers are round.

"I knew it all along," Zgrbnys assured his partner. "I just wanted to see if *you* knew."

"I knew it, too," Gthrmnys defended himself. "I didn't say anything because I didn't want to make *you* feel bad."

"Then why didn't you answer the question on *Jeopardy!*?" I taunted. "Instead, you busted up the show and punched Alex Trebek in the mouth."

Both Smarty-Pants buried their faces in their ties.

"Quiet, earthling," mumbled Zgrbnys. "We are pondering the most difficult problem of the new millennium, the escalator handrail paradox. It is far too complex for your primitive, Q-class mind."

"We're not Q-class," Mr. Slomin insisted, but this time he was smiling. His "Class A, All the

Way" was the new tourist slogan for Earth, and
he was pretty proud of that.

And he was extra happy because this trip
proved he'd been right all along.

"I *knew* there were UFOs landing on Earth!"
he said with deep satisfaction. "I *knew* there
were alien races visiting us! Everybody called me
crazy, but I knew it was true! When I tell the
rest of the UFO Society—"

"Whoa!" I said quickly. "Mr. Slomin, I'm thrilled that you turned out to be right and all that. But this whole thing has to be kept secret."

"Absolutely not!" declared our teacher. "This is the breakthrough the UFO Society has been waiting for! We're going to put this story on the front page of every newspaper in the world!"

"But then Stan would get arrested!" I protested. **"The Air Force would do all kinds of—like—experiments on him!"**

Mr. Slomin folded his arms. "I can't let that stand in the way of the UFO Society," he said stubbornly.

Oh, *no*! Just when it seemed like we were out of the woods, here was a terrible dilemma.

"What are we going to do?" I whispered to Stan.

"Devin," he chided me, "don't panic. We have two Smarty-Pants with us. And they're even smarter than before because now they know why manhole covers are round." He turned to Zgrbnys and Gthrmnys in the pilots' chairs. "Can you use your mega-intelligence to think of a way to stop Mr. Slomin?"

"Naturally," said Zgrbnys. "We will focus a beam of pure energy to scatter the molecules of his brain over a million light-years of deep space."

"And," continued Gthrmnys, "we will fill the hole in his head with a cantaloupe. Then he will remember nothing about Pan."

I groaned. If you want a stupid answer, always ask a Smarty-Pant. "Any other ideas?"

I ALWAYS SUSPECTED MY TEACHER WAS A MELON-HEAD.

"You've got worries of your own, young man," Mr. Slomin informed me. "Your social studies project is overdue, and you haven't even chosen a topic yet."

"I have a solution," Stan said sadly. "I, Stan, am the problem. I must not return to Earth."

What? No Stan? My exchange buddy had only been around for three weeks, but he already felt as much a part of the family as Lindsay or Roscoe. Actually, *way* more than Roscoe. "But Earth is the new vacation planet!" I protested. "You have to get ready for all the tourists!"

"The Pan-Pan Travel Bureau will appoint another agent." He lowered his eyes. "I, Stan, have heard that Shakespeare is looking for a new job."

"Shakespeare?!" I almost spat out the name. **"That cheater isn't fit to carry your jock-strap!"**

"Devin," my exchange buddy chided me, "Shkprnys may not be a very honest Pant. But when it comes to the travel business, he has no equal."

"But who'll break all my Rules of Coolness?" I babbled. "Who'll eat our old phone books? Who'll pick his nose in front of everybody at school? Who'll be the biggest dweeb in Clearview?"

"I, Stan, will miss you, too," said my exchange buddy warmly.

"There might be another way," suggested Mark McGwire. "After we drop off Devin, Stan, and Fungus, we can take Mr. Slomin for an extra spin around the sun. This creates a small time warp. That way, Mr. Slomin will arrive on Earth a few minutes *before* he left."

Trying to understand time travel makes my brain hurt.

"And he won't remember anything," Stan said excitedly, "since it won't have happened yet! That's brilliant!" He turned to the Smarty-Pants. "Can it work?"

Zgrbnys looked disgusted. "Well, I suppose it can. Not as well as replacing his brain with a cantaloupe, of course. But it's worth a try."

By this time, Earth had appeared on the ship's screen, all blue, white, and breathtaking. Pan is okay, I thought to myself, but as planets go, **Earth is a supermodel**.

"You'll never know how close you were to the icebox, old buddy," I told the world.

And then we were going down. I watched the view change: continent, country, state, town, neighborhood, and finally my front yard. Home, sweet home never felt sweeter.

As soon as we stepped off the ship, Fungus beat a hasty retreat to his doghouse. I honestly wished I could have gone with him. I sure wasn't looking forward to explaining all this to my folks.

Then I heard my dad's voice from inside the house. "Why did Devin and Stan just bolt out of here?"

"Because they're crazy?" suggested Roscoe nastily.

The Smarty-Pants were right! The whole trip had taken only a few seconds! We were back at

the night Zgrbnys and Gthrmnys had gone on *Jeopardy!* In Earth time, we had just left the room.

I was about to stick the garage-door opener back in the Honda when I froze. For there, sitting cross-legged in our driveway, was Mr. Slomin.

"How could he be *here*?" I hissed at Stan. "We just left him on the ship! He can't be in two places at once!"

"The time warp!" Stan explained. "Since he went back in time a few extra minutes, he got here *before* us!"

I had to find out for certain. "Mr. Slomin," I asked, "are you okay? Do you remember what happened to you?"

The teacher was dazed and confused. "I'm not sure," he began shakily. "I was on my way to your house, and then—" He shrugged, eyes wide. "The next thing I knew I was here in your driveway." He winced in pain. "With a splitting headache."

"That's a common side effect of time travel," Stan whispered triumphantly.

Mark McGwire's plan had worked! That guy was wasting his time with baseball. He was a *genius*.

Mr. Slomin shook his head. "I have a few other memories, but they don't make any sense— something about underpants—"

That's what you get for journeying 85,000 light-years without a change of underwear.

"You probably meant to go home and change them," suggested Stan.

Our teacher thought it over.

"Yes. Yes, of course." His brow knit. "I seem to recall one last thing—an excellent presentation on the achievements of the human race."

I got a great idea. "Oh, that was our social studies project," I told him.

"Right," said Mr. Slomin fuzzily. "It took up your whole garage—"

Three sets of eyes turned to the garage. You could see through the window it was empty.

Mr. Slomin frowned. "What happened to your project?"

"We presented it already." I winked at Stan. "Don't you remember, Mr. Slomin? You gave us an A-plus!"

Someday when I'm ninety, and my best friend, Stan Mflxnys, is 228, I *just might* admit that we didn't really deserve that social studies grade.

But when you think about it, we saved a whole planet. If that isn't worth an A-plus, what is?

YOUR MUMMY is a NOSE PICKER

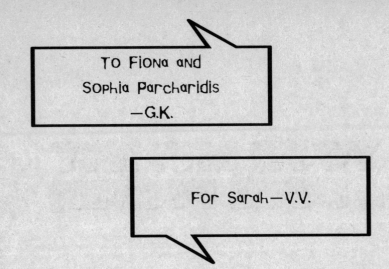

CONTENTS

Chapter 1

THE SCHNOZ•AHOLIC

✳ DEVIN HUNTER'S RULES OF COOLNESS ✳

☛ **Rule 25:** Don't give up, even when time is running out on you.

There could never be a better example of that than right now. The National Student Exchange Program was over. For the past three weeks, most of the fourth graders in our school had been hosting kids from other states. Now, as the visitors lined up to get on the bus to the airport, there were some emotional good-byes. Calista Bernstein hugged her partner, Wanda, and promised to E-mail her in California every day. Sam, a soccer nut from Minnesota, was heading a ball back and forth with his host, Tanner Phelps. Cody from Texas presented Joey Petrillo with a really cool brass belt buckle in the shape of the Lone Star State. And my exchange buddy, Stan Mflxnys, had his finger up his nose.

"Oh, *yuck!*" exclaimed Calista. "Stan, cut it out!"

Tanner groaned. "You're wasting your breath, Calista. The kid's a schnoz-aholic. Lucky for us, he'll be back in Pan tonight, where nose picking is the official town sport."

Tanner was our class bigmouth. But he was wrong on four counts. First, Stan wasn't a kid; he was a 147-year-old alien. Second, Pan wasn't a town in Illinois; it was a planet in outer space.

People from Pan are called Pants. Their president is the Grand Pant. His assistants are the Under-Pants. Their planet orbits a star in the constellation of the Big Zipper. It may sound like a comedy routine, but it's one hundred percent true. Stan even took me there once. I saw it with my own eyes.

Third, Stan wasn't really picking his nose. He was operating the tiny supercomputer that Pants have up their nasal cavities. A single nasal processor is stronger than all the

OF COURSE!

2

millions of computers on Earth put together. It does a lot more than word processing and surfing the Internet. With it, you can cut your lawn without ever touching a mower, or do your homework like magic. A nasal processor can cook a three-minute egg in a trillionth of a second. It's also a built-in cell phone—one that can call anywhere in the galaxy. Even home to Pan, eighty-five thousand light-years away.

Last but not least, Stan wasn't leaving. His assignment here on Earth had just begun. Stan was a travel agent, which is a very important job on Pan. Pants are the greatest tourists in the universe. They work two weeks per year and go on vacation for the other fifty—all except the employees of the Pan-Pan Travel Bureau. They spend all their time searching for new places for Pants to visit.

Stan was a great travel agent, too. Thanks to him, Earth was now Pan's newest resort planet, even though no one on Earth knew about it except me. Pants go on vacation in secret. Even now, there are Pant tourists on thousands of planets, pretending to be locals and taking in the sights.

Shhh! I'm goINg ON vacaTioN. . . .

These days, Earth was the hot spot. Every comet, nebula, and quasar in the galaxy had a billboard encouraging Pants to spend their hard-earned pantaloons on a trip here. Each day, spaceship loads of tourists were landing on every continent, ready to explore, relax, and party. And Stan was in charge of it all.

But now that the exchange program was over,

Stan had no reason to hang around Clearview anymore. He was supposed to leave, but he needed to stay. My house was his base of operations. I was the only Earthling who knew what Stan really was, so I was the only one who could work with him. A copy of my Rules of Coolness was being sent by nasal processor to every single Pant tourist. That was really important, because even though Pants are far more advanced than

we humans are, they really aren't very cool at all. They need help passing as Earthlings. I mean, even though Stan was my best friend, I had to admit that I'd never met a bigger nerd in my whole life.

It wasn't just the nose picking. Fashion was a little backward on Pan, too. Crew cuts were all the rage, along with glasses so thick that they make your eyes look like fried eggs. Pants' favorite food is paper. Their most popular leisure-time activity is sneezing—it has something to do with having a supercomputer up your nose. The hottest style in clothes is white dress shirts and polka-dot ties. A few of the Pants who have been living on Earth for years have learned to fit in a little better. But after a whole month here, **Stan still looked as if his picture belonged in the dictionary next to the word _dweeb_.**

So that was the problem. How could we keep Stan in Clearview to continue his work as the head travel agent on Earth?

Chapter 2

A MODEL PARENT

The last-minute handshakes were in full swing as we said good-bye to the visitors. Except Stan, that is. When you spend so much time with your finger up your nose, nobody wants to shake your hand.

HErE, shaKE MY gLOVEd haNd!·

Uh-oh! The other exchange buddies were filing onto the bus. I shuffled Stan to the back of the line. But what would we do once everybody else was on board?

Our teacher, Mr. Slomin, blew his whistle. "It's been a wonderful month," he announced. "I hope you'll go back to your home states and tell everybody about the warm welcome you received in good old Clearview, a very classy town—Stan, stop picking your nose!"

Stan dropped his hand. "Sorry, Mr. Slomin."

But of course Stan wasn't really picking. He was surfing the Pant Internet, the Overall. We had to find a Pant on Earth who was willing to come and pretend to be Stan's parent. Then he or she could ask Mr. Slomin if Stan could please remain in Clearview longer.

"Any luck?" I whispered.

"I, Stan, put out an APB."

I was impressed. "You mean an All Points Bulletin—like the police?"

He shook his head. "This is an All *Pants* Bulletin—wait!" He turned away from our teacher and stuck his finger up his nose again. "Good news. Agent Crfrdnys has responded to my APB. She's on her way now."

"I hope you told her to *hurry*," I hissed. "There's only one person in line ahead of you!"

Then it was Stan's turn. I broke about ten of my rules of coolness trying to stall for time. "Oh, Stan!" I wailed. "Don't go!"

I tried everything. I cried. I hugged him. I even threw myself to the ground and clamped my arms around his ankles. Then and there, I thought of a new rule to add when I got back to

my notebook: ☞ **Rule 102:** Don't make a fool of yourself in front of your entire class.

"All right, Devin," ordered Mr. Slomin. "That's enough. People have flights to catch." He disentangled me from Stan and led him onto the bus.

"One last thing," our teacher announced. "Since many of you will be flying on planes today, you'll have an excellent chance to watch the sky. We in the UFO Society have observed a great increase in spaceship activity lately. If you see anything, please call 1-888-UFO-SPOT."

Mr. Slomin also happened to be the president of the Clearview UFO Society. He stayed up all night every night, peering into his telescope for spaceships, and phoning to warn the Air Force. Luckily, the Air Force thought Mr. Slomin was a crackpot.

"Well," he told the driver, "it's time to go."

The doors of the school bus folded shut. Through the tinted windshield, I caught a panicked look from Stan. What were we going to do?

Chapter 3

THE OUT·OF·TOWNERS

"*Wa-a-a-ait!*" came a voice behind us.

Everybody wheeled around. A long silver stretch limo screeched into the parking lot.

"Stanley! Don't go! It's me—Mom!"

I let out a long breath. Crfrdnys had come through! We were saved!

A uniformed chauffeur got out and opened the passenger door. Out stepped Stan's "mother." I gawked. Everybody did. Mr. Slomin nearly swallowed his whistle.

It was supermodel Cindy Crawford!

I thought the bus would tip over from everyone rushing to one side to stare at Cindy Crawford. The kids on the lawn burst into applause. The goggle-eyed bus driver let Stan out.

"You mean Cindy Crawford is an *alien*?" I whispered incredulously.

Stan shrugged. "You didn't think a mere Earthling could look like that, did you?"

"Wow," I said. "I never knew you Pants were such an attractive species."

"It's simple technology," Stan explained in a low voice. "Before a big fashion show or photo shoot, Crfrdnys programs her nasal processor to make her extra-gorgeous."

I'd better explain how all this was even possible. When Pants come to Earth, they pose as normal humans. But since they have nose

computers, they're so fantastic at their Earth jobs that a lot of them become famous. Other Pants living on Earth include Michael Jordan, Mark McGwire, Leonardo DiCaprio, Regis Philbin, and two of the four Teletubbies.

Tanner was bug-eyed. "How can Cindy Crawford be your *mother*?" he asked Stan. "You don't even have the same name!"

Or the SOME MOLE!

"Oh, my real name is Cindy Mflxnys," Crfrd-nys explained. "I go by Crawford professionally. All the big modeling agencies are looking for girls with vowels in their last names."

Calista sidled up to Stan. "Do you think you could get your mom to give me an autograph?" she whispered.

"I, Stan, will try."

"Me, too!" added Joey. "Thanks, buddy!"

"No fair!" I exploded. "Five minutes ago everybody was making nose-picking jokes! Now you all act like Stan's best friends just because you found out his mom's famous!"

Mr. Slomin handed Cindy a piece of paper and a pen. "It's for my nephew," he gushed. "I'm—I mean, he's your *biggest* fan. Make it out 'To my favorite teacher, love and kisses, Cindy.'"

"Of course," she said, handing him the autograph. "Now I need a favor from you. I have some photo shoots coming up in Paris, Tokyo, and Neptune—"

"*Neptune?*" repeated the teacher.

"Neptune, *Vermont*," I put in quickly. "Big modeling community. Lots of photographers."

"So I can't be at home to take care of Stanley," Cindy went on. "Would it be possible for him to stay here a few more weeks?" She fixed her supermodel eyes on our teacher. "Please, pretty please, do this little favor for me?"

Mr. Slomin was the toughest teacher in school. He would stand up to Cindy Crawford. Heck, he would stand up to Godzilla! I held my breath.

"Of course, of course!" Then he added with a sneaky smile, "I'd be happy to keep an eye on that son of yours a little while longer."

So *that's* what our teacher was up to. Mr. Slomin didn't know Stan's true identity. But he had always suspected that there was some

Whoa, Mama!

connection between my exchange buddy and his UFO sightings.

After the bus left, Cindy stuck around to be "Class Mom" for the rest of the day. Then her chauffeur drove us home. I thought up a new rule of coolness on the spot: Limos rock! Man, this was the life!

"Excellent work, Agent Crfrdnys," Stan was saying. "I, Stan, am grateful. Now you merely have to convince Devin's family to let me stay."

The supermodel stuck her finger up her nose to fix her makeup. "Understood, Agent Mflxnys. Are they reasonable life forms?"

"Not really," Stan admitted. "But they have an Earth dog named Fungus who is very pleasant to talk to. He has a terrific sense of humor."

Nasal processors have something called a Pan-Tran translator, which allows Pants to speak any language, including Dog. According to Stan, Fungus was a regular laugh riot. I had to take his word for it, of course. To me, Fungus was the only member of our family who drank out of the toilet. If that little habit showed wit and intelligence, I just didn't get it.

I was kind of hoping that some of the neighbors would be out to see us pull up in a limo, but the block was deserted. Didn't it figure? There were always plenty of spectators on hand when Stan was drilling for oil up his schnoz. But now that we had something cool going on, no one was around.

I let Stan and Cindy into the house ahead of me. "Mom!" I called. "Guess what? Stan has company from—uh—out of town!"

"I know," came my mother's voice from the living room.

"You *know*?" How could she know? **Did they report on CNN that Cindy Crawford is the mother of a notorious nose picker?**

"I'm in here with Stan's uncles right now," Mom called.

"Not his uncles, his *mother*!" I exclaimed.

I stopped short. Side by side on the couch, each drinking a cup of tea and chewing on a paper napkin, sat a pair of Pants named Zgrbnys the Extremely Wise and Gthrmnys the Utterly Clever. We had told my parents they were Stan's uncles Zack and Gus, but they were really Stan's bosses from Pan. If they were here, that meant something was up. Something big!

DIDN'T I TELL YOU TO KEEP YOUR PANTS OFF THE COUCH!

Chapter 4

CUFFS WILL ROLL

Zgrbnys and Gthrmnys were members of a renowned group of supergeniuses known as the Smarty-Pants. Only the Grand Pant and his assistants, the Under-Pants, are more respected on Pan. To be a Smarty-Pant, you need an IQ so large that even you can't count that high. Stan once showed me a copy of the final exam at Smarty-Pants University. I would have flunked in a heartbeat. You have to recite the infinity times table, take apart a spaceship engine in minus one second, and figure out a way to move a class-A pulsar using nothing but duct tape, paper clips, and a number-two pencil.

"Hi, Uncle Zack! Hi, Uncle Gus!" I exclaimed, winking at the two Smarty-Pants. "Guess who's

here—Stan's mom! Your *sister*!"

"I have no sister," frowned Zgrbnys.

"And neither have I," added Gthrmnys.

I rolled my eyes. For a couple of geniuses, these guys could be thick as bricks.

"I, Stan, can explain—" my exchange buddy began.

But Cindy saved the day. "I'm actually their sister-in-*law*. Stanley's father—my husband—is their brother."

That's when Mom got her first look at Agent Crfrdnys. I thought her eyes would pop out of her head. *"Cindy Crawford!"* she cried. Then, to Stan, "She's your *mother?*"

Luckily, my family was so blown away at finding a supermodel in the house that Stan got the okay to stay as long as he wanted. They liked him anyway. In spite of his dweebiness, he was a really great guy. My parents were convinced he was a positive influence on me. Ever since he'd arrived, my room was clean, the leaves were raked, and all my household chores were done to perfection. Of course, Mom and Dad had no way of knowing it was all the work of an alien schnoz.

"I can't believe they bought it," I whispered to my exchange buddy. "Not one person has raised a single doubt that you're Cindy Crawford's son. Not even Roscoe."

My older brother gave me a hard time about everything. But today he was following Cindy around like her private butler, opening doors for her, and offering her stuff to eat and drink. He practically broke his neck climbing up on two chairs to get Mom's silver tray for her snack. It was pretty funny, because all he could find to put on it was a handful of stale Fritos.

"Since they can see no other reason why a famous model should be in their home," Stan concluded, "they must accept our fabricated explanation."

He had a point. Our story was pretty far-fetched. But could you imagine trying to explain who Cindy *really* was? ☛ **Rule 25:** Never resort to the truth when a good lie can save your bacon.

Dinner was a little wacky that night. Fungus, our cocker spaniel, spent the whole meal telling knock-knock jokes and doing his famous imper-sonation of the Grand Pant speaking Dog. This had Cindy and Stan howling with hysterics, but naturally, we humans only heard a lot of barking and laughing.

Who NEEdS TV?

The Smarty-Pants didn't get any of the jokes, so Fungus had to do plenty of explaining.

"Bad dog," scolded my little sister, Lindsay. "You shouldn't be so yappy when we've got company."

"That's quite all right," said Zgrbnys, swallowing

his napkin and wiping his mouth with his pork chop. "But I still can't understand why the answer to 'Knock, knock' is always 'Who's there?' Why not 'Your antigravity zircon booster is submerged in swamp water,' or 'Please retrofit my alpha phase modulator with banana-peeling capabilities'?"

Why didn't I think of that?

"Or even 'Rigellian armpit bacteria don't wear contact lenses'?" added Gthrmnys.

My dad was cracking up. "Zack, Gus, you slay me."

After dinner, Cindy left for the airport. She had a night flight to Paris for a fashion show. Stan and I went up to my room with the Smarty-Pants.

"Welcome Zgrbnys and Gthrmnys," said Stan. "May the Crease be with you. What's the news from Pan?"

"Not good," Zgrbnys said gravely. "We intercepted a message from the Pan-Pan Travel Bureau complaint department in the Crab Nebula."

"From the Wide Wale himself?" asked Stan, impressed.

Gthrmnys nodded grimly. "We haven't seen so many dissatisfied customers since the Big Dipper sprang a leak during SoupFest. Thousands of unhappy tourists are tearing at their belt loops and demanding their pantaloons back. The Wide Wale has received a snootful of the worst reports possible."

I had to ask. "Bad weather? Lousy food? Seedy hotels?"

"Even worse," said Zgrbnys. **"The nonhaving of fun."**

"That's serious!" exclaimed Stan. "Cuffs will

roll over this! What tourist attraction is creating such terrible problems? Have the lights gone out again on the Galactic Tour so nobody can see the dark matter?"

Zgrbnys shook his head. "The complaints are coming from right here. On Earth."

Chapter 5

WHY DID THE CHICKEN CROSS THE ROAD?

"On *Earth*?" Stan was appalled. "How can any Pant not love Earth? There are so many wonderful things to do here! Haven't they been caught in traffic jams, bitten by mosquitoes, and been forced to go to the dentist?"

Every tourist's dream!

"Yes, and they've enjoyed those merriments," confirmed Zgrbnys. "Especially having their teeth drilled. But the main reason why Pants came here was for the allergies. And so far, no one has sneezed."

"But Earth has tons of stuff to be allergic to," I protested. "We've got it all—dust, weeds, pollen, mold, and pet hair. We're practically the Disneyland of allergies. If you can't sneeze here, you won't sneeze anywhere!"

Gthrmnys looked down his nose at me. "Your primitive Q-class mind cannot begin to understand the capabilities of Smarty-Pants. We have beamed our nasal processors off an orbiting satellite to scan the entire Earth. No material on this planet will cause an allergic reaction in a Pant."

"Well, how about we give them all a cold then?" I persisted. **"Maybe we could find some sick guy to sneeze on the silverware at the hotel they're staying at."**

"Impractical," said Zgrbnys. "Too many tourists, too few germs."

My exchange buddy was really upset. "But I, Stan, researched this. I looked back as far as the time of Ptlnys the Unbelievably Magnificent, the first Pant ever to reach Earth. He visited what Earthlings call ancient Egypt. According to his journals, he never stopped sneezing for five minutes due to a severe allergy to Nile Delta goldenrod."

"Do you think he could have been lying?" I asked.

The Smarty-Pants looked at me like I had just

accused Santa Claus of Grand Theft Reindeer.

"Devin-shhhh!" Stan scolded me. "You can't disrespect Ptlnys the Unbelievably Magnificent. He's Pan's most revered hero. He invented the nasal processor. He founded the Smarty-Pants. He was even important in Earth history. Who do you think it was who told Alexander the Good, 'If you really want to make your mark, *Good* just doesn't cut it. You're going to have to be *Great*'?"

TONY the Tiger?

"Sounds like quite a guy," I commented.

Stan nodded. "He might have been even more successful, but he couldn't get around so well. Ptlnys walked with a terrible limp until the day he died. Some say it was from an infected in-grown toenail that would never heal."

"How did he get that?" I asked.

My exchange buddy shook his head. "Nobody knows. It's one of the great zippered mysteries of the universe. Like, how did the Sphinx of Egypt lose its nose? Or, why did the chicken cross the road?"

"You mean, to get to the other side?" I asked.

There was a moment of stunned silence, and

then Stan and the Smarty-Pants were locked in a joyous embrace.

"'To get to the other side!'" crowed Gthrmnys. "That's brilliant! It completely illuminates the chicken's motivation!"

"This is the first zippered mystery revealed since that glorious day when all Pantkind came to realize why manhole covers are round!" Zgrbnys added breathlessly. "It'll be the feature story of *Seams to Me* magazine!"

"Hey! *Hey!*" I interrupted. "We're talking about the tourists, remember? What happens if they don't pick up some allergies?"

My exchange buddy hung his head. "The Pan-Pan Travel Bureau will eat my contract and I, Stan, will be fired."

I couldn't believe it. "Over *sneezing*?"

"Over false advertising," Zgrbnys corrected. **"You can't promise sneezation when there's nonsneezation."**

"Customer satisfaction is the most important thing in the travel business," Stan explained. "Why, if the unhappy tourists all E-mail their complaints, they could jam the whole Overall. A single nasal processor can send up to twelve thousand messages per second, Devin. Who knows what might happen next? They might even start a letter-writing campaign. Then the people at the Pan-Pan Travel Bureau would develop heartburn from eating so much hate mail. That would be a public health disaster."

Personally, I couldn't have cared less about a bunch of nose pickers with acid indigestion. I was worried about Stan. "But could you stay here on Earth?"

Stan shook his head sadly. "I, Stan, will be called back to Pan, where I'll be demoted to the bargain basement of the Pan-Pan Travel Bureau. There, I'll take my place on the out-of-fashion slacks rack."

"But I'd never see you again!" I wailed.

"Not true," my exchange buddy said bravely. "I, Stan, will work hard until I achieve the status of travel agent again. This should take no longer than sixty years."

DON'T hold your breath!

"*Sixty years?!*" Stan would be 207 by the time he came back, which was still pretty young for a Pant. I mean, on Pan you can't even vote until you turn 250. But in sixty years, I'd be an old guy who had spent his whole life missing his best friend!

That did it. I couldn't help breaking ☞ **Rule 3: Never panic.** "We've got to scrounge up some sneezing! A sniffle! A chill! Sinusitis! *La grippe!* Allergic rhinitis! A postnasal drip! *Anything!*"

"Impossible, Earthling." Gthrmnys sounded impatient.

"It's not impossible!" I insisted. "That Ptlnys guy was allergic to Nile Delta goldenrod! My dad says you can't kill weeds with an atomic bomb!" Frantically, I yanked a book called *The Ancient World* off the shelf over my desk. "There's a whole chapter on Egypt! It's got to say what happened to the goldenrod!"

I handed the book to Stan, who held it out to the Smarty-Pants. Zgrbnys put his finger in his nose and gave a quarter-twist. A beam of light shot out from his nostril, shining a gleaming square on the table of contents. Suddenly, the pages began to turn, speeding up until they were almost a blur. With a *whoosh*, he was done.

"Ah, fascinating reading," smiled Zgrbnys. "You Earthlings are even more backward than I thought. Imagine building an entire temple out of ancient grease."

"Not grease—*Greece!*" I exploded. "It's a country!"

A VEry SLippEry LaNd.

Zgrbnys was sarcastic. "Oh, yes. Of course you're right and I'm wrong! After all, you're a mere child on a Q-class planet, and I'm *only* a Smarty-Pant, who can think in six dimensions, seven if you include hyperspace."

"But did you find out what happened to the Nile Delta goldenrod?" Stan asked urgently.

"Oh, that." Zgrbnys dismissed this with a wave of his hand. "That's all gone."

"What?!" Stan and I chorused.

"Three thousand years ago," Zgrbnys explained pleasantly, "Pharaoh Wheezinhotep IV developed such a strong allergy to the stuff that he ordered every single goldenrod plant in all of Egypt to be pulled up, placed in a humongous vessel, and sunk to the bottom of the Nile."

"No-o-o-o-o!!" I howled in agony.

Chapter 6
BACK IN TIME

"Calm down, Devin," said my exchange buddy soothingly. "We have two of the greatest minds in the galaxy to call upon." He turned to the Smarty-Pants. "Can you use your ultra-intelligence to determine the best course of action?"

"Naturally," said Gthrmnys. "You must travel back in time to the day that you recommended Earth as a possible vacation planet."

"Instead, you will select asteroid B-806 in the Great Slime Nebula of Orion," continued Zgrbnys, "famous for its six-foot cockroaches, electric quicksand, and the only professional hockey league for trees in the galaxy. You will not promise sneezation, or anything more exciting than perhaps getting hit with a slap shot by a forty-foot defenseman named Jacques LaMaple."

Is that ON PLANET SYRUP?

34

"But I, Stan, love Earth," Stan protested. "And asteroid B-806 is a terrible place for a vacation."

"Hold it, hold everything." I turned to the Smarty-Pants. "Did you just say *travel back in time*?"

Gthrmnys chuckled. "Ah, yes. You Earthlings haven't mastered time travel yet. Along with several other of the simplest achievements of science, such as repealing the law of gravity, harnessing the power of the coleslaw molecule, and spinning gold into straw. How quaintly primitive."

I let that pass. "Well then, what's stopping us from time-traveling to ancient Egypt, picking a

35

load of Nile Delta goldenrod, and bringing it back to make the tourists sneeze?"

You could almost hear the *boing!* as those two so-called geniuses realized that they'd missed something.

"There must be some flaw," Stan said, scratching his head. "Otherwise two Smarty-Pants could not possibly have overlooked such a brilliant plan."

"Naturally," agreed Gthrmnys, his finger up his nose. "The flaw is—uh-uh . . . " His voice trailed off.

"The flaw is that there *is* no flaw," concluded Zgrbnys. "And since there's no such thing as a completely flawless plan, there obviously must be a *hidden* flaw. But I wouldn't expect a non-genius to understand."

I was exasperated. "Listen, nobody cares that you didn't think of it! How do we *do* it?"

"Nothing could be simpler," said Zgrbnys. "When high speed and gravity come together, a time warp is created. For example, by flying a tight orbit around your sun, our spaceship would go back in time approximately four minutes."

"Four minutes?" I repeated. "That won't do any good! We need to go three thousand years!"

"In that case, we would merely circle the sun several times," said Gthrmnys. "Three hundred ninety-four million, four hundred seventy thousand times, to be exact."

I'M gETTiNg dizzy just thiNKiNg abOut it.

"Allowing for leap years," Zgrbnys added smugly.

"Wow," I said. "You guys have really thought this out."

"That's our job," nodded Gthrmnys. "We're thinkers. **That's why we get paid the plus-size pantaloons**."

An excited Stan was already herding us out of my room. "Let's get to the spaceship!"

"Hold it," I said. "You think my folks are going to let me fly off to ancient Egypt on a school night? What am I supposed to tell them?"

"Nothing, Earthling," snickered Zgrbnys. "Since we are travelling to the *past*, everything we do there will take no time in the *present*, since it will already have happened thousands of years *before*."

"Then we simply return to this exact moment,"

finished Gthrmnys. "To your parents' eyes, you will walk out, and then immediately walk back in."

"Is that too complicated for the simplicity of your Q-class brain?" added Zgrbnys in genuine concern.

"At least I understand knock-knock jokes," I muttered under my breath. "And so do most kindergarten kids."

We tiptoed downstairs. As a cover, I bagged up the kitchen trash, called, "Mom, I'm taking out the garbage," and slipped through the front door.

On the porch, I glared at Stan and the Smarty-Pants. "This had better work. Otherwise it's going to say on my tombstone that my last words were, 'I'm taking out the garbage.' Now, where's your spaceship?"

The two geniuses looked completely mystified.

"Oh, come on!" I blew up. "You forgot where you left it?"

Gthrmnys was annoyed. "This is top security, Earthling. We conceived of a hiding place so ideal that not even we could find it."

"Dazzling logic!" Stan marveled.

"It was my idea," Zgrbnys said modestly.

"No, it was *my* idea," argued Gthrmnys.

I pointed. "Hey, isn't that your spaceship over there?"

It was at a parking meter on Main Street—a Button-Fly 501 space cruiser from the first fleet

of His Most Tailored Majesty, the Grand Pant. It was shallow and eight-sided, like a giant stop sign, but with a long shiny pipe sticking straight up on top. To be honest, it looked pretty ridiculous in the middle of a line of cars.

"That's your brilliant hiding place? *That?!*" I was furious. "A nearsighted baboon couldn't miss it! If Mr. Slomin had driven by here, he would have called the Air Force on us in a second!"

"It's the perfect spot," argued Zgrbnys. "No one in his right mind would search for an alien spacecraft in the middle of the street. Therefore, that is exactly the correct place to hide it."

Brilliant! "As you can see, nobody noticed it," added Gthrmnys as we approached the spaceship.

"Oh, yeah?" I reached under one of the sixteen windshield wipers and pulled out a small piece of paper. "You two geniuses got a parking ticket—thirty bucks for an expired meter!"

Zgrbnys plucked it from my hand. "We don't have to pay this." He tossed it over his shoulder.

"But the Grand Pant honors all traffic citations," Stan reminded him. "From anywhere in the Milky Way galaxy."

"That's the advantage of a superior intelligence," smirked Gthrmnys. "I have used my limitless brainpower to determine that there's no possible chance that word of this could ever get back to the Grand Pant."

Zgrbnys stuck his finger in his nose. Instantly, the spaceship lifted up off the road and hovered above the cars. A tiny dot appeared in the side. It grew larger, yawning open into a round door. A silver staircase descended to the street, and a red carpet unfurled along it.

I'd seen this before, but it still blew me away. Pants can be pretty goofy, with their fingers up their noses, and all that Big Zipper stuff. But their technology is nothing short of spectacular. They are ahead of Earth in every way. They just happen to be very weird.

Stan followed the Smarty-Pants up the stairs. "Come on, Devin," he called down to me. **"This is an emergency. More tourists are *not* sneezing every minute."**

I picked the parking ticket up off the pavement and jammed it in my pocket—I couldn't risk having the police trace it back to my family. Then I ran up the stairs into the spaceship and into the unknown.

No . . .

Chapter 7
SPITTOON

Takeoff in a Button-Fly 501 space cruiser is like falling from a skyscraper in reverse. One second you're on the ground, totally stopped. The next, you're ten miles high, and the town below you seems like a sprinkling of tiny Monopoly houses. What else is down there? Oh, yeah. Your stomach. I'll bet you never get used to it, even if you do it every day.

DO THEY PUT barf bags ON THOSE SPACEShips?

A moment later, we were so far away that the whole planet looked about the size of a golf ball.

"Unbelievable," I breathed.

"Yes," agreed Stan. "Since the sun is only ninety-three million miles away, we must use extra-slow speed so we don't overshoot our target."

It sure didn't feel very extra-slow to my stomach and me.

"Now," he went on, "I, Stan, have to warn you about SPITTOON."

I gave him a blank stare. "Spittoon? You mean those funky ashtrays cowboys spit chewing tobacco into?"

"SPITTOON stands for Special Priority Intergalactic Time Travel Orders On Noninterference," he explained. "When you visit the past, you must be very careful not to do anything that might change the future."

"How can anybody do that?" I scoffed.

"It's no laughing matter," Stan said gravely. "Time travel can present a very serious problem. For example, what if, by accident, our spaceship lands on somebody? If that person's destiny was to become a great hero, or king, or president, that wouldn't happen, since he would be dead. So the future would change because he would no longer be in it."

I still didn't see what was such a big deal. "So we'll remind the Dummy-Pants to watch where they park the flying saucer."

"I heard that," called Zgrbnys from the controls.

"It's not so simple, Devin," Stan insisted. "Even something as tiny as stepping on an ant can affect the future. That ant might have been just about to bite an evil inventor. If his foot had become swollen, the inventor would have had to stay home from his lab. But he didn't, since the ant never lived to bite him. And that day, the inventor might create a terrible weapon that never should have existed." He was deadly serious. "So time travelers must be sure not to change even the slightest detail when they're in the past."

"We'll just get our goldenrod, pack up, and leave," I promised.

"Entering solar orbit in five seconds," called Gthrmnys. "Four—three—"

We were streaking in toward the sun, closer and closer until the entire view screen was white-hot fire. Solar flares reached for us with exploding fingers of flame. I was positive we would plunge inside and be roasted.

"Hit the brakes!" I howled.

The Smarty-Pants ignored me. "Hang on to

your belt loops!" cried Zgrbnys from the controls. "We're jumping to time-warp speed!"

I felt like a tiny pebble inside the tire of a race car that's driving two hundred miles per hour. The spinning action whipped me up against the wall. Going that fast, it's tough to see; everything is enveloped in a bright white haze. My lips went numb, followed by my fingers and toes. There was a churning in my stomach as if someone had taken a jackhammer to my belly button from the inside. I tried to scream, but the muscles in my jaw wouldn't move.

And just as suddenly, it was all over. With nothing pinning me to the wall anymore, I

collapsed to the floor. Slowly, my vision cleared, and I stared at the view screen. There, dead center, hung Earth.

"Aw, come on!" I exploded. "After all that, we just went *home*?"

"This isn't home, Earthling," Gthrmnys informed me as we started to descend through the atmosphere. **"We have completed approximately four hundred million solar orbits at one hundred million times the speed of light."**

"Yes, this is Earth," added Zgrbnys. "But it's hardly the Earth you know. The year is 1000 B.C."

Stan jumped up, eyes wide. "Then we did it," he said excitedly. "We're in the past."

"Nile Delta goldenrod, here we come!" I cheered. "Hey, what does that stuff look like, anyway?"

Gthrmnys was as blank as a movie screen with the projector switched off. His partner was even blanker, if that was possible.

I wheeled to face Stan. My exchange buddy didn't have a clue either.

I blew my stack. "You mean we just traveled three thousand years into the past, and nobody bothered to find out what we're searching for?"

There was an embarrassed silence. On the view screen, the northeast corner of Africa was hurtling up to meet us.

"Well," suggested Zgrbnys, "after we land, maybe we can find another book—"

"Books won't be invented for two thousand five hundred years," Stan reminded him gently.

"Oh, right," Zgrbnys said lamely. "I forgot."

I seethed all the way down to Earth. I know ☛ **Rule 26** says: What's done is done; don't be a baby about it. But I was really sore.

I was still muttering under my breath when the space cruiser touched down. I slapped my fist into my palm. "Darn it, there must be some way to recognize Nile Delta goldenrod!"

The tiny dot spiraled out into a door. A stiff breeze of hot, dry air blew into the ship. And suddenly, all four of us were sneezing our heads off!

PUT SOME NAME TAGS ON THOSE WEEDS!

Chapter 8

THE NOT·SO·GREAT PYRAMIDS

My three companions were overjoyed. There's nothing a Pant likes more than sneezing through his nasal processor. According to Stan, every single one of your trillion gigabytes tingles. He says no earthling feeling could ever be so awesome.

"*Sneezation!*" howled Zgrbnys. "This is—*achoo!*—fantastic!"

"I, Stan—*achoo!*—told you it was worth coming to—*achoo!*—Earth for!"

"It sure beats—*achoo!*—thinking all day!" added Gthrmnys.

"But what's—*achoo!*—causing it?"

I was sneezing so hard I couldn't stay upright. "It—*achoo!*—must be—" Finally I managed to crawl to the door and get a look outside. I'll bet my eyes bulged just like in cartoons. "*Nile Delta goldenrod!!*"

It had to be! We were in the middle of a vast field of the stuff—two-foot-high weeds with small yellow spiky flowers. It went on as far as the eye could see in all directions. "Boys," I wheezed happily, "we just hit the goldenrod jackpot."

Stan came up behind me. "There's enough here for every tourist on Earth," he gasped, and then collapsed to the floor sneezing.

We headed down the red carpet. In the middle of the field, the sneezing got even worse, complete with runny nose and itchy, watery eyes. The three Pants rolled around the goldenrod, loving every minute.

I was getting annoyed. I mean, fun is fun, but we were here to save Stan's career. I suppressed another sneeze. "Come on, we've got work to do. Can't you guys take some allergy medicine?"

Zgrbnys looked at me. "Allergy medicine?"

"So you'll stop sneezing!"

"*Stop* sneezing?" Stan repeated, as if I had just suggested they should cut their own throats. "Devin, Pants are willing to travel trillions of miles and spend thousands of hard-earned pantaloons just to *start* sneezing! Why should we do anything to make us—*achoo!*—stop?"

It became so impossible to do anything outside that we had to go back into the ship and seal the door so we could talk about our plan.

I took charge. "Okay, let's start yanking up

goldenrod. It shouldn't take very long for three nose computers to pick a bunch of weeds."

"Devin," Stan said patiently, "a nasal processor could never harvest goldenrod."

"Sure it could," I countered. "It cuts the lawn, right? Why can't it do the same with this stuff?"

"When I use my nasal processor to cut the grass," Stan explained, "it automatically transports all the clippings to Dimension X. But we *need* these goldenrod clippings. And we especially need the seeds. I, Stan, will keep a warehouse in an orbiting satellite. This will automatically reseed the planet whenever the Earthlings get out the weed killer." He turned to the two Smarty-Pants. "Earthlings don't like sneezation."

TEαcher, MY hOMEWOrk is iN DiMENSiON X.

"Primitive," muttered Gthrmnys under his breath.

"You mean—" I was horrified. "—you mean we have to pick this stuff *by hand*?"

"Exactly," confirmed Gthrmnys. He turned to his partner. "Feel like doing some sight-seeing?"

"Don't I always?" grinned Zgrbnys.

I couldn't believe it. "You mean you're not even going to *help*?"

"We're thinkers," Gthrmnys chuckled. "Laborious tasks are best left to the doers." He activated the ship's main screen and began flipping around different views of the area, humming under his breath. "Now, what looks interesting? Ah!"

My jaw dropped. "Those are the Great

Pyramids! We learned about them in social studies!"

I was thunderstruck. The ancient wonders looked brand-new. Come to think of it, they *were* brand-new—*now*. The biggest one wasn't even finished yet. As we watched, an army of Egyptian laborers and engineers worked ropes and pulleys to maneuver the top stone into place.

Gthrmnys made a face. "Good heavens, they certainly botched that job."

"Are you nuts?" I howled. "It's totally perfect!"

"That shows what you know, Earthling," Zgrbnys sneered. "It is a full three sixty-fifths of a millimeter off to the left. I'm amazed the whole thing doesn't come crashing down."

PICKY! PICKY!

I was really mad. "The pyramids are one of the most spectacular achievements of the human race."

"Devin," Stan chided gently, "you don't really believe the *Egyptians* built the pyramids, do you?"

"Of course they did. They're doing it right now. Look."

Stan shook his head. "The Great Pyramids were designed by Ptlnys the Unbelievably Magnificent while he was here on Earth. He was the chief engineer on the entire project."

"That's impossible!" I snapped. "And it doesn't make sense. Why would an alien need to build three humongous stone triangles in the middle of nowhere?"

"Ptlnys hadn't invented the nasal processor yet," Stan explained. "So he had no way to communicate with Pan. The pyramids were a message. When viewed from a spaceship, they spell out, 'Arrived safely. Wish you were here,' in Pant shorthand."

That's what I call using big words!

"Let's get over there!" Zgrbnys said excitedly. "Maybe someone will introduce us to Ptlnys the Unbelievably Magnificent!" And they opened the door and rushed out into the goldenrod, sneezing and bickering over who should be first to shake hands with the great Pant hero.

I turned on Stan. "How come you didn't give *them* the lecture on SPITTOON?" I demanded. "Aren't you worried that those two idiots will mess up the future?"

"Devin, they're Smarty-Pants," he scolded me. "They can move a pulsar with duct tape. Every step they take, their superbrains will be guarding against changing history. Trust me."

With the Smarty-Pants off playing tourist, we the "doers" got down to work. I won't try to sugarcoat it. Picking goldenrod is total slavery. Backaches, muscle aches, blisters, not to mention sunburn—when Mr. Slomin taught us about ancient Egypt, he never mentioned it was a hundred and ten degrees in the shade. Painful, exhausting, torturous—to those adjectives, I have to add just one more: *gross*. It's not much fun to have a runny nose thirty centuries before the invention of Kleenex.

After four mind-numbing, backbreaking, sweat-drenched, sneezing, wheezing hours, I finally stuffed the last armload of goldenrod into the hold. Stan tweaked his nasal processor, and the cargo door spiraled shut and winked out of existence.

The two of us collapsed to the ground, totally exhausted. I checked my watch. It was two-fifteen—but I couldn't be sure if that was in Egypt or in Clearview, 1000 B.C., or A.D. 2000 What it did mean was that the Smarty-Pants had been gone for four and a half hours.

"Oh, great," I moaned. "Two morons wandering around ancient Egypt. If somebody busts the Nile, we'll know who to blame."

"Smarty-Pants don't 'wander,'" my exchange buddy lectured me. "They follow carefully calculated paths decided by the supreme logic of their superbrains. I, Stan, am sure they'll be back soon."

But at sundown there was still no sign of the Smarty-Pants.

Chapter 9
MUM'S THE WORD

"Where are they? Where are they? *Where are they?*" I was freaking out.

By this time, even Stan was frowning. "They must have discovered a monumentally important task. They're too busy to check their nasal processors. I've put four APBs out."

"Can't you buzz them directly?" I nagged.

"Well, no," he replied. "Not if they've hung out the *Do Not Disturb* signs on their virtual nose knobs. They're probably doing research that will change our view of ancient Earth. Or they could be repairing some damage to history in keeping with SPITTOON—"

"Or those two boneheads got themselves lost and now they're wandering in the desert somewhere," I suggested.

"We can't wait around to find out," Stan decided. "The longer we stay here, the longer we risk that our ship will be spotted. We could never explain it to the Egyptians without affecting history."

"But what can we do?" I asked. "Our pilots are gone!"

"I, Stan, took Introduction to Flying, part 1 before I flunked out of Smarty-Pants University."

Just what I always wanted: a ride with a failed pilot.

"You mean," I was thunderstruck, "we're just going to leave them *stranded*?"

"Of course not," Stan replied. "We'll go back to the future and distribute our goldenrod among my fellow travel agents on Earth. Then we'll return here to pick them up."

"And you know where 'here' is?" I sure didn't.

"It's programmed into the navigational computer," Stan assured me as we climbed back into the ship.

When the door sealed, we stopped sneezing. But we were still a mess, with watery eyes and runny noses. So while Stan got us out of first

Egypt and then Earth's atmosphere, I scoured the space cruiser for some Kleenex. There was none in any of the supply closets. But I opened up a drawer marked "Snack Foods" and found ten boxes.

> And LOOK FOr NEW, iMProVEd NachO chEESE KLEENEX iN YOUr grOcEr's FrEEEZEr.

"Oh, delicious," said Stan at the controls, stuffing a handful of tissues in his mouth. He burped. "No more, thank you, Devin. I, Stan, wouldn't want to eat too much and get sleepy while I'm flying."

In answer, I blew my nose so hard I'm amazed I didn't blast a hole in the side of the space cruiser.

I couldn't tell if Stan was a great pilot or not. I still got slammed up against the wall when we whipped around the sun. But he had one really good idea. To avoid being seen, he set us down in a small clearing in the woods at the end of my street.

"Not bad," I commented as we walked down the staircase and headed for home. "What grade did you get in that flying course, anyway?"

"K-minus," he replied.

Top of the class? Low average? Total flunk-out? Anybody's guess is as good as mine.

We stepped out of the clearing and stopped dead. I goggled. I gagged. I did a reality check and never even came close to anything real.

Our house was there, all right. But in a way, it wasn't. Oh, there was the same white wooden siding with green trim, but it wasn't a two-story square anymore. It was a *pyramid*! My horrified eyes moved to the faded blue and a little bit rusty vehicle in the driveway. It wasn't our Honda. It was a motorized four-wheel *chariot*! The blue spruce on the front lawn, the old oak with the tree house, the lilac bushes close to the porch- they were gone. Instead, tall papyrus plants towered everywhere.

I looked around. All the other houses were pyramids, too. The streetlights were shaped like scarab beetles. The fire hydrants were miniature mummies. I blinked a few times, but when my eyes opened again, all that *stuff* was still there.

NOW ENTERING thE TWiLight ZONE!

My brother Roscoe stepped out the door. He was wearing a dress! Well, not a lady's dress, but some kind of tunic. In place of his usual baseball

cap was an Egyptian headpiece. **"Hey, guys! Want to play Hounds and Jackals?"** He squinted at us. "What's with the weird outfits?"

"Is it by any chance . . . *Halloween?*" Stan asked hopefully.

"No!" I snapped. "But even if it was, you don't dress up your *house* to go trick-or-treating!"

Stan put his finger in his nose. "Location: Clearview, Earth. Time: A.D. 2000 Life form: Earthling, Roscoe Hunter, age thirteen-point-two."

"That's right!" I hissed. "So why is everything *wrong*?"

"Insufficient data," Stan informed me. But he looked worried.

Things went from bad to worse. My mother turned out to be a priestess of the Nile. Instead of Barbies, my little sister Lindsay played with Nefertiti dolls. My dad worked for a company called Mum's The Word. They manufactured an automatic wrapping machine for mummies. There wasn't much demand for that in the Clearview I remembered. But he told us business was booming.

Our TV was pyramid-shaped, so the picture was a triangle. It would be pretty lousy for watching football. You'd never see any touchdowns since neither end zone would fit on the screen.

I shouldn't have worried. There *was* no football. Instead, we watched *Monday Night Crocodile Wrestling, Alexandria Hills
90210, Everybody Loves Ramses,* and
Battle of the Monster Chariots.

DON'T bE a couch papyrus!

"Pssst," whispered Stan. "Was TV always like
this?"

"Of course not!" I seethed at him.

The crowning moment of the evening came
when Pharaoh Tutankhamen the 53rd give his
State of the Empire speech. I've never seen a hat
that big in my life!

"My fellow Egyptians . . ." he began.

Lindsay pointed to the doorway. "Here comes
Fungus."

Fungus! Well, at least one thing was normal.
"Come on, Fungus," I beckoned. "Here, boy."

Into the den slithered a small black poisonous
snake.

Chapter 10
FREAK SHOW

I hit the ceiling. "Hide! Get a rake! Kill it! Call the cops!"

My mother chuckled. "Very funny, Devin. Fungus has only been our pet asp for five years."

"Pet *asp*?!"

"Of course," she replied. **"Asps are man's best friend."**

"No, they aren't!" I squawked. "Dogs are!"

"*Dogs*? Dogs are wild animals running around the hills in packs. They could never be domesticated."

"Have you all gone crazy?" I yowled. "Dogs make perfect pets. A disgusting viper like that could never do what dogs do!"

"Hey, look," chuckled Roscoe, pointing at the

open bathroom door. "Fungus is drinking out of the toilet again."

I stood corrected.

The asp slithered back into the den and wrapped himself around Stan's ankle. He stuck out a forked tongue and hissed. Stan hissed back.

"He's a pretty nice guy," Stan told me later that night when we were alone in my room. "He doesn't have a great sense of humor like Fungus the dog. But, as asps go, he's quite pleasant."

> EVERY SNAKE has his day.

"I don't want a pleasant asp," I complained. "I don't want *any* asp! I want my dog back. What happened to my life?"

"I, Stan, am also confused. It seems the entire world has become a modern version of ancient Egypt. However, my nasal processor indicates that the rest of the galaxy is completely normal, even the planet Pinkus, which is almost never normal. It's just Earth that is, as you say, screwy."

"But how?" I wailed.

"There is only one possible explanation," said Stan, very pale. "We must have committed a SPITTOON violation. Somehow, we changed history when we were in ancient Egypt."

"No chance," I said firmly. "We barely left the spaceship the whole time—" And then it hit me. "The Dummy-Pants!"

"Oh, no, Devin," Stan said firmly. "That could never happen to Smarty-Pants. They're far too intelligent."

"There's only one thing to do," I decided. "We've got to go back to ancient Egypt and fix whatever went wrong."

Stan made a pained face. "Time travel is so tricky. We might even make things worse. Are you sure you can't get used to *this* Earth? Asps aren't so bad, you know. **They can't fetch sticks, but they can impersonate them.** And they're wonderful at discouraging burglars. My nasal processor says that robberies have dropped down to zero in this society because every house is protected by an asp."

"I hope you're joking, Mflxnys," I growled. I lay back in my "bed," which was a mummy case propped against the angled pyramid wall. "Man, there's no way I'll ever sleep in this! It's a coffin! What do they think I am, a vampire? Let's go back to ancient Egypt before bedtime."

YOU'LL SLEEP LiKE THE dEAd!

"That would be unwise," my exchange buddy said seriously. "Until we know exactly what the damage to history is, it will be difficult to fix it."

"Can't your nose computer figure it out?" I asked.

Stan shook his head. "This is Earth history. My nasal processor can only get information about Pan. We'll need to learn more before we can risk time traveling again."

What a lousy night! My bed gave me nightmares. I couldn't take my eyes off a grotesque

stuffed animal with a person's body attached to the head of a hawk. My mother assured me it was my favorite toy as a toddler. I must have been some little sicko in this world.

Stan, of course, slept like a baby, snoring the microwave-oven hum of his nasal processor. Sure—it wasn't *his* planet that had turned into a freak show.

The next morning, I went through the Egyptian clothes in my closet to find something to wear to Pharaoh Akhenaton the 106th Academy—

formerly Clearview Elementary School. I finally picked out a tunic with gold-leaf stripes from Papyrus Republic. Luckily, there weren't any rules of coolness against guys wearing miniskirts—who could have imagined it would ever happen?

Stan chose a white tunic with a black-and-white polka-dot tie. You can stop history, but you can't stop Stan Mflxnys from being a dweeb.

I thought I looked pretty cool in an Egyptian kind of way. But when I got to school everybody laughed at me.

"Oh, Devin," giggled Calista. "No one dresses in *chariot-wear* anymore." This from a girl who looked like she was wrapped in the living room drapes.

"I pledge allegiance to the flat stone tablet of the United Empire of Egypt, and to the dictatorship for which it stands. One kingdom under Ra, uninvadable, with chariots and mummification for all."

No kidding, that's how the pledge went. I almost choked when I heard what the other kids were reciting. I was never a big fan of my old

71

school, but today really taught me some appreciation. To start with, our classroom was at the very top of the pyramid. Every time I got up from my desk, I smashed my head against the sloping wall.

I had flunked three tests by 10:30 in the morning because everything was in hieroglyphics. It was all Greek to me—or at least Egyptian. Stan used his Pan-Tran translator to help me. But that meant he had his finger up his nose practically full-time. Nose picking wasn't any more popular in this world than it was in the real one. Mr. Slomin, whose tunic bore the crest of the UFC Society (Unidentified Flying Chariots), sent him to stand out in the hall.

From there, my faithful exchange buddy beamed signals from his nasal processor back into the class to translate my Rules of Coolness notebook, which I found in my desk.

I watched in wonder as the hieroglyphics slowly came apart and rearranged themselves first into letters, and then into words.

Chapter 11

THE CLASS JACKAL

I couldn't believe it. My precious rules were all twisted. ☛ **Rule 15** was supposed to be: *Never wear white after Labor Day.* Now it was: *Never wear white after the third eclipse past the Festival of Ra.*

And there was some stuff in there that was totally out in left field, like ☛ **Rule 21:** *Let sleeping crocodiles lie;* ☛ **Rule 34:** *A guy's home is his pyramid;* and ☛ **Rule 60:** *Don't believe everything you read on the obelisk.*

It was all downhill from there. At lunch, when I asked for a hot dog, the cafeteria lady didn't know what I was talking about. When I pointed, she scowled, "Why didn't you just say you wanted a 'hot asp'?"

And when I tried to pay with a dollar bill, she made a big stink about it. With a sinking heart, I

looked around. Everybody else's money was brightly colored, with a picture of Pharaoh What's-His-Name on it.

"You're a counterfeiter!" she accused.

By this time, half the school had gathered around to watch me get chewed out.

"It's—Monopoly money!" I stammered. "I stuck it in my tunic instead of back in the game box—"

Eventually, the assistant principal came and ordered me to empty my pockets. He confiscated all my cash—$4.71; not a fortune, but who likes to throw money away? All I got to keep was a few pieces of linty candy, an old comb that looked like it had been used to clean the cooties out of a Sasquatch, and the Smarty-Pants' parking ticket. I also wound up with a week of detentions for trying to pass funny money.

"Don't worry," whispered Stan, "since this is all part of an incorrect future, your detentions aren't technically real."

"So I suppose it was just a dream when the assistant principal was screaming in my face," I mumbled. "He had onions for lunch. Yuck!"

We slipped into Mr. Slomin's room just in time for our Dynastics lesson.

"Today," the teacher was saying, "we're going to learn about the empire we live in."

He pulled a large hanging map down in front of the board. It was a totally normal map of the world, except that there were no borders, and it was all one color. A single word was written in hieroglyphics across the whole thing. I'd learned to recognize it by now. It said: EGYPT.

I raised my hand. "But what happened to all the other countries?"

That got a big laugh.

"Devin, stop being the class jackal," the teacher scolded. "You know perfectly well that Egypt swallowed up all the

> YOu gOt thE WhOLE WOrLd . . . iN ONE cOUNTry . . .

other countries a long time ago. Ever since Yemen surrendered in A.D. 16. That's why the whole world is Egypt today."

Suddenly, Stan kicked me hard under the table.

"Ow!"

I glared at him, but he just kicked again.

"Ow!" Then, in a lower voice, "What did you do that for?"

Stan raised his hand. "Mr. Slomin, can we be excused for a few minutes?"

The teacher scowled at him. "Absolutely not, Stan. Dynastics is your second-most important class-after Egyptology, of course."

But my exchange buddy wasn't so easily discouraged. Up went his finger into his left nostril. Instantly, the faucet at the back of the class sprang to life. But instead of running into the sink, the stream of water shot clear across the

A NOSE-PICKING CLaPPEr!

room, turned left to avoid Joey Petrillo, and drenched Stan and me.

Stan removed his finger, and the faucet shut off.

"All right, Devin and Stan," ordered Mr. Slomin. "Go dry yourselves off. And stop in to ask the custodian to check our sink."

In the hall, I grabbed Stan by his polka-dot tie. "What's the big idea of turning Niagara Falls on us?"

"That's it! That's it!"

He was leaping up and down with excitement. If we couldn't fix history, I was going to have to add a new rule of coolness: No jumping in an Egyptian tunic unless you want to show the whole world your underwear.

"That's what?" I asked.

"That's where history got changed," Stan explained. "The *real* Egypt was conquered, but this one went on to take over the entire planet. We must have done something to make ancient Egypt too strong."

"Can we fix it?" I asked nervously.

"We must try," he said somberly. "This is a severe SPITTOON violation. But first—" He put his finger up his nose. Out of the other nostril, an enormous blast of hot air practically knocked me over. In a split second, my sopping wet hair and clothes were completely dry.

"Thanks—I think," I mumbled while my exchange buddy turned the nostril on himself.

I felt kind of uneasy marching out of school in the middle of the day. I reminded myself that this Egyptian school—this whole Egyptian *world*—

was nothing more than a mistake. A mistake that we were on our way to correcting.

> A mistake that couldn't be fixed with a red pen . . .

The spaceship was still in the woods where we left it—no tickets or anything like that. Stan took us up and out of the atmosphere. This time I stayed close to the wall. It was a good move. I didn't get bounced around nearly as much when we circled the sun.

Suddenly, the ship lurched. I came off the wall like I'd been shot out of a cannon.

Crack! I bumped heads with Stan, who had been pitched out of the pilot's seat. Through the bright white speed-haze, I could see sparks shooting out of the control panel.

"It's the navigation computer!" Stan cried. "We're losing power!"

"How bad is it?" I shouted back.

"We have to make the ship lighter!" came the reply. "Otherwise, we'll break up and fall into the sun!"

Chapter 12
THE SOLAR SNEEZE

"Fall into the sun?"

I only got a C in science, but that didn't sound too healthy to me. I ran around the ship, looking for heavy things to get rid of. It was no use. All the furniture was bolted down.

"Breakup in ten seconds!" exclaimed Stan. "Nine—Eight—"

Then it came to me. "The cargo bay door! Open it!"

We were bouncing around so badly that it took precious seconds for Stan to find his nostril with his finger.

"Quick!" I howled.

Suddenly, our view screen filled with Nile Delta goldenrod. It seemed like space itself was full of the stuff. It billowed around our ship like a yellow nebula—four agonizing hours of bending, and picking, and cramming! We watched the cloud take on a funnel-shape as gravity began to suck every last seed and flower into the fiery sun.

"We're stabilizing," reported Stan, relieved.

There was a huge disturbance on the solar surface. A colossal flare exploded out like a flaming battering ram. The whole ship shook as it burst past us.

"It *sneezed*!" I exclaimed. "The sun is allergic to Nile Delta goldenrod, too!"

"*Gesundheit*," said Stan.

His ultrapolite manners could be annoying at times. But somehow, that was exactly the right thing to say.

We headed on to Earth—the ancient one, that is.

I was feeling pretty sour as we began our descent to the Egyptian desert. "I'm *so* not in the mood to start picking goldenrod again. All that work just to have the stuff burn up in the sun. What a waste!" I added, "Then again, if something has to burn, let it be the goldenrod, not us."

Stan set us down in exactly the same spot as the last time. The portal spiraled open, and I felt a blast of that arid desert air. I was halfway out the door before I realized that something was missing. I wasn't sneezing, and neither was Stan.

I looked down. We were supposed to be in the middle of a vast field of knee-high weeds. Instead, there was nothing but sand as far as the eye could see.

"Stan, what happened to all the goldenrod?"

My exchange buddy put his finger in his nose. "Uh-oh. Due to our computer malfunction, we have landed in ancient Egypt five years *later* than last time."

"You mean that Pharaoh Wheezinhotep guy has already gotten rid of it?" I asked, horrified.

"We have bigger problems than that, Devin," Stan said, agitated. "We may have arrived too late to repair the damage done to the past. Aw, twill!"

We had to be in pretty big trouble for Stan to use the T-word. Remember, he's a very polite guy.

Not the T-Word!

"Couldn't we just go back and fly around the sun a few million more times?" I asked hopefully.

"Not until we can repair our navigation computer. Only the Smarty-Pants can do that." He wrung his hands together nervously. "I, Stan, can't imagine how this could be any worse."

"Yoo-hoo," came a voice. "Hello up there."

I looked down. There, waiting for us at the bottom of the stairs, stood a bedraggled, down-on-his-luck Egyptian. Oh, *no! This* was how things could be worse! We could never explain our ship and ourselves without breaking the laws of SPITTOON and scrambling the future even more!

"Go away!" I stammered. "We're a mirage! A figment of your imagination! You're seeing things! It's the desert heat!"

The poor old wretch listened patiently to my babbling. Then he said, "May the Crease be with you."

"A *Pant*!" cried Stan in delighted relief.

Chapter 13

THE BIGGEST NOSE PICKER IN HISTORY

We rushed down to the newcomer.

"I am Agent Mflxnys of the Pan-Pan Travel Bureau," Stan introduced himself. "On Earth I am called Stan. This Earthling is Devin Hunter. He knows the pleated ways of our world."

The ragged Pant said, "My name is Ptlnys."

"Ptlnys the Unbelievably Magnificent!" Stan snapped to a rigid salute, ending with his finger up his nose. "What an honor! I, Stan, feel like a short Pant of seventy again! I must be blushing to the tips of my cuffs!"

Ptlnys seemed confused. "Unbelievably Magnificent? I am not known by this title. I am Ptlnys the Very Average."

EVErYbODY has to start SOMEWhErE.

"You may be average now," Stan assured him. "But you will go on to become the greatest hero of all Pant-kind!"

Surely there was some SPITTOON law against telling a guy about his own future. But here was Stan, blabbing away like a kindergarten tattletale.

The famous Pant's eyes narrowed. "How could you know all this?"

Stan spilled what was left of the beans. "We're time travelers from the future."

"Time travel!" exclaimed Ptlnys. "Remarkable! If—" he added, "if it's all true."

I spoke up. "I can prove it."

I pulled the Smarty-Pants' parking ticket out of my tunic and placed it in Ptlnys's dirty hands. "Check out the date—April 16, 2000."

"I'm flabbergasted!" said Ptlnys. "Tell me about the future."

"Which one?" I asked sourly. "There's a really cool one with MTV, NASCAR, and the World Wrestling Federation, but there's also one where you have to watch commercials about crocodile repellent with your pet snake. Now, if you'll excuse us, we've got a really big problem to take care of."

Stan pulled me aside. "Devin," he hissed, "we can't leave him like this!"

"Like what?" I asked. But I knew exactly what he meant. The guy's robes were torn and ratty, and he had no sandals to protect his feet from the hot desert sand. He was dirty and—no offense to Pan and its greatest legend—he smelled pretty bad. "Hey, Ptlnys, how'd you like to come on board our ship and, you know, take a shower or something."

Stranded thousands of years before the invention of deodorant!

Ptlnys looked surprised. "I am producing odoriferous emanations?"

"You reek," I confirmed as kindly as I could.

"You stop noticing when you live in the desert. Everything smells like sand." He seemed depressed. **"I have become a soiled Pant in need of the Great Dry Cleaner of the universe."**

"How can the designer of the pyramids come upon such hard times?" Stan asked in concern. "You were the master engineer for Pharaoh Wheezinhotep IV."

Ptlnys lowered his eyes. "Alas, great Wheezin-hotep has gone to the House of the Dead," he said mournfully. "In recent years, the new co-Pharaohs have stopped all pyramid-building. Their interests lie more in scarab racing, redecorating the palace in wicker, skinny-dipping in the Nile, and replacing the statues of the gods with balloon animals." He looked disgusted. "I have never met two bigger idiots in my life."

"We are searching for colleagues from the future," my exchange buddy told him. "Would you like to assist us?"

Ptlnys shook his head. "My time on this world is nearly finished. That's why I approached you. I thought your ship had come to take me back to Pan. In the meantime, I've been planning a new project called the nasal processor."

"*The nasal processor!!*" I thought Stan would launch himself clear on up into orbit.

Ptlnys didn't share his enthusiasm. "It isn't going very well. I don't think it's going to work. I'm considering giving it up."

"No!" cried Stan. "It *will* work! The nasal processor will revolutionize all Pant-kind! And in gratitude, the Grand Pant will promote you to the top drawer and declare you the very first Smarty-Pant!"

Ptlnys brightened. "Would you like to see my sketches for the working model?"

Stan glowed. "There could be no greater honor. Where is your schematic diagram?"

"Turn around," invited the great inventor.

We did. I gawked. There was something new to this area since our last visit. Something *gigantic*.

We followed Ptlnys around to the other side of the mammoth structure.

I nudged Stan. "I thought you said Ptlnys had a really bad limp. This guy walks just fine."

"You're right," Stan confided in a whisper. "Do you think the legend of the Unbelievably Magnificent's ingrown toenail could be false?"

Before I could answer, I got my first look at what Ptlnys was leading us to. I thought my eyes would pop right out of their sockets.

It was the Sphinx—the famous one we had learned about in social studies! It towered over our ship, surveying the desert with blank stone

eyes. But in our millennium, the Sphinx's nose had disappeared over the centuries—even Pants called it a great zippered mystery. Here the thing was almost new, with a schnoz that looked like it should have had a fake mustache and glasses attached to it. And—I gawked—**the Sphinx had one giant carved finger up its massive nostril!**

We were looking at the biggest nose picker in history!

Ptlnys led us up a series of rickety bamboo ladders to the colossal face of this wonder of the ancient world. I was terrified that a weak rung would break, pitching me to my death in the sand hundreds of feet below. But Stan was so psyched he was practically sprinting up the ladders. I remembered ☞ **Rule 22:** Don't be a spoilsport, and climbed on.

There I was, clinging to a piece of bamboo, Ptlnys's smelly feet about three inches from my face. I leaned over to examine the Sphinx's nose. Writing was scribbled all over the smooth surface of the rock—equations, and calculations, and circuit diagrams, not to mention thousands of notes like: LEFT NOSTRIL COMMUNICATIONS ARRAY CONNECT HERE, and NOSE HAIRS MUST BE COMBED AWAY FROM MAIN POWER RECEPTOR and IN CASE OF DEVIATED SEPTUM, PULL NASAL PLUG.

Even I was impressed. Stan was totally blown away.

"Ptlnys," he breathed, "this is fantastic—"

Suddenly, a voice bellowed, "Put your hands up, and step away from the nose!"

Chapter 14

THE CO·PHARAOHS ARE IN

I looked down. A patrol of Egyptian soldiers was gathered at the base of the Sphinx, waving swords and spears at us. Their captain cried, "Congratulations, lads! We've captured the foul scum who have been vandalizing the Sphinx!"

"It's not vandalism!" I called down. "It's—" How would you describe it? Diagrams for a nose computer? Oh, I don't think so.

Did I say it was hard climbing *up* those ladders? Well, try going *down* while being watched by a pack of armed ancient warriors. I noticed Ptlnys sticking the parking ticket in a small pocket in his rags just before they arrested us.

"Ptlnys," sneered the captain as his men shackled us together with heavy chains around our ankles. "I should have known you'd have sour grapes over getting fired from your cushy pyramid-building job."

"The co-Pharaohs are nothing but a couple of papyrus pushers!" Ptlnys said defiantly. "The tallest structure in all Egypt was an anthill before I got here! You tell *that* to your bosses."

The captain uttered a cruel laugh. "You can tell them yourself. The mighty ones want to pass sentence on the Sphinx terrorists personally!"

He ran a critical eye over the Button-Fly 501 Space Cruiser, which stood behind the Sphinx. "What manner of carriage is this? What happened to the horses that pull it?" When no one answered, he said, "Call the tow-chariot. I'm impounding this vehicle in the name of the co-Pharaohs."

With an ominous clang, our chains were attached to the back of one of the chariots. The captain cracked his whip. "To the palace!"

The chariot lurched forward. We were able to run along behind it for about three steps before we fell. Then they dragged us all the way to the capital city of Thebes. You know how you can't spend a day at the seashore without getting sand

in your bathing suit? Well, by the time we reached Thebes, I felt like I had a whole beach in my tunic, complete with shells and soda cans, and about fifty dollars in loose change.

"On your feet, maggots!" ordered the captain. He was a lot like a modern-day drill sergeant.

Dazed and choking, we struggled upright and

tried to brush tons of sand and dust out of our clothes. Before us loomed the great palace, huge and intimidating. Mr. Slomin had taught us about this place in Social Studies. It was designed to make ambassadors return to their home countries and tell their kings, "Don't mess with Egypt." It sure was having that affect on me. I'd never been so scared in my life!

Stan looked nervous too. "Ptlnys," he asked, "do you happen to know the penalty for defacing a public Sphinx?"

"The prisoner is given a choice," Ptlnys explained. **"Death by hanging, death by beheading, death by disemboweling—"**

"I get the picture," I interrupted. "The key word is"—I shuddered—"death. Thanks a lot, Mr. Good News."

"Don't worry," promised Ptlnys. "Before our execution, I intend to give the co-Pharaohs a piece of my mind."

Oh, wow. That would show them. I felt *so* much better now.

"Move!"

I felt a spear-point pressing against my back,

so I started forward. Into the palace they marched us, past glittering rooms filled with treasure, guarded by hundreds of soldiers.

> It's a NiCE PLaCE TO visit, but I WOULdN'T WaNT TO bE UNdEr arrEST ThErE!

"Listen, Stan," I whispered. "You know Rule 9?"

He put his finger in his nose. "Never rat out your friends?" He had all my rules of coolness stored on the septum-drive of his nasal processor.

"Right," I confirmed. "Well, delete it. When they bring us to the co-Pharaohs, I'm going to rat Ptlnys out. Remember, neither of *us* wrote on that Sphinx."

Stan was shocked. "Devin! What about SPITTOON? Ptlnys the Unbelievably Magnificent must go on to be the greatest hero in the galaxy."

"Ptlnys is toast either way," I argued. "We can't get dragged down with him. SPITTOON has to protect *us* too! We're not supposed to die in ancient Egypt. Heck, we're not even scheduled to be *born* for thousands of years!"

The guards stopped us at a huge set of golden doors. Out in front stood a tall shirtless guy who didn't have a single speck of hair anywhere on his head, his chest, his arms, or even his eyebrows. His skin gleamed with perfumed oil. He was holding up an ornate scroll with a message written in hieroglyphics.

"What does it say?" I whispered to Stan.

Stan put his finger in his nose to activate his

Pan-Tran translator. "'The co-Pharaohs are in,'" he told me. "If you flip it over, it probably tells you they're out."

Baldy put down the scroll and began to beat deep mournful kabooms on a kettledrum. "You are about to enter the chamber of the twin sons of heaven," he intoned dramatically. "Wielders of the mighty sword of Egypt, brothers to the gods themselves . . ."

The massive doors began to swing open.

"Kneel before the great co-Pharaohs, you maggots!" ordered the captain, aka the drill sergeant.

The guards shoved us to the hard marble floor. When I looked up, I was staring into the faces of the co-Pharaohs themselves.

I'm amazed I didn't have a heart attack right there in front of their wicker thrones.

They were none other than our missing Smarty-Pants, Zgrbnys and Gthrmnys!

YOU'rE KiddiNg!

Chapter 15
SPIES

The "co-Pharaohs" were snacking on sheets of papyrus and bickering over who would get to wear the crown next. They seemed pretty surprised to see us. After all, Stan and I had dropped them off in the past just yesterday. But to them, five long years had gone by.

"Oh, hello," Zgrbnys said weakly. "Fancy meeting you here."

I can't remember ever being so mad. I scrambled up in a blind rage. "You *idiots*! You stupid, lamebrained *morons*!"

Even Stan couldn't stick up for the Smarty-Pants this time. I mean, I knew they had messed up history. But I always figured it must have been by accident! Forget it! There was nothing accidental about getting yourself put in charge of an empire.

A huge young Egyptian with a jeweled breast-plate not quite hiding a barrel chest turned to the co-Pharaohs. "You know this boy?"

Gthrmnys held the two-piece scepter of Egypt, the crook and flail, in the shape of an X is his lap. "Oh, no, Prince Tutansweet," he replied airily. "Never seen him before in my life."

It was sort of true. I had first run into the Smarty-Pants in A.D. 2000, which wasn't for a long, long time yet.

"Maybe so," I snarled. **"But three thousand years from now you're going to be the stupidest person I ever met in my life!"** I shifted my blistering gaze to Zgrbnys. "In a first-place tie with *you!*"

"Prince Tutansweet is the son of the late Pharaoh Wheezinhotep IV," Zgrbnys explained pleasantly. "He was kind enough to let us have his throne."

What a guy!

He and Gthrmnys sang a rousing chorus of "For He's a Jolly Good Fellow." I guess that's how you thank a guy for letting you be king.

"But—" Stan's voice was full of bewilderment. "—you didn't follow the code of SPITTOON! You were supposed to avoid all contact with Egyptians! Becoming king counts as contact!"

"Well, that's just being nitpicky," said Zgrbnys in a crabby tone.

Ptlnys was dismayed. "You mean the two missing colleagues"—he pointed to the co-Pharaohs—"are *them*?"

I was pretty close to losing it. "But you said you were thinkers, not doers!" I wailed. "If getting crowned Pharaoh isn't *doing*, what is?"

"We're thinkers for our *job*, Earthling," Gthrmnys corrected me. "We can still be doers in our spare time."

"You *numbskulls*—"

Prince Tutansweet held out a meaty palm like a policeman directing traffic. "Be silent, boy." He reminded me of an old-fashioned year 2000 WWF wrestler, one with an Egyptian theme. He sure had the build for it. "The co-Pharaohs are not numbskulls. Nor are they idiots or morons. In fact, the only unpleasant thing about

THEY'RE NASAL ENGINEERS.

them is a single bad habit. Alas, the mighty ones engage in nasal excavation."

Nasal *what*?! "You mean nose picking?"

"We choose to overlook this," the prince went on, "in the case of two such gifted inventors."

"Inventors?" Fat chance! Those two couldn't discover ice in the freezer. And then it began to come together in my head. Inventors . . . nose picking . . .

I turned blazing eyes on the Smarty-Pants. "You've been using your nasal processors to give them stuff, right? Advanced technology from the future. That's why they let you be co-Pharaohs."

Busted!

"It's a filthy lie," proclaimed Zgrbnys. "Oh sure, we may have dropped a few *hints* to help our friends build a few things ahead of time. Like the microwave oven—"

Stan was horrified. "Microwave oven?"

"We needed it to make the low-fat popcorn," added Gthrmnys reasonably. "You can't expect us to be stranded in the past without a few of the necessities of life."

I folded my arms. "What else?"

Zgrbnys blinked. "Well, there's the Mickey Mouse night-light, the Weedwacker, the Chia Pet, the Clapper, and that's pretty much it, you know—unless you want to count the B-52 Strato-fortress bomber."

I choked. **"You gave an *ancient civilization* a B-52?!"**

Gthrmnys shrugged. "There was this rampaging army of Mesopotamian invaders—"

"No wonder Egypt never lost any wars!" I exploded. "It wasn't much of a fair fight! On one side, clubs and arrows! And on the other? A *B-52*!" I rolled my eyes at Stan. "'Oh, they couldn't possibly mess up history,'" I mimicked savagely. "'They're Smarty-Pants?' Well, I've got four words for you, pal: *I told you so*!"

Stan was too shocked to reply.

Prince Tutansweet was wide-eyed. "Are you saying that the mighty co-Pharaohs aren't even real Egyptians?"

Uh-oh. Me and my big mouth.

"Spies!" cried the prince, snatching the crown from Zgrbnys's head. He tried to take the crook and flail away from Gthrmnys, but the stubborn Smarty-Pant wouldn't let go.

"We're loyal Egyptians!" Gthrmnys grunted as the tug-of-war continued, the colorful fly whisk flapping back and forth between them. "Didn't we give you the electric egg-cooker and the Nintendo PlayStation?"

"*Guards!*" barked the prince.

Ever wonder how many ancient Egyptians it takes to beat up a couple of Smarty-Pants? Six.

Four to hold them down, and two to chain them
to Ptlnys, Stan, and me.

Tutansweet set the crown on his own head
and sat on one of the wicker thrones. "I, Tutansweet, son of Wheezinhotep, take my rightful

place as Pharaoh of Egypt. The names Zgrbnys and Gthrmnys will be carved from the face of every tablet and megalith in the land. So it shall be written; so it shall be done."

"But what about us?" asked Stan.

"As for the foreign spies," the new ruler went on, "including the ex-co-Pharaohs, **I sentence them to be mummified alive and buried under the heaviest pyramid in all Egypt.**"

Ouch!

Suddenly, life with a pet asp didn't seem that bad.

Chapter 16
MUMMIFICATION

Everybody has heard of the three Great Pyramids of Giza. But not a lot of people know about the massive Trump pyramid, which is larger than all the others combined. That was where we were taken to face our punishment for the crime of spying against the Egyptian Empire.

It was a pretty big show, too. In modern times we have baseball fans and hockey fans and horse racing fans. Well, the ancient Egyptians had execution fans. It seemed like the whole country showed up—all except Pharaoh Tutansweet. He found mummifications boring, and stayed home with his Nintendo PlayStation. He was probably whipping up some low-fat popcorn in the microwave, too.

The crowd was cheering like crazy. You would have thought this was the Super Bowl. They even had snack guys selling jackal chips and Croco-Jacks. They were also doing a booming business in T-shirts with a slogan written in hieroglyphics.

"What does it say?" I whispered to Stan.

"'Mom and Dad witnessed a mummification and all I got was this lousy tunic,'" my exchange buddy translated.

"Get your souvenir programs here!" barked another vendor. "You can't tell who's being mummified without a program!"

I know ☞ **Rule 33** says: **No groveling.** But when I wrote my rules of coolness, I wasn't exactly expecting to get executed. If there ever was a time for groveling, this was it.

"I'm too young to be a mummy!" I pleaded. "I'm not even supposed to be born for three thousand years! Please, *please* don't mummify me!"

The crowd only cheered louder. To an execution fan, watching someone grovel is like getting to see a grand-slam home run.

Do I need to say it? Mummification isn't much fun. First they paint you all over with this disgusting gluey stuff. Next you're wrapped from head to toe with supertight cloth bandages. Then you're placed in a mummy case where all that stuff starts to harden. When I was seven, I broke my arm, and the cast took three days to dry. It was cold and clammy and totally gross. Well, this was twenty times worse because it was all over me.

Once I was wrapped up and shut inside, I couldn't see what was going on. But judging from the roar of the crowd, my fellow prisoners were getting mummified, too. I remember Stan's voice quavering, "I, Stan, regret that I have but one nose to give for the Pan-Pan Travel Bureau." The Smarty-Pants were arguing over who would be a more intelligent mummy. Ptlnys the Unbelievably Magnificent must have gone to his fate in dignified silence, because I never heard a peep from him.

I was aware of my mummy case being lifted up and placed on a horse-drawn cart.

"All right!" bellowed the chief executioner.

"The show's over! Go on home! Nobody's allowed at the burial site!"

There was a loud chorus of boos, followed by sounds of the crowd breaking up. The cart began to roll forward.

"I, Stan, am most sincerely sorry, Devin," came a voice from the mummy case next to mine.

I should have been out of my mind with rage. I should have been cursing the day Stan Mflxnys came rolling out of the baggage chute at the Clearview Airport.

But when I opened my mouth, I had no harsh words for my exchange buddy. "Are you kidding?" I crowed. "Thanks to you, I've seen things most Earthlings only dream about. I barely even knew there was a galaxy out there before you and your magic nose came along. And now I've—"

Hold it! That was the answer! I couldn't believe I hadn't thought of it sooner. There *was* a way out of this mess. It was as plain as the nose on your face! Or at least, the nose on *Stan's* face!

You have to use your head—or your NOSE.

"Your nose!" I cried. "Stan, can't you use your nasal processor to get us out of here?"

"My nasal processor would be most helpful," Stan replied, "but I, Stan, have no way to reach it. My hands are immobilized."

112

Uh-oh. Stan needed a finger to work his nose computer. And his arms were tied up across his chest, the same as mine.

"Well, what about the Smarty-Pants, then? Anybody got a free hand?"

"Quiet, Earthling," came Zgrbnys's voice from my left. "I am calculating the amount of air we will have in our mummy cases once we are buried. I estimate three-point-two minutes."

"Not even close," chortled Gthrmnys from the other side of Stan. "The correct number is two-point-nine minutes."

Were there ever such idiots? I guess their pea brains only held one thought at a time. How else could they squabble over how long the air would last without considering what would happen when it ran out?

The carts stopped. I was aware of being lifted up and placed on rough earth. Then I was sliding down what must have been a tunnel. Until that moment I could still sense a little light coming in under the lid of the mummy case. Suddenly, I was in total darkness, so I knew I was under the Great Pyramid. I heard the

sound of shovels working, and then nothing.

Cold panic seized me. I squirmed as if I could break through the tape, the mummy case, and the thousands of tons of pyramid above me.

"Let me out!" I shrieked. There was a ripping sound, and my hand broke through the heavy bandages.

I WANT MY MUMMY!

114

I pushed the mummy case door open and felt through the loose dirt until my hand reached the casket next to mine. I knocked, "Stan?"

His muffled voice was incredulous. *"Devin?!"*

"I can slip my hand into your coffin." This was a sentence most fourth graders never have a chance to use. "But you're going to have to tell me what to do."

Yes, it was true. In order to get out of this pickle, I would have to break one of my oldest and most precious rules of coolness—the classic

☞ **Rule 5:** You can pick your friends, and you can pick your nose. But you can't pick your friend's nose.

Is he saying what I think he's saying?

Chapter 17

A TICKLISH SITUATION

I wedged my hand inside the opening in his mummy case and patted around. Wouldn't you know it? Stan was ticklish. His taped body trembled. Snickering laughter bubbled out of the mummy case next to me.

"Stop it!" I hissed. "You're wasting air!"

"Sorry," he gasped. "We Pants are a very ticklish species. Our fabric is known to be delicate."

He did his best to hold still. I was able to find his neck. From there it was easy navigation: chin, mouth—jackpot! Carefully, I eased my finger through the sticky tape covering his nose and dug into a nostril.

Eureka!

Was it gross? Disgusting? Nause-ating? Repulsive? Amazingly, not at all. There was nothing but machinery up there. It

116

was no different from sticking your finger into the printer port on a computer—only a lot more complicated. There were thousands of tiny buttons, levers, and switches. How was I ever going to figure out the right ones?

A breath caught in my throat, and I choked. We were starting to run out of air!

"I told you it was two-point-nine minutes," said Gthrmnys smugly.

Well, I just started pressing away—anything and everything. If I could feel it against my finger, I hit it. I was puffing now. "How am I doing?" I rasped.

"You just ordered an extra-large pizza with double anchovies to be delivered to the Ring Nebula."

"Stan, I'm not going to make it in time!" I gasped. "The air is getting thinner—"

"Move your finger to the left," Stan ordered briskly. "To the right . . . straight up . . . now in a little half-circle . . ."

I followed his directions word for word. Inside his nose, I could feel buttons pushing, switches flipping, dials turning. And then—

The desert itself trembled as the colossal Trump pyramid lifted itself ten feet straight up off the ground. The sand above us disappeared in a whirlwind.

"Hang on!" cried Stan.

Stan and I, Ptlnys, and the Smarty-Pants were lifted up out of our mummy cases by a force that was both gentle and unstoppable at the same time. Round and round we spun as the bandages flew off us. But my finger never left Stan's nose, like a strong magnet was holding it there.

"How is this *possible*?" cried Ptlnys.

"Behold the power of the nasal processor!" announced Stan.

I could have sworn that his Munchkin voice sounded a little deeper just then.

It was amazing! Stan and I had wriggled out of some tight spots before, but nothing like this. "Mflxnys, I *love* you!" I bellowed. "Put 'er there!" Right there in the shadow of the hovering pyramid, I grabbed his hand and shook it.

For a split second, I couldn't understand the look of pure horror on Stan's face. Then it hit me: my finger was out of his nasal processor.

There was nothing holding up the pyramid anymore!

"*Run!*" I wailed.

Desperately, the five of us hurled ourselves away from the falling pyramid.

BOOOOOOOM!! It slammed back down to the desert with the force of thousands of tons of solid rock. The impact kicked up a cloud of sand a quarter-mile high.

"YEEEEEEEE-OWWWWWWWW!!!"

The mighty Trump Pyramid landed right on the very tip of Ptlnys's big toe. Pan's greatest hero jumped back as if he'd been launched from a slingshot. Up and down he hopped, holding his injured foot and howling in pain. "Aw, the nail's split off!" he complained. "It's already swelling up! It'll never heal right!"

He was lucky it was ever going to heal at all, I thought to myself. Six inches to the left and his whole foot would have been flat as a pancake. Another yard and *adios, Mr. Magnificent*.

Stan shot me a look of complete understanding. At least now we knew how Ptlnys got his legendary ingrown toenail. A ten-year-old Earthling accidentally dropped a pyramid on it. Another great zippered mystery solved.

"We'll get you to a doctor," Stan promised.

"Never mind about me!" Ptlnys exclaimed. "Watching your nasal processor in action was the biggest thrill of my life! I'm on the verge of the most important invention of all time! I've got to get back to my drawings!" And he limped off in search of a ride to the Sphinx, complaining, "How come you can never find a sedan chair when you need one?"

ANCIENT CIVILIZATIONS SURE AREN'T WHAT THEY USED TO BE.

"Gthrmnys and I have pooled our natural supergenius to analyze our situation," Zgrbnys informed us. "We have weighed every possibility, counter-possibility, and counter-counter-possibility. We have decided that the best course of action is to *get the heck out of here!*"

"Not yet," I said grimly. "First we have to go back to the palace and bust up every single thing from the future that you two gave the Egyptians."

"It's the only way to repair history and avoid a SPITTOON violation," Stan added.

"But we were co-Pharaohs for years," protested Gthrmnys. "We'll be recognized in a nanosecond in the palace."

"Just act intelligent," I told them. "Trust me, no one will know it's you."

Okay, that was pretty mean. But getting through to those Dummy-Pants could be like drilling into an anvil with a Popsicle stick. I mean, we weren't going to knock on the palace gates and say, "Can we please come in and break things?" Obviously, we were going to sneak in.

We had to walk back to Thebes—three hours, barefoot all the way, mostly on hot sand. **When you get mummified, you're not allowed to keep your sandals.** By the time we crouched in the bushes outside the palace, the four of us were limping as badly as Ptlnys. Even my blisters had blisters.

We climbed in through a small window in the guards' dressing room. Jackpot! Nobody was around and there were racks and racks of soldiers' uniforms. There must have been some pretty short guys working at the palace, because even Stan and I found stuff that fit. Disguised as sentries, we darted off in search of tools we could use to smash things. I picked up a long-handled battle-ax from the armory room.

The Smarty-Pants were busy drawing mustaches on each other with a piece of charcoal.

"You look so entirely different that I must use

my nasal processor to confirm it's really you," chortled Zgrbnys.

"I'm not one-hundred percent certain that I *am* me," agreed Gthrmnys. **"And you're a total stranger."**

We stepped out of the armory into the foyer, where a uniformed guide was leading a class of Egyptian schoolchildren on a palace tour. "And on our left you will notice a statue of Alexander the Great made out of balloon animals. And on our right, we see the co-Pharaohs with a little dirt smudged under their noses."

"Weren't they mummified for spying?" asked one of the kids. He looked about kindergarten age.

"At first we were," stammered Zgrbnys, "but we pleaded guilty to the lesser charge of driving a chariot without a license. So our sentence was reduced from mummification to community service."

"And while we were out painting the tomb of Queen Hatshepsut," Gthrmnys added, "we got drafted. So here we are, ordinary guards, and not fugitives from—*ooomph*!"

I whipped off my headdress and stuffed it in his mouth. Stan grabbed Zgrbnys, I grabbed Gthrmnys, and we ran.

"What should we smash first?" panted Stan.

"The microwave oven," I decided. "Where is it?"

"The royal antechamber," supplied Zgrbnys.

I hacked the microwave in two with one stroke of my battle-ax. Then I pounded the low-fat popcorn into cornmeal, and crushed the egg cooker. Boy, that ax was heavy. It makes you respect those ancient warriors who could swing them around like yo-yos. I was already winded, and the room still had a fax machine, an electric toothbrush, and a Lava lamp that all needed smashing.

I turned to Stan. "Don't just stand there! Help!"

My exchange buddy put his finger in his nose and twitched slightly. The fax melted, the toothbrush evaporated, and the lamp turned to dust.

I grinned at him. "Your way is better, but mine is more fun."

ANYthiNg YOU caN do, MY NOSE caN do bETTer.

All through the palace we stalked, destroying everything that didn't belong in ancient Egypt. Nobody hassled us. There were hundreds of guards around; we were just four more.

I bashed up the karaoke machine, the stapler, the Slinky, and the paperweight that, when you shook it, showed a snowstorm at the black hole of Cygnus X-1. Stan's nose fried the Etch A Sketch, the toilet brush, the VCR, and the gumball machine. While Stan took care of the Cuisinart, I found a pin and popped every balloon animal in the Hall of the Gods.

"I think that's everything," said Zgrbnys.

I pointed down one last gilded hallway. "What about in there?"

"Those are Tutansweet's private chambers," whispered Gthrmnys.

And then I saw it. There, right on the new Pharaoh's bed, sat the Nintendo PlayStation.

Chapter 18

THE SUSPENDERS

"We can't go in there!" hissed Zgrbnys. "It's too risky."

"But the PlayStation contains computer technology," protested Stan. "It would be a gross violation of SPITTOON to leave it here."

That's why Stan and I wound up standing over the Pharaoh's own bed, preparing to destroy Tutansweet's most prized possession.

"Okay," I whispered. "One—two—three—"

"Hello, Your Great Imperial Royalness," came Gthrmnys's loud voice from the hall. "We're just two humble guards who happen to look a lot like the old co-Pharaohs."

Wham! My battle-ax came down on the PlayStation, while Stan's nose shot a bolt of lightning that set the pieces on fire.

"What's that noise?" Suddenly, Pharaoh Tutansweet was in the doorway, staring in horror at the flaming wreckage on the bed.

"My PlayStation!!" The wrestler-sized king drew a massive sword and pulled it back like a baseball bat.

His sword came forward in a home-run swing. Desperately, I got my ax in the way.

SNAP! My weapon broke in two and clattered

to the floor. The Pharaoh swung again, ready to slice us in half.

The razor-sharp blade was an inch from my neck when Stan got his finger in his nose. All at once, the sword went as soft as a wet noodle and drooped to the angry king's sandals.

"*Guards!!*" bellowed Tutansweet in a blind rage.

We bolted. What a footrace! Four of us against hundreds of soldiers. Every time I looked over my shoulder, there seemed to be more Egyptians running after us. By the time we sprinted out the palace gates, it seemed like half the Egyptian army was hot on our heels. A flaming arrow sizzled past my ear, missing by inches.

"Where's the ship?" I howled. But as I rounded the corner, I spotted the main holding pen for impounded vehicles. Behind a low fence grazed horses, oxen, camels, elephants, and— hooray! **Our Button-Fly 501 space cruiser floated among the livestock.**

Without missing a step, Zgrbnys put his finger in his schnoz to lower the staircase and red carpet. It had to be history's very first full-speed galloping nose pick. We hopped the fence and darted in and around the animals, dodging hooves, and hurdling elephant droppings. Up and into the craft we sprinted. A split second after the door spiraled shut, a volley of arrows rained against the metal of the ship where the opening used to be.

Zgrbnys threw himself into the pilot's seat. "Prepare for liftoff—"

"Not yet!" cried Stan. "There's a malfunction in the navigation computer!"

Gthrmnys tugged at a nostril. "Diagnostic check!" he ordered.

The ship's computer sprang to life like a Christmas tree full of blinking, colored lights. A mechanized voice announced, "There is a used Kleenex wedged in the navigation console."

I was embarrassed. "Mine," I admitted. It had to be. Pants *ate* Kleenex; I was the only one who had any other purpose for them. I found the guilty tissue and yanked it out. " Sorry."

"Imagine using delicious Kleenex to blow your nose into," harrumphed Zgrbnys. "Earthlings are barbarians." He hit a switch, and we lurched a thousand feet straight up, quick as a hiccup.

"Okay," I said. "Now we need a new shipment of Nile Delta goldenrod."

"But that's all gone!" protested Gthrmnys. "It's at the bottom of the Nile in a giant watertight container!"

"We can still get it," argued Stan, "using the Suspenders."

"Suspenders?" I repeated.

"A robotic cargo-handling system," explained Stan. "It was invented by the Smarty-Pants and built by the Designer Jeans. The Suspenders could pluck out the whole barrel."

Zgrbnys focused the ship's scanners on the Nile. "Hmmm. I see fish, seaweed, Cleopatra's barge, and—aha! A giant piece of Tupperware three hundred feet wide."

"Tupperware?" I turned blazing eyes on the Smarty-Pants. "Where did the ancient Egyptians get Tupperware?"

Gthrmnys shrugged. **"Just because they're ancient doesn't mean they don't deserve to keep their leftovers crunchy and fresh."** He pulled a lever. "Activating Suspenders."

Two long elastic straps plummeted from the bottom of the ship, clips open. They disappeared into the waters of the Nile. Then, a moment later, they sprang out again, clamped to a dripping, mud-covered pink Tupperware tub as big as a football stadium. I don't know how we lifted it. I mean, our ship wasn't a fiftieth the size of that container. But Pant technology was like magic sometimes. The Suspenders clamped the thing to our ship with nothing more than a faint *wump*, and we just kept on flying.

THEY shOuLd cALL iT thE SNEEZY-BOWL!

"That was easy," I said, pleased and surprised. I mean, we had our goldenrod, and our Smarty-Pants, and we were heading back to the future. But I couldn't shake the feeling that we'd forgotten something.

Zoom!! A deadly heat-seeking missile shot past our ship, missing us by inches.

A *missile*? In *ancient Egypt*?

Then we flew out from behind a cloud, and I saw it. It was the B-52, filled with angry Egyptians!

"Prepare for light speed!" Zgrbnys exclaimed.

"No-o-o!" howled Stan.

My exchange buddy's eyes were locked on the main view screen. Dead ahead of us was the Sphinx. There, perched on top of the great stone head, was Ptlnys, chiseling away at his schematic drawing on the nose.

"We can't save him!" cried Gthrmnys. "We've got to get out of here!"

"If that diagram gets lost, the nasal processor might never be invented!" Stan argued. "Then the future of the whole *galaxy* would be changed!"

Suddenly, the heavy stone nose lurched. Ptlnys lost his footing and fell over forward. We watched, horrified, as the nose, and on top of it, Ptlnys, broke away from the statue and plummeted off the face of the Sphinx.

Is that what they mean by nose drops?

Chapter 19

ESCAPING BY A NOSE

"*Ptlnys!!*"

Heroically, Stan leaped for the controls, knocking Zgrbnys to the floor. The ship shot forward, and the ceiling above us began to open. I saw a split second of the Egyptian sky, and then—

"Heads up!" I hurled myself out of the way just as the giant nose of the Sphinx crashed into the ship, crushing the chair I'd been sitting in. Ptlnys rolled off the stone and landed right in my lap in a shower of dust and pebbles. So much for the great zippered mystery about what happened to the Sphinx's schnoz. In a million years I never would have guessed it was this.

Ptlnys's eyelids fluttered. "Am I dead?"

I shook my head. "You escaped by a nose."

"Oh, no!" cried Stan. "They fired again!"

"Evasive action!" I cried. But when I checked the screen, I could see it was no use. The missile was coming straight at us.

"We're goners!" cried Zgrbnys.

"Now I'll never get to donate my magnificent brain to the Pantsonian," added Gthrmnys tragically.

I closed my eyes.

KA-BOOOOOOM!!!

The explosion was even louder than I expected. But somehow we didn't blow apart into a million pieces. What was going on here? We were supposed to be dead!

I opened my eyes. A dense yellow fog had replaced the bright blue sky. All of Egypt was covered by a thick cloud—*of Nile Delta goldenrod*!

Of course! The missile hadn't hit the ship! It had slammed into the colossal Tupperware container!

Stan closed the roof, but not before a spray of airborne goldenrod covered us. We dissolved into *achoos*.

The Strato-fortress engines sucked in goldenrod.

Pow! Pow! Pow! Pow! Pow! Pow! Pow! Pow!

One by one, all eight of the B-52 jets exploded. Parachutes appeared as the crew bailed out. There were major-league fireworks as the Strato-fortress bomber burst into flame, and blew itself to bits.

Zgrbnys looked embarrassed. "Oh, yeah, we might have given them the parachute, too."

"And a few other items that probably won't change the future," added Gthrmnys. "The TV dinner, the pink flamingo lawn ornament, and—*achoo!*—the handy-dandy radish curler."

The Smarty-Pants replaced Stan at the controls, and we flew up and out of Earth's atmosphere. By this time, the air filters had started to clean up the goldenrod pollen, so we could all breathe again.

Ptlnys regarded us with wide-eyed amazement. **"If you four are a sample of what the future is going to be like, I'm glad I live in the past.** I can't handle the excitement!"

DON'T BE SUCH a WUSS!

"Ptlnys, please don't judge the future by us," my exchange buddy pleaded. "Wonderful things lie ahead, and you are destined to be the greatest hero Pan will ever know. I, Stan, assure you that today was not a typical day."

For once, the Smarty-Pants agreed. "A typical day has much more thinking in it," Zgrbnys explained, "and far less running, yelling, escaping, and narrowly missing getting killed."

"Statistically speaking," added Gthrmnys, "after all we've been through, we won't be due for another big scare for several decades."

No sooner were the words out of his mouth than a spaceship careened into orbit right in front of us, hurtling at light speed on a collision course.

"Look out!" I bellowed.

Zgrbnys dove at the controls and we swerved out of the way. The other ship missed us by a hair.

"More aliens going to ancient Egypt?" I mused. It's amazing they had any room for the Egyptians.

Then I saw the other craft in the view screen. It was flat and eight-sided—another giant stop sign. More visitors from Pan.

"A Button-Fly 1 space cruiser," said Gthrmnys, impressed. "The first of the Button-Fly series. That's quality workmanship. They don't make them like that anymore."

"It's the ship I was waiting for when I found you!" Ptlnys exclaimed excitedly. "My ride back to Pan!"

We docked with the Button-Fly 1, and Stan

and the Smarty-Pants used their nasal processors to move the Sphinx's nose to the other cargo hold. Weird, huh? Nose computers transporting a diagram for the nose computer— which hadn't even been invented yet. If you think about it long enough, it makes your brain hurt. Kind of like calling up Alexander Graham Bell long distance and telling him how to build the first telephone.

What if you got a busy signal?

Since I didn't have a nose computer to do the heavy lifting, I helped the other crew perform first aid on Ptlnys's foot. Let me tell you, I wouldn't have traded places with that poor guy for a billion dollars. His toe had swollen up to the size and color of a plum tomato.

"Well, Ptlnys," said Stan when it was time to leave. "I, Stan, will never forget our time together. May the Crease be with you."

"And with you, Agent Mflxnys," smiled the great hero. "It's refreshing to know that the children of the future are as intelligent and resourceful as you and your Earthling friend." His brow darkened. "I wish I could say the same for your colleagues, the co-Pharaohs."

"We're terribly sorry we fired you from your pyramid-building job," Zgrbnys apologized. "If we had known that you were Ptlnys the Unbelievably Magnificent, and not just another smelly Earthling, we never would have done it."

"All that my partner says is true," added

Gthrmnys, "except he forgot to mention that the whole thing was his idea."

"*My* idea?" cried Zgrbnys. "I didn't even want to be Pharaoh in the first place. I told you we should have taken those jobs as high priests of the Temple of Osiris. But no, you had to be top banana!"

"Oh, yeah?"

"Yeah!"

"Remarkable," commented Ptlnys. **"Centuries pass, worlds transform. But stupidity is eternal."**

He may not have been Unbelievably Magnificent yet, but the guy had a way with words. I stole his line—word for word—for my rules of coolness.

Chapter 20
THE *REAL* FUTURE

As we spun around the Sun, reversing the time warp, I started to get really nervous. In a few minutes, we would be back in the year 2000. What if the future wasn't fixed right? What if it was still Egypt, or something even more awful? We could be savages, living in caves. Fungus could be the only saber-toothed tiger who drinks out of the toilet! Or worse, my family might never have been born at all. I'd be all alone. I might even just disappear the minute we hit Clearview.

"**Come on, Earth,**" I muttered under my breath. "**Be normal.**"

Stan was worried, too. "There's more than just Earth at stake here, Devin. If we allow history to change too much, all of SPITTOON could collapse. We'd have people going back in time just to get a bargain on a dozen eggs, or to bet on horses that they know are going to win. Time traveling would be as common as taking a crosstown bus. The future would get changed so often that you couldn't even tell what it was supposed to be in the first place."

"What a couple of worrywarts," sneered Zgrbnys from up at the controls. "Of course the future is secure. You had Smarty-Pants intelligence telling you exactly what to do."

"Don't give me that!" I snapped. "You two were ready to leave without taking care of the B-52! It was pure luck that they attacked us, or you wouldn't even have remembered it was there."

Earth grew larger and larger in the view screen. And suddenly, we were in the clouds, cruising for Clearview. The knot in my stomach got tighter and tighter until I thought I would pass out from the tension. As we came through the cloud cover, I could make out flashes of my hometown. But I couldn't tell if it was back to its old self.

All at once, we were there, hovering low over Clearview. My heart in my throat, I risked a look out the window. Relief washed over me like a wave. There were houses out there instead of pyramids. Cars, not motorized chariots, zipped around on the streets.

"It's okay, right?" I barely breathed.

Stan was too choked up to speak, but he managed to nod.

As we passed over my house, a blond long-eared dog went racing across the lawn. It was Fungus, out playing with Roscoe in the backyard. We were home! Home to the *real* future.

The Smarty-Pants cracked open a roll of toilet paper to celebrate, and even Stan joined them for a square or two.

Break out the Champagne Napkins!

But all at once, I found myself feeling really sad.

Yeah, I know I should have been overjoyed. It was nothing short of a miracle that we had fixed the future without getting ourselves killed in the process. But I just couldn't get into the party mood. And it had nothing to do with the fact that toilet paper wasn't my idea of a feast.

Stan put a friendly arm around my shoulders. "This is the best we could have hoped for, Devin," he said soothingly.

"But we didn't do what we set out to do," I mourned. "We never brought back any goldenrod to make the tourists sneeze. And we sure can't risk going again. Time travel is like juggling atomic bombs! One slipup and the whole future is wrecked." I had to struggle to keep from breaking ☞ **Rule 18: Whining is for wimps.** "And now I'm going to lose my best friend for the next sixty years."

Stan's fried-egg eyes looked pained. "I, Stan, will get here sooner," he promised. "With good behavior, perhaps I can be back to Earth in as little as forty-five years."

A MErE SLap ON thE wrist.

"Don't worry, young Earthling," put in Zgrbnys. "We will visit often. Each century we Smarty-Pants sponsor a being less gifted than ourselves."

"Just the way we did in the 1900s with that Swiss patent clerk," added Gthrmnys. "The one who played the violin. What was his name?"

"Albert Einstein," Zgrbnys supplied. **"Not a very smart fellow.** But his hair-cut was so stylish."

Stan practically glowed. "See how lucky you are?"

"I'm a regular leprechaun," I mumbled. If there was one thing worse than losing Stan, it was looking forward to a lifetime of visits from the Dummy-Pants. I pictured myself at age thirty-five, explaining those two idiots with their fingers up their noses to my wife and kids.

Didn't it figure? The Smarty-Pants refused to take my advice to land the ship in the woods. They insisted on setting us down in the *same* parking space as before—right in the middle of a line of cars.

"But you got a ticket last time," I protested.

"Which we didn't have to pay," Zgrbnys said smugly. "Why is your primitive Q-class brain so fixated on this?"

"Well, at least put a quarter in the meter," I persisted.

"We only have Egyptian money," Gthrmnys reminded me cheerfully. "I'll tell you what. We'll flip this coin. Tails, we pay; heads, we don't."

I stared at the silver piece in his hand. His own portrait was stamped onto the face of it, beside the hieroglyph for pharaoh. But when he turned it over, Zgrbnys's picture grinned at me from the other side.

"Hey, wait a minute," I said angrily. "They're both heads."

Zgrbnys shrugged. "Well then, I guess we don't pay. Let this be a lesson to you, Earthling, for the next time you think you can match wits with Smarty-Pants."

The door spiraled open and we started down the staircase.

"Achoo!" sneezed Stan.

"Achoo! Achoo!" That came from Zgrbnys and Gthrmnys.

I frowned. What was going on here? And then—

"Achoo!" I sneezed, too.

I looked around. There were yellow spiked flowers amid the weeds in Clearview Park. Flecks of yellow could be seen in every lawn and garden. I gazed down the street to where the woods began. There was almost as much yellow as green in there!

It was—it was—

"Nile Delta goldenrod!" I gasped. "But—but *how*? We lost it all in ancient Egypt!"

I watched Stan's confusion change to understanding and finally delight. "When the B-52 shot down the giant Tupperware, billions of goldenrod seeds were sent flying for hundreds of miles. They must have planted themselves! And over the centuries, they've spread across the en-tire—*achoo!*—planet!"

"Do you think the tourists have been sneez-ing?" I asked excitedly.

Stan put his finger in his nose. I waited with bated breath.

This was the big moment. Now we were go-ing to find out if Stan would be called back to Pan in disgrace, or if he could keep his job.

"They've been sneezing like crazy!" my ex-change buddy crowed triumphantly. "Customer satisfaction is higher on Earth than any other spot in the galaxy—even higher than the beach at Mizar 2, which has a binary sun, so you can get a two-sided tan." He reached out to me. **"Give me an elevated five."**

"That's 'high five,'" I corrected, slapping his hand. "Congratulations, Stan!"

"I, Stan, have been promoted to the second drawer from the top, and my contract has been sprinkled with red-hot chili peppers so it can never be eaten," my glowing exchange buddy went on. "I'll be on Earth as long as there are tourists—and that'll be a long time!"

We were clamped together in a joyous embrace, pounding each other on the back. I'd long
since changed ☛ **Rule 8:** No hugging to No hugging
unless you've just pulled off a miracle. So we were
safe, coolness-wise.

Then I noticed that the Smarty-Pants both
had their fingers up their noses, frowning.

"What's wrong?" I asked.

"My nasal processor shows that we have an

unpaid parking violation from Clearview, Earth," scowled Zgrbnys.

"I knew you were going to get in trouble for that ticket!" I exclaimed.

"But how could an Earth fine get back to the Grand Pant on Pan, eighty-five thousand light-years away?" said Gthrmnys in perplexity.

I snapped my fingers. "Ptlnys had it! He stuck it in his pocket so the soldiers wouldn't get it when we were arrested for writing on the Sphinx. He must have brought it back to Pan."

"I suppose we'll have to pay it," grumbled Zgrbnys. All at once, he turned pale. "Wait a minute! This fine is over eight million dollars!"

"It was only a thirty-dollar ticket!" wailed Gthrmnys.

I laughed in their faces. "Yeah—when you first got it. But Ptlnys handed it in during the time of ancient Egypt. It's been collecting interest and late fees for three thousand years!"

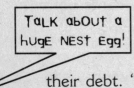

It didn't take very long for those two Dummy-Pants to hatch a scheme to get the money to pay their debt. "We will travel back in time to the age of the dinosaurs," said Zgrbnys decisively, "where we will invest seventy-five cents in Pterodactyls 'R' Us on the Jurassic Stock Exchange."

"Which will be worth millions when we return to the present!" raved Gthrmnys. "Brilliant! I'm glad I thought of it!"

I peered over at Stan and noticed in alarm that he was taking this idea seriously.

"You can't let them do that!" I hissed. "They'll mess up the future twenty times worse than before!"

"Devin," he began patiently, "they're *Smarty-Pants*! They didn't invent thinking, but they perfected it!"

I sighed. Oh, sure, I would probably never be able to convince him that his precious Smarty-Pants were a couple of interstellar airheads. But now that Stan's job on Earth was safe, at least I'd have plenty of time to try.

INVASION of the NOSE PICKERS

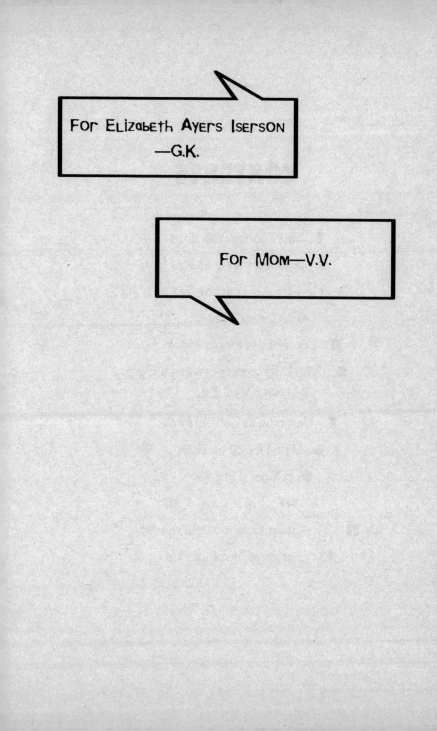

CONTENTS

Chapter 1

YOU SNOOZE, YOU LOSE

✳ DEVIN HUNTER'S RULES OF COOLNESS ✳

☛ <u>Rule 23</u>: Never let yourself be pushed around by a six-year-old girl.

But when the six-year-old girl is my rotten sister, that's easier said than done.

Lindsay was a picture of defiance on the cafeteria bench. In each hand she clutched a peanut butter and jelly sandwich.

"Come on, Lindsay," I wheedled. "Those belong to Stan and me."

"Finders keepers, losers weepers!" she jeered at us. **"You snooze, you lose, pal."**

I'll bet my face was bright red. "You know darn well that Mom only gave them to you because Stan and I had to carry our fly-fishing poles

1

for the field trip tomorrow! Don't be a jerk! Hand them over!"

Obediently, she held the sandwiches out to me. Then, just as I reached out, she crammed them both into her mouth.

"Stan! Quick!"

Stan put his finger into his left nostril. Instantly, both sandwiches sprang out of Lindsay's mouth, danced a figure eight in the air, and landed in my arms.

Lindsay's eyes bulged. "What the—"

You're probably wondering how a kid could do

all that just by picking his nose. The answer is that Stan Mflxnys was no ordinary kid. He was a 147-year-old alien from the planet Pan. And he wasn't picking his nose, either. He was operating his nasal processor, a superpowered minicomputer built right into his schnoz.

"You're in trouble, Lindsay!" I snarled. "I'm telling Mom!"

"Oh, I'm *so-o-o-o* scared!" she taunted us, as we stormed away.

Back on the fourth-grade side of the cafeteria, Stan and I examined our food. The sandwiches were mangled— crushed and gross.

ABC FOOD—ALREADY BEEN CHEWED.

I sighed. "I guess we're buying lunch today."

My best friend frowned. "I, Stan, don't understand it. My nasal processor should have retrieved the sandwiches long before Lindsay could have bitten them."

"I guess alien high technology is no match for a first grader with a bad attitude," I said, laughing without humor.

Stan shook his head. "I must perform a complete system diagnostic on my nasal processor."

"Sounds technical," I commented.

He nodded. "It's one of the most complex operations in Pant science."

Pants—that's what people from Pan are called. Trust me, it gets weirder. Their president is the Grand Pant. His assistants are the Under-Pants. Their top thinkers are the Smarty-Pants. Their planet is in the constellation of the Big Zipper. No lie.

I faced him. "What do you have to do?"

"I, Stan, must see how long it takes to cook a three-minute egg."

I was blown away. "What if there doesn't happen to be an egg handy?"

"Thousands of years ago, Smarty-Pants scientists were able to splice a strand of chicken DNA into the Pant gene code," Stan explained. "If there's no egg handy, we can lay our own."

Like I needed to know that. A new rule of coolness began to form in my mind: ☞ If you can lay eggs, keep it to yourself.

The cafeteria lady was pretty surprised when Stan told her he wanted to buy a raw egg. But when we promised we weren't going to throw it

at anybody, she held out the carton.

Stan took the egg, ducked behind the cutlery rack, and put his finger up his nose. Instantly, a bolt of lightning shot out of the other nostril, enveloping the egg in an energy field. I tapped it with a spoon. Soft-boiled to perfection.

"Did you time yourself?"

Stan nodded. "One billionth of a second."

5

Chapter 2
A GIANT FLYING SAUCER

I whistled. "Wow, that's fast!"

He looked horrified. "Fast? Devin, the standard time for a nonsneezing nasal processor should be one *trillionth* of a second."

I blew my stack. **"B i l l i o n t h ! T r i l l i o n t h !** Who cares which one it is? If you can't wait that long for a soft-boiled egg, you're a pretty impatient guy!"

"One billionth of a second is a thousand times slower than one trillionth of a second," Stan explained patiently. "It may seem like small potatoes to an Earthling, but to a Pant, it's very large potatoes indeed. It means my nasal processor is not functioning properly."

Or an Idahoan . . .

6

That *was* serious. A nose computer was a pretty handy thing to have around. For example, tomorrow our whole fourth-grade class was going on a camping trip to Calhoun Gorge. Stan's nasal processor could fight off an angry bear, or pick nuts and berries if our food supply got pushed off a cliff. But not if it wasn't working right.

Mr. Slomin, our teacher, appeared at the entrance to the cafeteria. "Let's go, fourth grade. Lunch is over."

My stomach rumbled. For those of us with terrorists for sisters, lunch hadn't even started yet. Out of the corner of my eye I saw Stan stuffing a stack of napkins in his mouth. Pants can survive on nothing but paper, but we Earthlings require something a little more nourishing.

We were halfway up the stairs when Mr. Slomin's beeper went off. Our teacher whipped his cell phone out of his pocket and dialed. Probably not that many teachers were wired for communication like that. But Mr. Slomin was president of the Clearview UFO Society. Talk about fate. The one UFO-crazy teacher in our school just so

CaLL 1-555-UFO-NUTS

happened to get a visitor from the other side of the galaxy in his class. Luckily, Mr. Slomin never quite realized he had an actual alien right under his nose.

"Slomin, here!" He was all business. "Uh-huh . . . uh-uh . . ." Suddenly, his eyes bulged. ***"A giant flying saucer heading for New York?!"***

He took the stairs three at a time back to the classroom. We had to scramble to keep up. "Hurry! Hurry!" he called back at us. "An alien spaceship just landed in New York harbor!"

It was amazing how fast Mr. Slomin turned our little classroom into UFO central. In no time at all, two UFO-spotters from New Jersey had faxed over a sketch of the spaceship, and Mr. Slomin had it up on the overhead projector. The teacher had his cell phone against one ear, and the regular phone against the other. On his belt, the beeper was going crazy.

I examined the sketch on the screen. It was a flying saucer, all right. A handful of dark bubbles on top gave the ship the appearance of a giant chocolate-chip cookie.

"Pssst," I whispered to Stan. "Is it one of yours?" There had been a lot of Pant ships in orbit lately. But they were usually careful not to be noticed.

"Negative," Stan replied, frowning. "But my nasal processor indicates that it's a perfect match for a Humongan ship."

"Humongan?" I repeated, shocked. "You

mean there are *two* kinds of aliens coming to Earth now?"

He scratched his head. "Humongans are two-hundred-foot-tall green robots—"

"What?" My blood ran cold. I thought about

☞ **Rule 51:** Sometimes it's better to be totally clueless than to know what's really going on.

"Don't worry," Stan soothed. "There's no way any creature as large as a Humongan could visit a crowded Earth city without being noticed. I, Stan, believe this is a hoax."

I allowed myself to breathe a little easier. Mr. Slomin and his UFO buddies were kind of a flaky bunch. Maybe Stan was right.

By the end of the day, no one besides the New Jersey UFO-spotters had seen any spaceship. The Air Force just laughed when Mr. Slomin asked them to declare a national emergency. Even the Secret Service phoned to order Mr. Slomin to stop faxing the president that picture of a chocolate-chip cookie.

"Fools!" croaked Mr. Slomin. "When are they going to realize that UFO safety is the greatest challenge facing our planet?"

I thought it was
personal hygiene.

The bell rang. Thanks to that UFO scare, we had done nothing all afternoon. And because tomorrow was the field trip, there couldn't be any homework either. High fives were flying everywhere as we got our jackets. Stan held up his hand but nobody slapped it. ☛ **Rule 67:** When you spend half your life with a finger up your nose, nobody wants to high-five you.

Chapter 3

COMING APART AT THE SEAMS

As soon as we got home, I made a point of ratting out Lindsay. "She did it on purpose, Mom!" I complained. "She ruined our lunches in front of the whole school! We're starving!"

"Inaccurate," Stan corrected. "I, Stan, have enjoyed a feast of succulent cafeteria napkins, with a side order of paper towels from the upstairs boys' bathroom. I even had a nip of my social studies textbook as a snack."

"Oh, Stan, you kill me!" Mom laughed. She glared at me. "Why can't you have a sense of humor about this, like Stan?"

He isn't joking! I wanted to tell her. But I couldn't blow Stan's cover.

"He's lucky enough to be an only child," I grumbled. "It isn't *his* sister who's turned into Godzilla Junior."

My mother sighed. "I'm sorry, Devin. I'm afraid your sister is just going through a phase right now. Six can be a very difficult age."

I thought she was more like Darth Vader with a touch of Lord Voldemort.

I was still griping about it when Stan and I went upstairs to the room we shared. Stan had started out as my buddy for the National Student Exchange Program. The program was over, but Stan had gotten special permission to stay longer. So he lived with us.

"If I pulled a stunt like that, I'd be grounded for a year!" I complained. "Mom and Dad let Lindsay get away with everything! She's their little darling. 'Just a phase!' What a crock!"

"I, Stan, disagree. Even Pants of the highest drawer go through a similar childhood phase at age sixty-five or so. It's called the 'phase of the knotted undergarments.'"

I frowned. "Why do they call it that?"

He shrugged. "It's when all Pants seem to

have their knickers in a twist. But because even the youngest Diaper-Pants have nasal processors, it's much more dangerous than an Earthling phase. After all, a temper tantrum with a nasal processor could knock down a building, or cause a tidal wave, or . . ."

He kept on talking, but I didn't hear a word he said. I was staring at his schnoz, which was suddenly *glowing*!

"Stan, are you all right?" I asked anxiously. "You look like Rudolph the Red-Nosed Reindeer!"

"My nose is illuminated?" Stan gasped. "This could be a Stitch-in-Time distress call coming in on an infrared frequency!" He looked at me seriously. "Pants can only use this frequency when they're truly coming

HELP! CaLL a taiLor!

apart at the seams!"

He put a finger up his nose. "This is Agent Mflxnys on Earth responding to your call. Please identify yourself! . . . There's too much interference! I, Stan, cannot hear you. . . ."

☛ **Rule 13:** In a crisis, don't just sit there; DO something!

Hey, I'd been hanging around Stan long enough to learn a few nose-computer tricks myself. I yanked the cable wire out of my small TV and stuffed the end into Stan's free nostril. Instantly, the set clicked on.

I could hardly see anything at first. The picture was flipping like crazy. But Stan fiddled with the cable, and the image stabilized.

"Greetings, Agent Mflxnys," came a voice.

Don't worry. Stan wasn't a galactic spy or

anything like that. He was a travel agent. Pants are the greatest tourists in the galaxy. They work two weeks per year and go on vacation for the other fifty.

Stan gawked at the small screen. "Devin," he hissed at me, "do you have any idea who that is?"

I shook my head. I didn't want to hurt Stan's feelings, but most Pants kind of look alike to me. They've all got crew cuts and thick glasses that make their eyes look like fried eggs. They wear white dress shirts and black polka-dot ties. Face it; they're a bunch of interstellar dweebs.

"That's the head Smarty-Pant!" Stan whispered in awe. "Only the Under-Pants and the Grand Pant himself have more authority on Pan!"

HE PUT THE 'GEE!' IN GENIUS.

Out loud he said, "Mr. Know-It-All! What an honor! I, Stan, assumed you'd be busy thinking on a fine day like today."

"There's no time for that now!" Mr. Know-It-All stormed, his tie flopping to and fro as he shook with anxiety. "Don't you realize what's happening here? Haven't you heard?"

Stan and I just stared at the TV. A wild scene was going on behind the head Smarty-Pant. Dozens of dweebs were running around, babbling. A blizzard of papers filled the air, as files were frantically emptied. Fried-egg eyes were wide with horror. Fingers bobbed in and out of noses like little jackhammers. It looked like Nose Picker Headquarters under siege.

"The whole planet's on high alert!" howled

Mr. Know-It-All. "The Grand Pant has given the order to fasten the Big Zipper! Every button, snap, and drawstring is tight as a drum!"

"But why?" asked Stan.

"Something," croaked the frazzled dweeb on the screen, "has been sucking all the power out of the Crease."

The Crease!

Is there an echo in here?

Chapter 4
CREASE PIRATES

Stan had told me about the Crease once. It's a little hard for us Earthlings to understand, but here goes.

There's a crease in the fabric of the universe. Through it flows a limitless supply of energy. That's where Pants get the power for their spaceships, their nasal processors, and almost everything on Pan.

"This is terrible, Devin!" Stan whispered to me. "Imagine Earth with dry oil wells, dead electricity, and no sun for solar energy. That would be like Pan without the Crease!"

What?! NO TV?!

I snapped my fingers. "That must be why your nose computer couldn't get those

sandwiches away from Lindsay in time."

"**We've switched all vital systems to our backup utility—Neptunian marathon gerbils on a wheel,**" Mr. Know-It-All reported grimly. "But they can't keep running forever. How about you, Agent Mflxnys? What can you tell me from your end?"

"*My* end?" My exchange buddy was confused. "I, Stan, have been here on Earth the whole time."

"Exactly," said the head Smarty-Pant. "That's where the energy theft is coming from. Something on Earth is sucking power out of the Crease."

"On *Earth*?!" cried Stan in disbelief. "But that's impossible! This is a Q-class world! Earth isn't advanced enough to know the Crease even exists! There's no technology here that could tap into the Crease."

Mr. Know-It-All looked angry. "My best thinkers pinpointed the problem. It was confirmed by a crack team of ponderers. And I personally confirmed the confirmation. Are you suggesting that we, the Smarty-Pants, are—dumb?"

"No!" Stan gasped. No Pant would ever say anything bad about the Smarty-Pants.

NO . . . JUST INTELLECTUALLY CHALLENGED.

All at once, it hit me. "The spaceship!" I turned to Stan. "Mr. Slomin's UFO buddies thought they saw a spaceship heading for New York last night. That must be who's doing this! The——what did you call them?—Humongans!"

"Sir!" my exchange buddy piped up. "I, Stan,

have reason to believe that a Humongan ship has landed here recently. Humongans would be capable of tapping into the Crease, wouldn't they?"

"Unlikely," Mr. Know-It-All replied. "Humongans are one of the most reasonable and level-headed species in the galaxy. Why would they become Crease pirates?"

"I, Stan, promise to track them down and ask them."

"It's too late for that. The Grand Pant has made his decision. While Pan still has enough power left for space travel, we must invade Earth."

I thought my eyes would pop clean out of their sockets. "**Invade *Earth*?** But that's no fair! We never did anything to the Crease!"

"The invasion force will need to devote full power to their engines," Mr. Know-It-All told Stan. "That means their navigation computers will be shut off. Your job, Agent Mflxnys, will be to direct the fleet to Earth."

"Don't do it, Stan!" I pleaded.

But Stan stood at rigid attention. "You can count on me, sir! I, Stan, will not let the waistband droop!"

I couldn't believe it! Stan Mflxnys—my best friend—was selling us out!

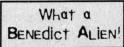

What a BENEDICT ALIEN!

Chapter 5
LOWER EAST HOOLA MOOLA

Stan removed his finger. The TV cable dropped to the carpet.

"You rotten, low-down traitor!" I cried accusingly. "I welcomed you like a member of the family! I fed you all the best newspapers and catalogs and phone books! I taught you my rules of coolness! **And *this* is how you repay me— by giving up Earth to an army of cosmo-nerds!"**

"But, Devin," Stan replied with a wink of one fried-egg eye. "I, Stan, promised to guide the invasion force *to* Earth. But I never mentioned *where* on Earth I'd guide them."

We ran to the globe that stood in the corner of the den. A few turns and then . . .

"Right here," said Stan. "Perfect."

He was pointing at the island of Lower East Hoola Moola, a tiny speck right smack-dab in the middle of the vast Pacific Ocean. There was nothing within a thousand miles of it in any direction.

"Won't they just move on when they realize they're in the wrong place?" I asked.

"Of course," said Stan. "But with their navigation computers off-line, that could take days.

Which gives us the time we need to track down the Humongans and straighten out this business with the Crease."

☛ **Rule 27: Give credit where credit is due.**

"Mflxnys, you're a genius," I assured him. "Quick, call that Know-It-All guy back."

I could tell the power drain was getting bad. While Stan was transmitting the coordinates, his nose computer made a whinnying sound like an old car trying to start on a cold morning.

"There's no doubt about it," he said sadly.

"We're in the middle of a full-blown Crease emergency. That's the second scariest thing that could happen to Pantkind. Only a factory defect in the Big Zipper could be more of a crisis."

"Look on the bright side," I coaxed. "At least Mr. Know-It-All was enough of a sucker to believe those fake coordinates. I'd love to see the look on his face when he winds up in Lower East Hoola Moola. What a dummy!"

"Devin!" Stan scolded me. "You're talking about the greatest mind on Pan! To become the head Smarty-Pant, you have to add up all the numbers in the universe without using a calculator or counting on your fingers! You have to do crossword puzzles in *pen*, and know the square root of a jar of peanut butter! You have to understand why the Jewish holidays always start at sundown the night before! It's *hard*!"

"Sheesh, sorry," I mumbled. ☛ **Rule 42:** Never make fun of your friend's friends.

Chapter 6

THE DIFFERENCE BETWEEN A GORGE AND NEW YORK CITY

The next morning, Lindsay went ballistic because she couldn't go on the camping trip with Stan and me.

"But you're only in first grade," my father explained reasonably. "When you're older, your class will go on exactly the same trip. Everybody does."

"Good. Then I'll go now and miss it later," she snarled.

"You'll just have to be patient," Mom told her gently.

"No-fair-no-fair-no-fair-no-fair-no-fair!!"

Dad drove us to school since we had our heavy duffel bags to carry. All the way there, he lectured us on how we

I wonder if she thinks it's fair?

28

had to be extra understanding of Lindsay because of the difficult phase she was going through.

"I don't know, Dad. Are you sure it's a real phase?" I asked. "When I look at Lindsay, all I see is a rotten kid pitching a fit."

Actually, I was pretty close to pitching a fit of my own that morning. Think about it. An alien invasion force was on its way to Earth. That makes it pretty tough to get psyched about your fourth-grade camping trip.

I leaned over to Stan. "How are we going to find those Humongans when they're in New York, and we're at Calhoun Gorge?"

"I, Stan, am working on it." My exchange buddy's finger was buried deep in his nostril. He looked strained, probably because he was low on power.

We pulled up in front of the school, and Dad helped us load our duffel bags onto the bus. There was an anxious buzz among the other kids assembled on the sidewalk.

"What's going on?" I asked Calista Bernstein.

"I think there might be a problem with our trip," she told me nervously.

Mr. Slomin stood at the front of the line, rifling through our itinerary. He was gawking from sheet to sheet, totally bewildered. "This is impossible!" he cried. "We're supposed to be going to Calhoun Gorge! This schedule is for a visit to New York City!"

My head whipped around to stare at Stan. He flashed me the "index-fingers-up" sign, which was kind of like thumbs-up for Pants.

Our bus driver, Mrs. Ford, was also confused. "My directions are for New York, too. Are you sure the plan wasn't changed?"

I thought Mr. Slomin was going to blow a gasket. "On the very morning of the trip? Without telling the teacher?"

Mr. Slomin even called the tour company on his cell phone. But when I saw Stan duck behind a bush with his finger up his nose, I already knew what their answer was going to be.

"What do you mean we were *always* going to New York?" the teacher howled. "I planned this trip myself! I've got twenty-five kids with sleeping bags and hiking boots and bug spray! We've been learning fly-fishing for three weeks! Where are we supposed to do that? In the city sewer system? . . . No, I won't hold! . . ."

Eventually, the principal himself came out to ask why we were standing around instead of loading the bus.

MAYbE thEY'LL catch SOME OF thOSE MUtANt aLLigatOrs.

"Well, uh—" stammered Mr. Slomin. You could tell he wanted to explain our problem, but he was afraid to look like an idiot in front of Dr. Bickleford. Thanks to Stan's nose computer, there wasn't the slightest clue anywhere that this had ever been a trip to Calhoun Gorge. I thought of a new rule of coolness for Mr. Slomin:

☞ Never let your boss think you don't know the difference between a gorge and New York City.

"Broadway, here we come," the teacher declared finally. "Everybody onto the bus."

Chapter 7
CAMPING IN CENTRAL PARK

The drive to New York took four hours, just about the same as Calhoun Gorge. Then, right outside the city, we got stuck in the biggest traffic jam I've ever seen.

Stan loved it. Pants have some pretty bizarre tastes. He was staring out the window, mesmerized by the scene all around us. It was like a giant parking lot. **"This is fantastic,"** he raved. **"Sitting for hours, yet barely moving!** It's almost as thrilling as going to the dentist!"

"We're not here to enjoy the traffic," I reminded him in a low voice. "How are we going to find the Humongans?"

Stan shrugged. "How difficult can it be to locate a two-hundred-foot green robot? It can't exactly blend into the scenery, you know. Oh, look. That cement mixer just cut us off. What fun!"

At last, we made it through the tunnel and onto the busy streets of Manhattan. Even I have to admit it was pretty cool—pounding on the bus windows, waving at all the taxis and limos that swarmed around us, and gawking up at the tall buildings.

Stan wasn't very impressed. "You told me New York had skyscrapers."

I stared at him. "Are you kidding me? The Empire State Building alone is over a hundred stories high."

"That wouldn't even come close to scraping the sky," he harrumphed. "On Pan, our tallest building, the Levi Strauss Center, is over four billion stories in height. The Designer Jeans had to run the elevator through a hyper-space shortcut or else it would take three weeks to get to the top."

Since all we had was camping equipment, our driver took us to Central Park. We stopped in a wide grassy field called the Great Lawn. Then came the hard part—setting up our tent. In no time, Tanner Phelps had somehow zipped his jacket into the zipper door. Calista was wrapped up in so much canvas that she looked like a mummy. Joey Petrillo held the stake steady for Ralph O'Malley to pound in.

Wham! Ralph swung the mallet down with crushing force onto Joey's thumb.

"Yeeeow!!"

And then Stan put his finger in his nose. With a *whoosh*, a great wind billowed from under the canvas, standing the big tent upright. Calista was demummified and launched right into the arms of a bewildered Mr. Slomin. The poles snapped smartly into place, and the stakes jumped up and hammered themselves into the ground.

We rushed to free Tanner, who was hanging by his jacket, still zipped to the front entrance flap.

There were *ooh*s and *aah*s from the class. Stan's nose computer had added a few extras to the tent, like a basketball hoop, a weather vane, and a welcome mat. A flock of city pigeons descended on the bird feeder.

I was impressed. Even at low power, the Crease sure could put on a show.

Mr. Slomin was confused, but he was still ready to take credit for what had happened—whatever *that* was.

"Uh—excellent work, people," he said approvingly, in a shaky voice. "I told you I could get this tent up."

We watched as a police car pulled up behind

the bus. A tall uniformed officer got out and approached the teacher.

"Hey, pal, what do you think you're doing? There's no camping here."

"But—but—" Poor Mr. Slomin had spent most of the day in a state of confusion, and things didn't make any more sense now. At a loss for words, he showed the officer our trip itinerary. The cop radioed the station house, and sure enough, a fourth-grade class from Clearview Elementary School had special permission to camp on the Great Lawn of Central Park for the next three days.

"Darnedest thing," the officer told Mr. Slomin. "I've been a cop here for thirty years, and no one's ever been allowed to do this. You folks must have a lot of clout. Is the governor's kid in this class or something?"

"Nope. Just a normal group of fourth graders," replied Mr. Slomin.

Plus one galactic travel agent with a magic nose, I thought.

Chapter 8
THE UNITED NATIONS

At the souvenir stand, everybody else bought T-shirts, key chains, hats, and stuff like that. Stan and I pooled our money and purchased a cheap pair of binoculars and an "I ♥ NY" transistor radio. During the whole two-hour bus tour, Stan scoured the city for signs of Humongans, while I listened to the radio for reports of two-hundred-foot aliens terrorizing New York.

There was nothing on the news, but maybe New Yorkers didn't get scared by alien invaders. They seemed like a pretty cool group of people to me. No one was fazed by taxis that drove ninety miles an hour and then screeched to a halt three inches behind the cars in front of them. Could it be that giant robots were no big deal either?

LOOK, Marge. It's the alien invaders again.

I leaned over to Stan. "Any chance the Humongans are hiding inside one of those big buildings?" I whispered.

"Impossible," he replied. "My nasal processor is equipped with a Pan-tastic alien life form detector. If there are Humongans inside these structures, it will pinpoint them and alert us."

The last stop on our tour was the United Nations. By that time, Stan and I were pretty nervous. We had driven all over New York, and we still had no clue where the Humongans might be hiding. We weren't even completely sure there *were* any Humongans!

The United Nations was really cool, but today it just made me feel even more worried. When Mr. Slomin showed us the spectacular display of the flags of all 188 member countries, it only reminded me of how much was at stake. Invaders were on their way to Earth right now. It was easy to look at Pants as a big joke because they've always got their fingers up their noses. But they had spaceships and technology that were light-years ahead of us. You bet it was scary.

The highlight of our tour was a visit to the famous General Assembly. It was a huge room set up sort of like a theater. Each country had a desk where its ambassadors and diplomats sat. I couldn't really figure out what they were voting on—catching codfish off the coast of Newfoundland, or something dull like that. I reminded myself of ☞ **Rule 39:** Just because something is boring doesn't mean it isn't important.

Suddenly, a small, slight man in brightly colored robes ran up to the podium at the front and

cried, "My friends, stop voting! I must alert you to a most horrible and beastly injustice going on in my home and native land!"

The secretary general stared at the guy. You could tell he didn't have a clue who he was. "And your country is . . . ?" he prompted.

The funny little man drew himself up to his full height and announced, "It is my honor to represent the government of Lower East Hoola Moola."

Uh-oh.

NATIONAL SYMBOL: HOOLA HOOP.

Chapter 9

GENERAL PUT·ON

"Lower East *what*?" chorused a number of diplomats.

"Hoola Moola," the ambassador said with dignity. "Including Lower East Hoola Moola itself and the islands of the greater Moola archipelago. At this very moment, my people—a brave people, a proud people—are being invaded."

"Invaded?" The secretary general was shocked. "By whom?"

"Pants!" cried the ambassador. "As we speak, platoons of GI Pants are hovering over my beloved island paradise in flying tank tops! Invaders climb down from suspenders that drop from the sky! Our president is being held in Pant-cuffs!"

What a Fashion victim.

Poor Stan looked like he wanted to crawl into a hole. We were so busy patting ourselves on the back for sending the invasion force to the middle of nowhere! I guess it never crossed our minds that this wasn't exactly going to be much fun for the Hoola Moolans.

I was nervous. I could just picture every country on Earth banding together to help the Hoola Moolans win back their island.

It was like watching a train wreck—you could see it coming, but you couldn't stop it.

Or could you?

I cupped my hands to my mouth. "Tell us about the invaders' weapons!" I called down.

"Devin!" Mr. Slomin scolded, horrified.

Stan looked at me in confusion.

I could see some of the delegates scanning the visitors' gallery. They could hear me!

"What are the invaders' weapons?!" I bellowed again.

Mr. Slomin was turning red. "Shhh!" he hissed. "You're interfering with important world affairs!"

But the Hoola Moolan ambassador answered

my question. "The Pants are unarmed," he admitted.

"Unarmed?" repeated the secretary general. "Then how have they managed to subdue your entire country?"

"With their noses," replied the ambassador.

There were snickers in the General Assembly.

A NOSE KNOWS.

"These are no ordinary noses!" the little man insisted, highly insulted. "They have been bewitched with special powers. To harness this

44

magic, an invader must merely insert his index finger into his nostril like so." And he actually did it, just like a Pant working his nose computer.

The United Nations erupted with laughter.

The ambassador was enraged. "Oh, so you think this is funny?" he shouted. "Let's see how amused you are after you view this videotape from the invaders!"

The lights dimmed, and a remarkable-looking Pant appeared on the big screen at the front.

Stan squeezed my shoulder hard enough to splinter the bone. **"That's General Put-On!"** he rasped in horror.

"Put-On?" I repeated. "That doesn't sound like a Pant name."

"His real name is Tnhrnys," Stan quavered. "But everyone calls him General Put-On because he puts on his trousers both legs at the same time! I, Stan, should have realized he would be selected to lead the invasion force. He's the supreme high commander of the Crease Police!"

Chapter 10
INSIDE OUT

"Even the Smarty-Pants are frightened of General Put-On," Stan raved, white to the ears. "He's the roughest, toughest, meanest stone-washed Pant in the galaxy!"

Stan filled me in. This Put-On guy was more than just a general. He was a planetary legend. Pant parents say to their little kids, **"Don't chew on the yellow pages or we'll tell General Put-On."** Almost like the bogeyman here on Earth! In addition to leading the Crease Police, he was the Under-Pant who oversaw teeth-gnashing and stepping on ants, the Smarty-Pant in charge of thinking up ways to break things, and a level five grandmaster at Candy Land. He *invented* frowning! According to Stan, before General Put-On, everybody smiled almost all the time.

It MUST have SEEMEd LiKE TELETUbbyLaNd.

I squinted at the screen. The general sat ram-rod straight in the saddle atop a large feathered—

"What's with Big Bird?" I asked.

"General Put-On always rides a Rigellian fire-breathing ostrich named Monty," Stan supplied. "It's standard issue for all seventy-four-star generals."

"He doesn't look so bad," I murmured. No-body in a polka-dot tie ever seems tough to me.

"You know the constellation of Gemini?" Stan asked.

I nodded. "The Twins."

"Well, there used to be only one guy," Stan explained, "until General Put-On got mad and rammed it with his spaceship so hard that it split into two. All because he couldn't get his parking validated. They sing songs about his temper in twenty different star systems."

The general looked like every other Pant ex-cept he wore a military helmet that magnified his fried-egg eyes into exploding suns. His white dress shirt had epaulets that extended a foot past each shoulder to fit his seventy-four stars. The ostrich burped and a shaft of flame shot out of its

mouth, roasting a nearby palm tree to ashes.

"Uh-oh," whispered Stan. "When he's in a bad mood, General Put-On feeds Monty nothing but chili with raw onions. A Rigellian fire-breathing ostrich can burn down a whole rain forest with a single hiccup."

SMOKEY BEAR says: ONLY YOU—and PEPTO-BISMOL—can prevent FOREST FIRES.

"Citizens of the Q-class planetoid known as Earth," the general began in a voice that echoed all around the United Nations. "I bring this warning from his Most Tailored majesty, the Grand Pant. If the force that is tapping energy from the Crease is not shut off by midnight on Friday, I vow to turn the planet inside out looking for it. **Now I must go and award myself some more medals**."

Then, just before the screen went dark, General Put-On snapped to a smart salute that ended with his finger up his nostril. There were howls of laughter in the General Assembly. Diplomats were rolling in the aisles. The secretary general was doubled over. Even Mr. Slomin, who saw aliens behind every door, exclaimed, "What a ridiculous hoax! Magic noses indeed!"

I leaned over to Stan. "See? That wasn't so terrible."

Stan stared at me. "Didn't you hear General Put-On? He's going to turn the planet inside out!"

"Oh, that's just an expression," I laughed. "My mom says it whenever she can't remember where she put something—'I'll turn the whole house inside out looking for it.'"

Stan shook his head gravely. "Turning a planet inside out is General Put-On's usual search procedure."

"**You mean—**" I was horrified, "**he's actually going to turn the whole Earth *inside out*?**"

Stan looked sheepish. "Sorry, Devin, but it's policy."

"But what's the point of that?" I complained.

"A couple of centuries ago, a band of interstellar jewel thieves stole the Grand Pant's royal pocket stud and hid it at the core of Saturn. It was a bold plan, but the criminals weren't counting on General Put-On. To remember where they'd stashed the loot, they'd established rings around the planet. Well, the general saw through that in a minute. He merely turned Saturn inside out to get the stud back. He left the rings up as a warning: Don't try to put on Put-On."

"Yeah, but Saturn's a *gas* planet," I reminded him. "It's easy to turn inside out. Earth is—*stuff*!"

Stan nodded apologetically. "It's a lot messier with a solid world."

"He's bluffing!" I cried. "How can he do all that? Pan is practically out of power. Your nasal processors sound like old cars, and you haven't even got enough juice to turn on a navigation computer!"

"Unfortunately," Stan replied, "it takes very little energy to turn a planet inside out. Earth's own gravity will be twisted around so that every-thing on the surface winds up in the middle, and vice versa."

I couldn't see myself, but I must have turned pale. Everything—supermarkets, hockey rinks, the Rocky Mountains, my house, not to mention 6 billion people—would get buried under solid rock! And talk about hot! The Earth's core was where all that lava came from! What didn't get squashed would get fried!

It would all happen in two days if we couldn't solve the mystery of what was tapping the Crease.

Chapter 11

THE GREAT GALACTIC
LEDERHOSEN

From the time we opened our eyes in the morning till the time we went to sleep at night, nobody could forget that we were in the Big Apple.

At dawn we awoke to hoofbeats on the horse trails by our tent. New York society was going for its morning ride. The trucks came next, followed by the taxis. By this time, the runners, the 'bladers, and the bikers were thick on the paths, and Mr. Slomin was choosing a group of volunteers to go buy fresh bagels for our breakfast. The campfire kettle was boiling up our hot chocolate. It would have been an amazing trip, if it wasn't for the fact that Earth was in terrible danger.

Stan had a morning routine of his own—a crisp new white dress shirt (heavy starch), polka-dot tie, ten deep knee bends, and then into the woods for a system diagnostic on his nasal processor.

That day I went with him.

"A twenty-thousandth of a second," he said dejectedly, handing me the soft-boiled egg.

"That's fifty million times slower than usual. I, Stan, fear the drain on the Crease is becoming critical."

I shook my head miserably. "What are we going to *do*, Stan?"

"Our best," he replied bravely. "We Pants have an old saying: **'Do your best, for better or worsted.'**"

The first stop on our schedule that day was the Museum of Natural History. There we stood in the dinosaur gallery, looking up at the skeleton of *Tyrannosaurus rex*, when Stan elbowed me in the ribs and whispered, "I don't see what everybody is so excited about. My nasal processor indicates that this life form has been dead for over sixty million years. What do they expect it to do—sit up and beg?"

YEah!

I was mad at him. "Don't waste your nose power on dinosaur bones! We're looking for aliens, remember?"

But Stan just couldn't seem to keep his mouth shut that day. In the planetarium show next door, our whole class got kicked out because my exchange buddy was heckling the narrator.

"This universe is all wrong!" he called out. "Where's the Big Zipper? You've got triple stars as double stars, and double stars as singles! Your black holes are only dark gray! What's more, you've left out the Asteroid Belt completely! **Without the belt, what's holding up the Great Galactic Lederhosen?**"

At lunch over real Manhattan pizza, Mr. Slomin gave us a serious lecture. "We didn't come to New York so you could insult people, Mflxnys." He frowned. "In fact, I'm not sure why we came to New York at all. We were supposed to be at Calhoun Gorge. But whatever the reason, we're here now, and you're going to be polite. Is that clear?"

"Yes, Mr. Slomin," mumbled Stan, his mouth full of napkins.

After lunch, we hit F.A.O. Schwarz, the famous toy store. The place is practically alive. You can't escape the bells, sirens, whistles, buzzers, computer voices, horns, and beeps in every pitch. Why, there was even a noise coming from somewhere that sounded exactly like Stan's nose comp—

I pinched him hard enough to remove the flesh from his bones. "Stan! That's you!"

But he was way ahead of me. His finger was buried up there to the second knuckle.

"Devin!" he hissed excitedly. "My Pan-tastic alien life form detector has located an alien!"

"A Humongan?" I asked anxiously. I looked around like I was expecting to see a two-hundred-foot robot standing there in the electric-train department.

Stan wiggled his finger. "I, Stan, can't tell. The signal is very faint."

Suddenly, wisps of smoke began to curl out of Stan's ears. I grabbed him by the elbow and yanked his finger down. "Careful! You're starting to overload!"

DOESN'T hE SEE thE NO SMOKING sigN?

"Oh, yuck!" Calista cried from across the store. "Stan's picking his nose again! And Devin's helping!"

We ignored her.

"I, Stan, must find a power booster for my alien life form detector!" Stan exclaimed urgently. "Quick, before the alien gets away!"

I took in our surroundings. We were in the middle of a toy store. It wasn't exactly Clearview Light and Power Company.

And then it came to me. I yanked a tiny locomotive out of the setup on the counter. I flipped it open, fished out a triple-A battery, and handed it to Stan. He grabbed it and shoved it, anode-first, up his nose.

Chapter 12

BATTERIES NOT INCLUDED

"Oh, that's better." The bottom of the battery stuck out of his nostril. It bobbed up and down as he talked. "The signal is quite close. And—" He frowned. "Devin, quick—another battery."

I was astonished. "What happened to that one?"

"It's used up."

"So *fast*?"

"Devin, this is the power of the *Crease* we're replacing," he explained. "To get my nasal processor up to full speed for even a few minutes, we would need at least seventeen thousand, eight hundred twenty-six and a half of those batteries."

"Seventeen *thousand*?" I echoed.

"Give or take eight hundred twenty-six and a half," he added.

That's a LOT OF ENERGIZER BUNNIES.

"Listen, Stan. Even if we could find that many batteries, so what? We have to chase down aliens! Can you carry seventeen thousand batteries? I can't."

"Hmmm. I see your point," he said thoughtfully. "However, I, Stan, know of a Pant who is in New York right now. He might be able to help us."

"Is he really strong?" I asked.

My exchange buddy nodded. **"His name is Stncldnys, but here on Earth he's known as Stone Cold Steve Austin."**

"Stone Cold Steve Austin?" I repeated. "From the WWF? *He's* an alien?"

Stan chuckled. "You didn't think a mere Earthling could wrestle like that, did you?"

I'll never get used to finding out how many famous people are actually Pants posing as Earthlings. When you think about it, it makes perfect sense. They have nose computers, so whatever they do, they're bound to be better at it than us humans. So, sure, they get famous. Shakespeare, Jerry Springer, even Michael Jordan—all Pants. And now Stone Cold Steve Austin.

That EXPLAINS it!

I handed Stan a battery. "Phone him up."

Stan put the triple-A in one nostril and his finger in the other. "Calling Stncldnys the Crushingly Powerful. This is Agent Mflxnys. Oh, sure. I'll hold." To me he whispered, "He's busy stomping someone."

"Maybe he's using his famous end move, the

Stone Cold stunner," I said reverently. "Here, take another battery."

"Stncldnys, this is an emergency," Stan said when the wrestler came back on line. "Meet me in front of F.A.O. Schwarz on Fifth Avenue in ten minutes." He tossed aside another dead battery. "He's on his way."

It was bizarre to think of a dweeb like Stan barking orders at the great Stone Cold Steve Austin. I had to remind myself that Stan was Pan's head travel agent on Earth, and that made him Stone Cold's boss. Weird, huh?

Then it was time to sneak away from the group to visit Stan's, *ahem*, employee. Mr. Slomin was so afraid of losing somebody in the big city that he was constantly counting heads. To escape his watchful eye, we were going to have to get low.

We crawled along the floor until we made it to the coolest toy in the whole place—a miniature Porsche Carrera, silver gray, with a real electric engine. We slipped into the seats—Corinthian leather. And before I knew it, Stan was steering us toward the exit.

"Don't hit anything!" I rasped. "The price tag says eleven thousand dollars!"

I kept my eye on the rearview mirror. PEANUTS! When Mr. Slomin disappeared behind the giant model of the Alps in the display for Ski Chalet Barbie, we ditched the car and ran outside.

Perfect timing. A limo pulled up and out stepped Stone Cold Steve Austin himself. He was even bigger than I expected. Huge muscles bulged through his black *Austin 3:16* T-shirt. And what came out of the mouth of the most famous wrestler of all time?

"Greetings, Agent Mflxnys. May the Crease be with you."

Chapter 13

FACE·TO·FACE WITH AN ALIEN

"Ah, yes, the Crease," Stan told Stone Cold Steve Austin. "That's the problem, Stncldnys. The Crease isn't going to be with any of us pretty soon."

He filled the wrestler in on the mysterious power drain.

Stone Cold nodded understandingly. "I noticed my nasal processor hasn't been working very well," he reported. "Usually, all it takes is a touch of my nostril and I've got my opponent flat on the mat, pinned. But lately, I've actually had to *fight* these people—which is no problem. But it makes you so sweaty!"

I didn't like to interrupt, but we needed to get

this show on the road if we were going to catch the alien. "Mr. Austin, we need seventeen thousand batteries, but we're not strong enough to carry them. Are you?"

"Triple-A's?" he asked, all business.

I nodded. **"Nostril size."**

He flexed his arm muscles. I almost felt a wind from the motion.

So we got the batteries. I know that sounds too simple. But when you're with Stone Cold Steve Austin, nobody gives you a hard time about things. He just signed an autograph for the security guard and asked to go to the warehouse. And they left us alone in there!

Stan and Stone Cold each took a battery to get started, and stuffed them into their nasal processors. That gave them enough power to send thousands of triple-A's floating off the warehouse shelves that stretched up forty feet high.

It was something to see! Giant rolls of masking tape soared into the air, wrapping the batteries end to end. Pretty soon, 17,856 single units had been turned into a cable of DC power over eight football fields long.

Stone Cold wrapped the whole thing into a giant coil, which he slung over his massive shoulders.

"Okay," he said, grunting under the strain of the weight. "Let's move out."

"Not so fast," I said quickly. "We can't just take these batteries. That's stealing!"

"Devin!" Stan was shocked. "We would never do that! We left an interstellar payment voucher backed up by the Grand Pant himself and our planetary bank, the Pocket."

I looked around for it. "Where?"

Stan chuckled. "Since Earth doesn't know that Pan exists, it was necessary for us to make the voucher invisible so as not to interfere with Earth's normal development. But you can rest assured that it's there, good as gold. You have my word as a Pant of the Second Drawer from the Top. Right, Stncldnys?"

"That's the bottom line," rumbled the big wrestler, "'cause Stone Cold said so!"

☞ **Rule 61:** Never argue with anyone who could snap your neck with a hiccup.

I was afraid that the alien might have buzzed off while we were setting up our power station. But when Stan plugged in the battery cable, his Pan-tastic alien life form detector started beeping again.

"This way!" cried Stan, pointing to a rear exit from the warehouse.

On the dead run, he headed out the door, with Stone Cold Steve Austin loping along behind him, lugging the seventeen thousand triple-A's. I brought up the rear. I was anxious to get out of there before someone accused me of Grand Theft Batteries.

As we ran down the narrow alley, I could hear Stan's nose beeping faster and faster. We were getting close! A feeling of dread started to grip at my chest. Were we about to come face-to-face with a two-hundred-foot robot? That was an alien monster even Stone Cold couldn't handle.

"Aha!" I heard Stan yell.

I rounded the corner and stopped dead in my tracks. There, trapped between the two Pants, a broken basket full of half-rotten apples, and the side of the building, sat a thin, gray—

"A *rat*?" I exclaimed.

Chapter 14

THE CHEESY WAY GALAXY

"Hey, buddy, who are you calling a rat?" the long-tailed creature snapped at me. **"I'm a *Ra'at* from the planet Rodentia Alpha in the Cheesy Way galaxy.** Show some respect."

"An intergalactic traveler!" exclaimed Stan. "What are you doing on Earth?"

"Isn't it obvious?" The Ra'at sunk his sharp teeth into the core of a Granny Smith near the top of the basket. "I'm getting my piece of the Big Apple."

I couldn't believe it! He wasn't a Humongan! He wasn't a Pant! How many different kinds of aliens were there on Earth? The next time I saw a mosquito, would it be a real bug, or a guy from Jupiter or something?

"Have you been messing with the Crease?" I demanded.

The Rodentian traveler was highly insulted. "Listen, pal, we Ra'ats have two directives we always follow. One: never fool around with another species' power source; and two: don't let your tail dangle too close to the paper shredder."

I was really upset. "You mean we got the wrong guy? Someone *else* is tapping the Crease?"

The Ra'at choked on an apple seed. "Someone's tapping the Crease? Man, I gotta get out of here before the Grand Pant sends General Put-On to turn the whole place inside out!"

He tried to scurry off, but Stone Cold delicately grabbed him by the tail.

"Hey, musclehead, what's the big idea?" he complained. "You're violating the Galactic Charter on the Treatment of Rodents!"

"Nobody likes a Ra'at who deserts a sinking ship," the big wrestler shot back.

"Earth is in big trouble," I informed the Rodentian. "General Put-On is already here. If you can do anything to help us—"

Stan had his finger up his nose. "Unlikely, Devin. My nasal processor indicates that Ra'ats are not known to have any special talents."

The intergalactic visitor was appalled. "Are you kidding? You'll never find a more talented life form than us Ra'ats! Dogs may be man's best friend on Earth, but we Ra'ats are best friend to species on thirty-six different planets, moons, asteroids, floating rocks, and clouds of space dust. Tie our tails together and you've got a pair of fur earmuffs that can sing to you in two-part harmony. When it comes to infesting, we're number three in the universe, after *Cockroachus maximus* and *Termitus munchus*. And we're unmatched anywhere when it comes to cheating at Candy Land."

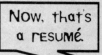

Now, that's a resume.

"Hold it!" I turned to Stan. "Didn't you say General Put-On likes to play Candy Land?"

"He's a level-five grand master," Stan replied. "He's never lost. His fireplace at home is over six miles long so he has room on the mantel for all his trophies."

"Let me at him," the Ra'at urged. "He's met his match with Ra'at A. Tooey—**king of the Lollipop Woods, master of the Gumdrop Pass, lord of the Molasses Swamp**. Where is he?"

"The island of Lower East Hoola Moola," I supplied.

Ra'at A. Tooey was surprised. "He'll never find any decent Candy Land competition way out there. They've got nothing but palm trees and tiki huts."

"And one Ra'at," I decided. "If you can get him involved in a long Candy Land tournament, that might buy us some more time to find out

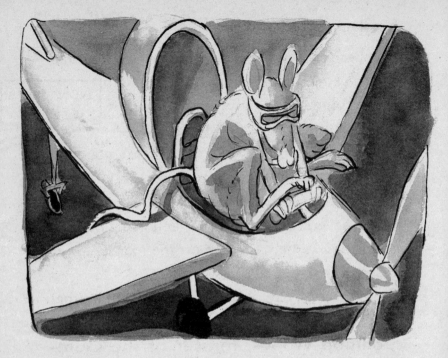

who's been messing with the Crease." I frowned. "But how can we fly you all the way to Hoola Moola?"

Stone Cold Steve Austin hefted the coils of batteries around his shoulders. "Kid, we've got *power*."

We went back into the F.A.O. Schwarz warehouse. Stan picked out a small remote control plane and opened the cockpit bubble. Ra'at A. Tooey crawled behind the controls and plucked a pair of goggles off the little plastic pilot. Stan held the engine up to his free nostril and snorted. The toy plane's propellers roared to life.

"How will we know if he makes it?" I asked Stan over the noise.

"I, Stan, have established a nose-to-nose cone communications link with the aircraft," my exchange buddy replied.

"It's in the bag!" the Rodentian called to us. "There are two things you can always count on with us Ra'ats: We never give up, and we always find a way to get in through your toilet pipes."

Zoom!! The small plane rocketed out of the warehouse and disappeared in the glare of the sun.

It's a bird.
It's a PLaNE.
It's a . . . rat?

Stan removed the end of the power cord from his nose. "Dead," he announced. "I, Stan, was forced to inject full energy into the plane's engine for the long trip to Lower East Hoola Moola."

Stone Cold Steve Austin had a Wrestlemania event in New Jersey that night. So he wished us luck and went to get ready. Stan and I snuck out of the warehouse back into F.A.O. Schwarz.

My head was spinning. Earth's safety depended

on a rat—excuse me, a Ra'at—flying halfway around the world in a toy plane to challenge an alien general to a game meant for six-year-olds.

Just when I thought things couldn't possibly get any scarier, I saw him standing in the games department, madder than fire. Mr. Slomin.

*"Where-have-you-been-we've-been-waiting-for-over-an-hour-we've-missed-our-matinée-of-*The-Lion-King*-thanks-to-you-two-immature-irrespon-sible-thoughtless . . ."*

It didn't end. As he yelled at us, the wind from his tantrum blew my hair into my eyes. I thought about how unfair all this was. Everything we'd done had been to try to save Earth. But how could we ever explain that to Mr. Slomin? UFO spotter or not, he'd think we were nuts.

"New York is *over* for you two!" he bawled at us. "As of this minute, *you're grounded*!"

Stan and I exchanged a look of sheer agony. If Ra'at A. Tooey couldn't make it to Lower East Hoola Moola, "grounded" was going to take on a whole new meaning.

Chapter 15

THE TIMES SQUARE JUMBOTRON

☞ **Rule 66:** Nothing can drive you crazy faster than sitting around twiddling your thumbs when there's important work to be done.

That night the whole class got to go to the Hard Rock Café for dinner and then on to Madison Square Garden for a New York Knicks game against the L.A. Lakers. Being grounded, Stan and I had to stay in the tent, eating instant macaroni over the campfire with Mr. Slomin. He was even madder at us than before because he was missing a great dinner and the game, while Mrs. Ford, the bus driver, got to use his ticket.

"Oh, it's okay, Mr. Slomin," I tried to assure him. "Stan and I can look after ourselves. We've learned our lesson now. If you take a taxi, you can probably catch the second half of the game."

"This never would have happened at Calhoun Gorge," the teacher muttered, not even answering me. "Now *that* would have been a field trip. I still can't figure out why we didn't go."

At 10:30 P.M., Mrs. Ford and the class came back, raving about "the most fun we've ever had in our lives." That got Mr. Slomin so riled up he couldn't sleep. So much for our plan to sneak away and continue the search for Humongans. Stan and I both dozed off while our teacher was still tossing and turning, muttering under his breath.

It was the middle of the night when Stan's crazed voice jarred me awake.

"Quick!" he exclaimed. "Get the mousetrap!"

I turned around in my bedroll. Stan was fast asleep, but his nose was blinking red, blue, red, blue. . . .

"We've got rats! Call an exterminator!"

I shook him. "Stan, shhhh! You're having a nightmare!"

He sat up and put a finger to his nose.

"Negative, Devin," he whispered. "I, Stan, am receiving a live transmission from the nose-to-nosecone communications link. Since my nasal processor was in 'sleep' mode, the signal was automatically relayed to my mouth."

"You mean—" I began.

He nodded. "Ra'at A. Tooey has reached the island of Lower East Hoola Moola. Those were the cries of the GI Pants as he infested their campsite."

Careful not to wake our classmates and our teacher, who was finally asleep, we crept out of the tent. I took my transistor radio and inserted the tip of the antenna into Stan's nose.

What a racket. There was a whole lot of crashing and shrieking going on, along with shouts of, "Get the broom!" and "What do you mean you left the rat poison on Alpha Centauri?"

"What a bunch of wimps," I commented. "You'd think they'd never seen a Ra'at before."

"Oh, they have," Stan assured me. "But it's very hard to tell the difference between a Ra'at and just a plain rat."

At that very moment, Ra'at A. Tooey bellowed, "I'll bet five brown apple cores and half a pack of Tic Tacs that there isn't a soldier in this army who's Pant enough to beat me at Candy Land!"

THEM'S FIGHTIN' WORDS!

"And if you win?" came a voice.

Sudden silence fell.

"The general!" Stan hissed. "Who else could quiet a crowd of soldiers when there's a rat in the barracks?"

"If I win," said the Ra'at, "you have to promise not to turn Earth inside out."

"General, we can't agree to that!" urged a GI Pant. "We could lose our only way to find the Crease Pirates!"

General Put-On chuckled. "I've never lost anything in my entire life—not my spaceship keys, not my lunch, not even my baby teeth. And certainly not a game of Candy Land. Mr. Ra'at, I accept your challenge. **May the best life form win.**"

"We've got to see this!" I exclaimed. "Earth's whole future is at stake!"

"Follow me!" exclaimed Stan, running for the park entrance.

I admit it. I was a little nervous. After all, how safe could it be for fourth graders to be wandering around New York City in the middle of the night? But even getting mugged didn't seem that bad compared with the whole planet being turned inside out. So I gritted my teeth and followed Stan.

We ran through dark and deserted streets, and then Stan turned the corner into Times

Square. We stopped in our tracks.

Thousands of flashing lights and glowing signs made the city bright as day. People packed the streets. Cars and taxis jammed the roadway. Here it was, one o'clock in the morning. But in Times Square, it might as well have been high noon!

Stan climbed onto a bench. From there, he swung himself over to a streetlight, where he began to shinny up the pole.

I was astonished. "What are you doing?"

Suspended above the crowd, Stan hung on with one arm. That left his other hand free to get a finger up his nose. "I, Stan, am programming my nasal processor to deflect the signal from Lower East Hoola Moola over to the TV."

I looked around desperately. "*What* TV?"

Then I saw it—mounted halfway up a building—the giant Times Square JumboTron, the largest TV screen in New York!

NOW I SEE thE big picturE.

Chapter 16

THE ICE CREAM FLOATS

Suddenly, there it was, right on the Times Square JumboTron—the island of Lower East Hoola Moola. Palm trees, sandy beaches, sparkling ocean, bright sunshine—

"But it's the middle of the night!" I protested.

"It's the middle of the night *here*!" Stan corrected me. "Hoola Moolan time is twelve hours ahead of New York. It's one o'clock in the afternoon there."

The Candy Land game was set up on a table on the beach. General Put-On, who was still mounted on Monty, the fire-breathing ostrich, pored over the board in intense concentration. Opposite him, Ra'at A. Tooey was perched atop a pyramid of coconuts.

The general picked a card—double blue. He

moved his gingerbread game piece to the second blue square, and punched the time clock. In the grandstand of bleachers, thousands of GI Pants cheered. A reporter from ESPN—Extremely Sporting Pants Network—jabbered excitedly into a microphone. An aide ran up to wipe the sweat off the general's medals, while another rearranged the stars on his shoulders into new and exciting constellations. Monty let fly with an enormous belch, which set the game board on fire. Instantly, a team of Fire Pants burst through the crowd to put out the blaze with their Panty Hose.

"You call yourself a Candy Land player?" Ra'at A. Tooey sneered right in General Put-On's face. **"You don't know the Peanut Brittle House from the Gumdrop Mountains!** My great-grandmother could beat you with four hands tied behind her back!"

"What's he trying to do?" I called up to Stan. "He's getting the general mad at him!"

"Well, he *is* a Ra'at," Stan reminded me. "You have to expect a certain amount of trash talk."

Ra'at A. Tooey was next. He picked a card

and flashed it for all to see. It was the Ice Cream Floats, the best card in all of Candy Land. It allows you to advance your gingerbread man to the Ice Cream Floats space—nine-tenths of the way to the Candy Castle! It was almost a sure win.

Na-Na-Na-Na. . . hEY, hEY, hEY! GOOd-bYE!

"All right, Ra'at!" I cheered. This rodent was a Candy Land superstar! Earth's safety was in the bag!

I wasn't counting on one thing—General Put-On's famous temper.

"Aw, twill!!!" he howled, picking

up the whole table and hurling it into the ocean. *"Twill! Twill! Twill!"* He jumped down from his mount and started kicking vast clouds of sand in all directions. Then he pulled a huge clove of garlic out of his uniform pocket and fed it to Monty.

"Ohhhhhhhh, no!"

There was a mad scramble as the entire platoon of GI Pants dove off the bleachers into the safety of the ocean.

A split second later, Monty let fly an enormous belch. The grandstand was engulfed in flames.

But the red-faced general didn't even seem to notice. He kicked over the pyramid of coconuts, sending his opponent flying. Then he grabbed poor Ra'at A. Tooey in midair and shook him by his tail.

I stared at the JumboTron screen. Hidden Candy Land cards were falling out of the Ra'at's fur and fluttering to the beach. They were all Ice Cream Floats.

The general raised an eyebrow. He said, "I smell a rat."

"You mean you smell a *Ra'at!*" the Rodentian corrected hastily. "Sorry, General. It was a long flight. Maybe I should take a shower. Nobody likes a dirty Ra'at."

General Put-On flew into a blind rage. *"Cheater!"* he bellowed. ***"Arrest this rodent!"***

A siren cut the air as sentry Pants came from all directions.

"Stan!" I called. "What's the penalty on Pan for cheating at Candy Land?"

"Six millennia of hard labor," came the reply. "But with good behavior, he might cut it down to four."

"This is our fault!" I cried.

If I'd learned anything from Stan Mflxnys, it was that all life forms are important—even slimy and disgusting ones like Ra'at A. Tooey. I wouldn't pick the guy to have tea with the Queen of England, but we had to save him from General Put-On.

Chapter 17

SAVE OUR SEAMS

Halfway up the streetlight, Stan put his finger to his nostril. "This is a Stitch-in-Time distress call for General Put-On! S.O.S.—save our seams!"

On the JumboTron, General Put-On reached up for his nasal processor and dropped the Ra'at.

"Run!" I howled at the screen.

Did he ever! The Rodentian's short legs were already pumping when he hit the sand. He made a sprint that would have left any NFL halfback green with envy. GI Pants dove at him every which way; nose computers shot lightning bolts at him. He dodged it all. The intergalactic traveler leaped into his plane and rocketed into the sky a split second before Monty barbecued the runway.

"Phew!" I let my breath out. "Man, that was close!"

Stan climbed down the pole. The picture from Lower East Hoola Moola disappeared from the JumboTron as soon as his finger left his nose.

We walked around for another hour, but Stan's Pan-tastic alien-life-form detector kept cutting in and out. So we had no chance of tracking down any Humongans. Eventually we just returned to Central Park and crawled back into the tent for a few hours' sleep.

In the morning, Mr. Slomin announced that the class would be touring Greenwich Village, going to a virtual-reality video arcade, and taking a ride on the Staten Island Ferry past the Statue of Liberty. He said it to everybody, but he was looking straight at Stan and me, trying to rub it in that we wouldn't get to go.

But today, Mr. Slomin threw us a curve ball. *He* would be taking the class on the bus; we were to be left with Mrs. Ford. I must have looked relieved, because he added, "If Mrs. Ford has anything to report about you two, you'll both have a month of detentions when we get back home."

"I'd be overjoyed to serve a month of detentions," I whispered to Stan, "if there's going to be an Earth to serve them on."

The class drove off, cheering and pounding on the windows of the bus. We were left to clean up the mess from breakfast. Mrs. Ford set us to work, then sat down on a campstool to do her needlepoint. Our bus driver set two stitches in a pink rose, and fell fast asleep.

> What a SPINE-TINGLING hobby!

"Stan!" I hissed. "Let's get out of here!"

He looked shocked. "But we'll be punished!"

"The whole planet's going to be punished if we can't find those Humongans! Come on!"

I tossed a plate of half-eaten bagels into the wire trash bin.

"Hey, what's the big idea? Can't a Ra'at enjoy his breakfast in peace?"

Chapter 18
THANKS FOR NOTHING

Stan and I both gawked. There was a rat in the garbage, chowing down on what was left of a honey bun. Not just a normal rat, but Ra'at A. Tooey himself, back from the island of Lower East Hoola Moola.

So help me, I was so glad to see the little guy alive and well, I reached down to pull him out of there. But he batted my hand away with a swipe of his tail.

"You again!" he snarled, beady eyes blazing. "Thanks for nothing, pal!"

"Hey," I said sharply. "If it wasn't for us, you'd still be under arrest. At least we got out of there."

"Yeah, sure!" the Rodentian exclaimed sarcastically. "Real quality transportation. That so-called airplane you got me ran out of juice over a split-level in New Jersey. Lucky for me those people had a trampoline in their backyard, or I'd be one dead Ra'at!"

"I, Stan, should have used a few thousand extra batteries while I had Stone Cold Steve Austin to carry them," my exchange buddy admitted. "My nasal processor has become very weak."

Shoulda, coulda, woulda . . .

The Rodentian looked disgusted. "Now he tells me. Listen, pal, we Ra'ats have some of the most advanced technology in the Cheesy Way galaxy. But on our own, we're pretty much left with scurrying. Ever try to scurry through the Lincoln Tunnel at rush hour? Those bus drivers have no respect for a long tail."

Band-Aids were wrapped all the way down the rear part of the thin tail. "Ouch," I said sympathetically.

"Tell me about it," he grumbled. "And I finally limp into New York with my caboose flattened by a twenty-ton bus just in time to wave goodbye to the spaceship that's supposed to be my ride home. This happens to us Ra'ats *every time!*

We go out of our way to help you nonrodent life forms. But we always end up getting treated like vermin!"

I felt guilty. "Well, couldn't you call for another ship?"

"Listen, bub," he sneered, "catching a spaceship to the Cheesy Way galaxy isn't like getting on a bus to Brooklyn. If you miss a flight to Rodentia Alpha, you've got a heck of wait till the

95

next one." He climbed out of the can. "Here, give me a hand with my luggage."

This turned out to be a dirty, crumpled Ziploc sandwich bag. Inside were half a jelly bean, a chewed pen cap, a mud-encrusted subway token, a chicken bone, a linty Gummi Bear, and a gleaming bright green Statue of Liberty key chain. "Souvenirs for the grandkids," he told me.

He's a Rat Packer.

Stan came over and held out his pinkie. "On behalf of the Pan-Pan Travel Bureau, I, Stan, would like to apologize for the terrible situation we've put you in."

Ra'at A. Tooey reached up and shook it. "I'm not a Ra'at who holds a grudge," he sighed. "You want my advice? Save yourself. I was there when Omega Twelve got turned inside out. Upside-down buildings everywhere—it took me a month to get the mud out of my ears! And dark! Just try to read a street sign! If it wasn't for that electric toothbrush, I never would have dug my way out! If I were you, I'd be long gone by the time noon rolls around."

"You mean midnight," I corrected. "That's

when they're turning us inside out. Midnight."

The Ra'at shrugged. "If you say so, pal. But the word on the street is it's going to happen at noon. And we Ra'ats are never wrong about the word on the street."

I glared down at him. "I was at the UN when they played the video. I heard General Put-On with my own ears. He said *midnight*."

All at once, Stan's eyes widened in horror. "Midnight *Hoola Moolan* time!" he exclaimed. "That's twelve hours *earlier* than here! Devin, he's right—it *is* noon!"

"But that's only three hours away!" I croaked, my blood chilling to ice water.

Ra'at A. Tooey dumped out his Ziploc bag and began sorting through his treasures on the grass. "Maybe I can trade some of this stuff for a grapefruit. **When a planet gets turned inside out, vitamin C is almost impossible to come by.**"

Stan picked up the shiny key chain. "The Statue of Liberty," he sighed. "It's known throughout the galaxy. I, Stan, really wanted to see it."

I wasn't in the mood. "Don't even think about it. We've got less than three hours to find those giant green robots. We don't have time for a giant green statue."

We stood there staring at each other, taking in what I'd just said. It was almost a silent instant replay.

And suddenly, the answer seemed so obvious that it was crazy we hadn't figured it out days ago!

Ra'at A. Tooey stared blankly at us. "Am I missing something?"

How could a two-hundred-foot green robot hide in New York City? By impersonating a two-hundred-foot green statue.

Chapter 19
DESTINATION: DOWNTOWN

Of course! The Humongan was on a giant pedestal in New York harbor, posing as the Statue of Liberty!

"Call General Put-On!" I crowed. "Tell him we've figured out who's tapping the Crease!"

> ELEMENTARY, MY dear Rat-SON!

Stan put his finger up his nose. I waited. Nothing happened.

"Uh-oh," the Ra'at said gravely.

"We'll find some batteries," I promised.

Stan shook his head. "That isn't the problem. I, Stan, believe that General Put-On has already begun warming up the Planetary Mega-Gravitron. That would block all messages coming into Lower East Hoola Moola."

"But how can we reach him?" I asked.

"We can't," Stan replied. "We must approach the Humongan directly and convince him to release his hold on the Crease."

"In other words," groaned Ra'at A. Tooey, **"we have to *talk* to the Statue of Liberty."**

"It's worth a try," Stan said seriously. "Humongans are renowned throughout this galaxy for their reasonableness."

"Well, what are we waiting for?" The Rodentian scampered up the side of my exchange buddy's pant leg and plopped himself in his shirt pocket.

With a quick check to make sure Mrs. Ford was still asleep, we sprinted out of the park and jumped into a taxi.

"Statue of Liberty!" I barked at the driver.

He eyed us in his rearview mirror. "That's an expensive ride from here, kid. Sure you've got enough money?"

Whoops.

Stan spoke up. "Would you consider accepting an invisible interstellar payment voucher, backed by the good credit of his Most Tailored Majesty,

the Grand Pant himself?"

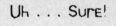

He kicked us out of the cab.

"Funny," Stan mused. "Usually, the Grand Pant's name opens doors all over the universe."

"The subway!" I yowled, pulling Stan toward the entrance. "We've got enough money for that!"

The New York City subway system is a crazy

thing. Even Stan, whose travel agent work had taken him all over the galaxy, couldn't figure it out. The map showed dozens of multicolored train lines crisscrossing each other like spaghetti.

LOOKS MORE LIKE LINQUINI TO ME. Or MAYBE ANGEL HAIR.

We did *everything* wrong. We went uptown when we needed to go downtown. We took the local when we wanted the express. We blundered through the exit door and had to pay again. When we finally got ourselves turned around, somehow we ended up on a train bound for Brooklyn.

I looked at my watch. It was eleven o'clock. "We've wasted almost *two hours!*" I glared at the tiny head poking out of Stan's shirt pocket. "I thought you said Ra'ats use the subway all the time!"

"I said *rats* use the subway all the time!" he retorted. **"We Ra'ats like to travel first class."**

I wanted to cry. There was no way we'd ever make it now.

And then a kind voice behind us said, "Statue of Liberty? Take the A train to Fifty-ninth

Street, and switch to the downtown Number One to South Ferry. That's where you get the boat for the Statue of Liberty."

I turned to look at the lady who had helped us, but she had already walked on past, her high heels clicking on the platform. I wanted to thank her. Maybe even tell her that she might have just saved the planet. But our train pulled up and we had to get on.

My exchange buddy was impressed too. "I, Stan, have witnessed many amazing things in my travels with the Pan-Pan Travel Bureau. I have watched the legendary evaporating pachyderms of Sirius trumpet proud blasts with their trunks and disappear into wisps of gray mist. I have heard the complaining of the famous disgruntled miners of the Coal Sack. I have looked on as the tireless moose-antlered hummingbirds of Antares have flapped valiantly in a vain attempt to keep their forty-pound heads aloft. But we have just seen one of the rarest and most wondrous creatures in the galaxy."

"What's that?" I asked.

"The friendly New Yorker."

Chapter 20

A KING·SIZE NASAL PROCESSOR

Eleven-fifteen. Eleven-thirty . . .

I gritted my teeth and tried to will our train to go faster. Every station stop seemed like an endless delay. I was a one-kid sweat bath by the time we pulled in to South Ferry.

Stan and I ran down the platform.

"Get out of the way!" Ra'at A. Tooey barked at the passengers ahead of us.

"What's the matter?" I said to a shocked man as we brushed past him on the stairs. **"Haven't you ever seen a talking rat before?"**

By now the sun was high in the sky, and the New York harbor gleamed like a sea of diamonds. As stressed out as I was, I couldn't help noticing the pure *energy* of the place—the towering sky-line, the rush of people and cars, and even the boats on the water. In Battery Park, the southern tip of Manhattan island, a real Hollywood film crew was shooting a movie. I stared. Behind the camera was none other than Steven Spielberg, the most famous movie director of all time.

The Ra'at pointed. "Look!"

We followed his beady-eyed gaze. There, across the harbor, stood the Statue of Liberty. If there was ever any doubt that it was the source of the power drain, it was gone now. **Miss Liberty was holding the tip of her torch up her nose!**

"Brilliant," breathed Stan. "The Crease energy is being diverted to a king-size nasal processor."

"Is that a Humongan?" I asked.

Stan put a finger in his nostril. "Impossible to tell. My Pan-tastic alien life form detector is completely off-line. It's definitely an imposter, though. This creature is one hundred sixty feet tall. The actual Statue of Liberty should only be one hundred fifty-one feet."

I was confused. "But I thought Humongans

were supposed to be two hundred feet tall."

"This must be a very short Humongan," Stan decided.

"An unhumongous Humongan," groaned Ra'at A. Tooey. **"What will they think of next?"**

"Okay," I said. "There's the ticket window for Liberty Island."

The line stretched as far as I could see. We ran

to take our place behind the last person. There, a small sign declared: FROM THIS POINT, THE WAIT IS APPROXIMATELY TWO HOURS.

"Two hours?" I cried. "We've only got twenty minutes!"

AND YOU thought SpacE MOUNTAIN was bad.

"Devin! Stan!" came a familiar voice. "What are you guys doing here?"

I wheeled around. Tanner Phelps was at the cotton candy stand. Behind him, I could see our entire class waiting at the entrance to the Staten Island Ferry.

"Duck!" I whispered to the Ra'at.

"Where?!" he asked excitedly.

"Get *down*!" Stan commanded.

The Rodentian was disappointed. "Too bad. Du'ucks are the greatest troubleshooters in the universe. There is no problem so large that a du'uck won't take a quack at it." And he disappeared inside Stan's shirt pocket.

"Tanner, keep your voice down!" I hissed at our classmate. "If Mr. Slomin sees us, we're cooked!"

"Where's Mrs. Ford?" he asked.

"Still in Central Park," I admitted. "Listen, Tanner, we need to sneak onto the ferry with you guys. It's our only chance to get close to the Statue of Liberty."

Tanner grinned with every tooth in his head. "What's in it for me?"

"My basketball card collection," I offered. "No? What if I throw in my Niagara Falls paper-weight?"

He smiled even wider. "Not enough."

I wanted to punch the guy. All life on Earth could get squashed because this big jerk got his jollies by busting our chops.

And then Stan Mflxnys—the guy who thought traffic jams and dentist appointments were big-time entertainment—came up with exactly the right thing to say.

"How about two free tickets the next time Wrestlemania comes to Clearview? Plus back-stage passes to meet Stone Cold Steve Austin."

All at once, the smirk disappeared from Tanner's face.

Chapter 21

TAKE ME TO THE HENHOUSE

Mr. Slomin stood by the door counting heads as we filed onto the Staten Island Ferry. I followed close behind Tanner, my face practically buried in the hood of his jacket. Stan was sandwiched so tightly between Ralph and Joey that I think they carried him most of the way.

"That's funny," murmured Mr. Slomin when we were all on board and the ferry had left the dock. "I'm coming up with two *more* kids than I brought."

"You musta double-counted a couple of 'em." The conductor shrugged. "Happens all the time."

The teacher shook his head. "Weirdest field trip I've ever been on. We're supposed to be at Calhoun Gorge, you know."

Stan and I broke from the class and took the stairs two at a time to the top deck.

The Statue of Liberty was a few hundred yards away and getting closer.

"Can you use your nasal processor to talk to the Humongan?" I asked urgently.

Stan put his finger up his nose. "Negative. All communication functions have shut down. I, Stan, must perform a system diagnostic."

I stared at him. "You mean the egg thing? *Now?* I can't believe you remembered to bring one along on this wild goose chase!

"I didn't bring one," my exchange buddy informed me. "I, Stan, will have to lay my own."

"What? *Here?*"

"Certainly not," Stan said primly. "A Pant needs privacy. **Egg-laying is a very personal thing.** Take me to the henhouse."

"The *henhouse?*" I repeated. "What are you, nuts? We're on a boat to Staten Island! There isn't any henhouse!"

We finally decided on the bathroom. It was a little cramped in there, but it was the only privacy on the crowded ferry. I stood guard outside. Even though ☛ **Rule 7:** was *listen to music; listen to reason; but never listen in on some poor guy in the bathroom*, I couldn't help positioning my ear up against the door. I have no idea what I expected to hear.

First there was a rustling sound, like a chicken resettling its feathers. That was followed by a soft clucking in a voice I recognized as Stan's.

Joey Petrillo came strolling down the deck. "Hi, Devin. Is that Stan in there?"

I was about to say yes when a series of sharp squawks rang out from inside the bathroom.

I'll bet my face was red as a tomato. I mean, I'd put up with a lot of humiliating uncoolness from Stan Mflxnys. Sometimes it felt like I spent half my life explaining away every dweeby thing he did. That's not even including his nasal processor, which made him come off as the biggest nose picker of all time. But this—*this* was beyond anything!

"That's not Stan," I said quickly. "It's—uh—some other guy."

At that moment, Stan said in his normal voice, "Eureka, Devin. The shell has appeared."

"Cluck harder," suggested Ra'at A. Tooey.

And the squawking started up again.

Joey rolled his eyes. **"Well, that chicken
sure does a great impression of Stan."**
And he ran off, calling, "Hey, Tanner! Stan's in
the bathroom with some dude! And he's pretending to be a chicken!"

After what seemed like forever, my exchange

buddy burst out of the bathroom, the soft-boiled egg in his hand. I'd never seen him so depressed.

"Three minutes!" he cried. "It took three full minutes to cook this! Do you know what that means? The power drain from the Crease has gotten so severe that my nasal processor is no stronger than a common egg cooker! Soon the energy level will be down to zero!"

I looked over the railing of the ferry. The Statue of Liberty was fifty yards away. It would never get any closer than this.

"What are we going to do?" demanded Ra'at A. Tooey. "If there's one thing we Ra'ats can't stand, it's wasting time. It comes from running down the street with the exterminator on your tail."

"There is only one possible course of action," my exchange buddy decided. "I, Stan, must blow my nose."

"You don't even have a Kleenex," I moaned.

Use an air hanky!

"Blowing your nose is a special emergency function of the nasal processor," he explained. "A

Pant is able to fire off all the remaining power in his nose in one final blast of energy. That just might be enough to launch us off this boat and get us close enough to talk to the Humongan."

Suddenly, an angry voice boomed, "Devin! Stan! What are you doing here? ***What have***

you done with Mrs. Ford?"

I spun around. Mr. Slomin was pushing through the crowd, his face an unhealthy shade of purple.

I checked my watch. It was ten minutes to twelve. Earth wouldn't make it through another chewing out by Mr. Slomin. Whatever we did, it had to be *fast*!

But how could we try anything with our teacher standing right there? "If only there was some way to create a diversion," I mumbled aloud.

"A diversion?" The Ra'at pulled himself upright in Stan's pocket. "Bub, if there's one thing we Ra'ats know how to do, it's create diversions! One diversion, coming up."

He bellowed, **"Look! A rat! A rat!"** Then he jumped down to the deck of the ferry and darted around the passengers' feet, slapping at ankles with his bandaged tail.

Pandemonium broke loose. A cry of "Ra-a-a-at!!" went up like an air raid siren. People were running and jumping and screaming. Some vaulted up on benches. Others tried to beat off the Rodentian with coats and brief-cases.

Best of all, Mr. Slomin totally disappeared in the crazy crowd. The coast was clear!

"Do it, Stan!" I urged. "Blow your nose!"

Chapter 22

CUTTER, CUTTER, PEANUT BUTTER

The last thing I remember was Stan with a finger plugging each nostril. His face turned red. His cheeks puffed out from the effort of his blowing. And then everything went nuts.

With a loud hissing sound, dense white mist encircled Stan and me like a thick fog. A powerful force picked me up by the seat of my jeans and lifted me clear out of the boat. Through the air I sailed, the waters of New York Harbor sparkling below.

"I hope you know how to land!" I called over at Stan, who was beside me.

He looked completely blank. "Land?"

Wham!

We came down in a small grove of juniper bushes. My clothes were torn, and I was scratched and bleeding by the time we managed to crawl out.

We looked up. There, right above us, loomed the "statue." I cupped my hands to my mouth. "Hey, you!" I bellowed. "Humongan! Down here!"

"It's no use," decided Stan. "We'll have to take the staircase up to the crown."

"Aren't you forgetting something?" I reminded him. "The *real* statue has a staircase. This isn't the real statue; it's an alien."

"Humongans started out as robots," Stan explained. "Their makers needed a way to get around inside their creations. So they installed stairs. And even though Humongans now are born and grow up like other life forms, staircases continue to be part of their bodies."

Sure enough, there it was—the entrance to the steps. There was a velvet rope at the door. A long line of people stretched down the path. I checked my watch. Eight minutes to go! We'd never make it if we had to wait.

I cried, *"Cutter, cutter, peanut butter!"* and the two of us barreled in to the head of the line. Then came the climbing—160 feet straight up a narrow, dark, steep, hot, cramped staircase, pushing past flocks of sweaty tourists the whole way.

"Excuse me . . . coming through . . . planetary emergency . . . excuse me . . ."

It was a major workout. I was drenched by the time we made it to the giant alien's kneecap. At belly button level, some little kid didn't want to let me by. When I pushed past him, he started shrieking. So much for ☞ **Rule 36:** Keep a low profile. The noise echoed all the way up and down the steps. I thought I was going to bust an eardrum!

NO PAIN, NO GAIN.

We were both exhausted by the time we made it to the top. I looked out the opening in the "statue's" crown. All of New York lay before us.

"Hey, Humongan!" I rasped with what was left of my breath. "Listen up!"

"Devin! Shhh!" Stan whispered. "Is that any way to speak to the most mature and reasonable species in the galaxy?" He cleared his throat and addressed the alien that was all around us.

"Pardon me, your Great and Extremely Enormous Massiveness. I am Agent Mflxnys of the Pan-Pan Travel Bureau, sometimes known as Stan. Might I take a tiny moment of your sizably vast, and hugely valuable time?"

I held my breath. Earth's whole future depended on what happened right now.

At first there was total silence except for the distant screaming of that little kid on the stairs.

Then a voice that came from all around us boomed, *"WHADDAYA WANT?"*

"Well, Your Largeness," Stan began, "you know how you've been tapping energy out of the Crease?"

"YEAH?" The voice was so loud I could almost feel it rattling my brain. *"SO?"*

"So I, Stan, was wondering if you could— well, you know—cut it out?"

There was the creaking of metal as the statue's giant brow furrowed. The Humongan was thinking it over!

"NO!" resounded our answer at last.

"No?" I repeated. "What do you mean, no? The whole future of the planet is riding on this!"

I'm pretty sure the Humongan frowned, because the ground bent under our feet, forming a little gully directly above the bridge of the "statue's" nose. Stan and I both lost our balance and conked heads.

"FINDERS KEEPERS, LOSERS WEEP-ERS!!" thundered the Humongan. *"YOU SNOOZE, YOU LOSE, PAL!!"*

This was the most mature species in the

galaxy? This guy reminded me of Lindsay!

My exchange buddy was genuinely bewildered. "I, Stan, don't understand it. Humongans are renowned for their reasonableness."

"Yeah, well, are you sure this is a real Humongan? This guy's about as reasonable as my rotten sister! Plus he's forty feet shorter than he's supposed to be. . . ."

Chapter 23
A NOT·SO·LITTLE BRAT

When it finally dawned on me, it was like a brilliant sunrise. I dragged Stan back to his feet by his polka-dot tie. *"That's it!"*

Stan looked blank. "You have information, Devin?"

I practically screamed it in his face. "This *is* a real Humongan! But it's just a kid! That's why he's too short—he's not fully grown yet! And he talks like my sister because he's going through a *phase!*"

Stan was amazed. "So you're saying that tapping the Crease is nothing more than—"

"Misbehavior!" I cried. "He's being *bad!*"

It was mind-blowing! Half a world away, a maniac on an ostrich was about to turn Earth inside out. Pan was going crazy. The whole galaxy was on high alert. And it was all because of one rotten kid!

This was like a five-year-old who digs up an anthill in his backyard. Does he ever think how the ants must feel? Of course not! He's just playing around!

That's what the Humongan was doing—playing! And we were the ants, about to lose our home—all six billion of us!

"If only I, Stan, had the enormous brainpower of a Smarty-Pant," my exchange buddy lamented. "Mr. Know-It-All would see what to do."

I was triumphant. "What do you do with a naughty kid? Tattle on him to his parents! I'll bet they're worried sick about this not-so-little brat!"

"But my nasal processor is stone dead!" Stan protested. "We have no way to send a message through deep space!"

I checked my watch. Two minutes to go. It was so frustrating I wanted to scream. We were totally out of power. Yet, just a few yards below us, the Humongan's torch was tapped into the greatest energy source in the whole universe!

I got an idea. I grabbed Stan and pushed him out the crown of the "statue," leaving him hanging on to one of the iron slats.

"Devin, what are you *doing*?" he hissed at me. "Without my nasal processor, I, Stan, will be killed if I fall!"

"Just hang in there!" I urged. Then I ran to the stairs and cried. "Help! Help! My friend went over the side! Quick! Give me your belts so we can pull him back in!"

It's amazing how fast cranky tourists can turn into a rescue squad. In a few seconds, I had twenty belts tied together and just as many volunteers ready to yank Stan back up to safety. I took the position at the front of the "rope" so I could block the others from seeing what we were really up to.

Stan grabbed hold of the first belt, but I instructed the men to keep lowering. I watched him climb down the face of the Humongan, rappelling against "Miss Liberty's" forehead like a mountaineer. When he was at the point where the torch was touching the Humongan's nose, I yelled, "Steady!"

My volunteers held fast. At the end of all those belts hung my exchange buddy, high above Liberty Island. His rope arm rested on the big green torch. The other was in its usual position, with Stan's finger up his nose.

He had done it! He was tapped into the Crease! But would the Humongan's parents get the message in time?

I looked at my watch. *Less than a minute to noon!*

AND a NEW YORK MINUTE at that!

Chapter 24

OOPS!

All at once, one of my volunteers pointed. "Look! Up in the sky!"

"It's a bird!"

"It's a plane!"

"It's a giant chocolate-chip cookie!"

A giant chocolate-chip cookie? Then I remembered. A Humongan ship!

"Stan, you did it!" I called. "They're here!"

Stan shinnied up the belts, and the men hauled him back into the crown.

"We're glad you're alive, son," one of the men said emotionally, choking back tears. "We thought you were a goner there and—*ugggh! Get your finger out of your nose!*"

I couldn't believe it. The Humongans were

here! But it was half a minute to noon!

The Humongan ship hovered low over New York Harbor for a moment. Then it disappeared under the water. After a few seconds, there was a titanic splash and a pair of two-hundred-foot-tall green robots arose from the waves.

"What the—" breathed the man who had pulled Stan inside.

"It's two more statues of liberty!" exclaimed another volunteer. "And they're *alive*!"

"*MOMMY?*" boomed the guilty voice of our Humongan. "*DADDY?*"

I checked my watch. Five seconds to go! Four . . . three . . .

"*DEAR ONE,*" thundered the mother robot, "*HAVE YOU BEEN A NAUGHTY LITTLE HU-MONGAN AGAIN?*"

Two . . . one . . . zero! Oh, no! I put my hands over my head and waited to be crushed like a bug.

And just like that, the Humongan took the torch out of his nose. "*I DIDN'T DO IT, MOMMY!*" he whined. "*IT WASN'T ME! IT MUST HAVE BEEN SOMEBODY ELSE! NO-*"

FAIR-NO-FAIR-NO-FAIR-NO-FAIR-NO-FAIR!"

Stan put his finger in his nostril. "Devin, it's Mr. Know-It-All! The hold on the Crease has been completely released!"

"You mean Earth won't have to be turned inside out?" I cried.

Stan nodded, beaming. "The Grand Pant has ordered the unfastening of the Big Zipper! General Put-On is feeding Monty Alka-Seltzer to soothe his stomach. The emergency is over!"

☞ **Rule 1:** Don't ever act excited—even when you're excited.

Well, who cares about Rule 1 when the planet's just been saved? I threw my arms over my head and started yahooing like a maniac. *"We did it! We did it! We—"*

And then everything tilted crazily this way and that. Stan, the volunteers, and I were tossed around like chicken pieces in a Shake 'n Bake bag. Outside, New York bounced wildly. My first thought was that crazy General Put-On was turning Earth inside out anyway. But then I realized what was actually happening.

Our Humongan had jumped off the Statue of

Liberty's pedestal, and was trying to run away from his parents!

"Abandon statue!" I bellowed.

That isn't exactly easy to do when the "statue" is moving. I think I fell down about half the stairs. And I had it easy. Picture what it was like for the families with baby strollers, or the teenagers with heavy backpacks. If Stan hadn't used his nasal processor to help, it would have been a total wipeout. As it was, Stan and I sprinted out of there just a second before the Humongan parents got hold of their naughty child.

"Ha!" I shook my fist up at him. "Now you're going to get it, you big baby!"

I had revenge in my heart. I was psyched for the great granddaddy of all spankings—it has to be heavy duty when the spankers are both two hundred feet tall. But I guess Humongans don't believe in that. Instead, they gave their kid a time-out—right at the top of a fifty-story office tower. While he was up there sulking, they fished the real Statue of Liberty out of New York Harbor. The "dad" carefully shook off the mud and seaweed, and placed Miss Liberty back on her

pedestal. Then the two giant robots turned to face the city skyline. *"WE APOLOGIZE FOR ANY INCONVENIENCE OUR CHILD MAY HAVE CAUSED THIS PLANET!"* boomed the "mom." *"AS WE SAY ON OUR HUMONGAN HOME WORLD, 'OOPS!'"*

And with that, they got their rotten kid down off the skyscraper, summoned their spacecraft up out of the water, and took off, towing Junior's smaller ship behind them. Then, just as they were about to pass over the Staten Island Ferry, they came to a dead stop in midair. There they hovered, just above the boat's top deck.

I squinted into the brilliant sky. "What's going on?"

A tourist standing next to me had a pair of binoculars. "It looks like they're picking up a hitchhiker—very short, kind of furry, long tail—" She made a face. "Oh, yuck, I think it's a *rat!*"

"Of course!" Stan exclaimed. "The Humongan home world lies in exactly the same direction as the Cheesy Way galaxy. The Humongans have volunteered to give Ra'at A. Tooey a lift." He beamed. "Have you ever seen such reasonable life forms?"

I was ready to strangle him. Reasonable? The whole planet came within a heartbeat of total disaster, and all those monsters had to say for themselves was "Oops"? Not to mention that half of New York City had ground to a halt to stare at the sight of giant robots punishing their kid atop a hundred-plus-story building. Why, the only people anywhere who weren't staring pop-eyed at the spectacle in the harbor were Steven Spielberg and his movie crew. They just kept on filming through the whole thing, like this was a typical day at the office.

I guess the famous director was following ☞ **Rule 16:** The show must go on.

Chapter 25
SPECIAL EFFECTS

The end.

Well, not *really*. A whole bunch of stuff happened after that.

Mr. Slomin practically killed us when we met back at the ferry terminal. And Mrs. Ford was so upset at being deserted in Central Park she refused to drive the class home. Our principal had to call on Mr. Slomin's cell phone and offer her a raise before she'd even tell us where she had hidden the keys to the bus. So the trip ended on kind of a downer—at least for everybody who didn't know how Stan and I had saved the world.

Nothing was changed when we got back home. Lindsay was still going through her phase, but it didn't bother me anymore. What did I care if she hogged the TV remote—just so long as nobody was going to turn the planet inside out because of it?

While the family tried to keep up with Lindsay's channel surfing, Stan barked away at Fungus, our cocker spaniel. Stan's nasal processor was equipped with a Pan-Tran translator, so he could speak Dog. He was going over all the highlights of the trip. I knew Fungus was really into the story. He was yipping and woofing through the whole thing.

"What's he saying?" I whispered.

"He believes he could have helped us," Stan translated. "Dogs are very good at handling statues."

"Dogs are very good at handling fire hydrants," I corrected. "One-hundred-sixty-foot statues are a little out of their league."

How do you say "bowwow" in Pant?

Suddenly, Lindsay flipped to a news program. Behind the anchorperson was a graphic of the New York skyline with the words MASS HALLUCINATION written across it.

"Turn it up!" I exclaimed.

". . . there's still no explanation for a very strange sight noticed by several thousand people in New York Harbor yesterday," the lady was saying. "Just after noon, onlookers claim to have witnessed two giant Statues of Liberty giving a slightly smaller Statue of Liberty a time-out atop a skyscraper. After that, all three climbed into two flying chocolate-chip cookies and disappeared. Police are baffled. One boy, however, has a theory."

They cut to their New York reporter in Battery Park, exactly where we had been the day before. Standing right next to her was—

"Devin!" Mom sat bolt upright on the couch. "That's *you!*"

I remembered giving this interview. But never in a million years did I think it would get on TV all the way back home in Clearview!

"Oh, it was pure special effects," I said on television. "None of it was real. They're shooting a science-fiction movie here. See? There's Steven Spielberg behind the camera."

"But—" My dad was bug-eyed. "But I thought you were at Calhoun Gorge!"

"It's a long story," I admitted.

"That reminds me," my exchange buddy added eagerly. "Along with Devin, I, Stan, have been awarded six months of detentions. It's quite an honor."

Fortunately, my parents were so blown away by the sight of their son on TV, that I didn't have to answer too many questions.

"Hey, Stan," I whispered. "What a lucky break that Steven Spielberg happened to be shooting a movie in New York yesterday. Otherwise,

COMING SOON TO a PLANET NEAR YOU.

we never could have come up with a decent explanation for everything that happened."

"Devin," Stan chided me, "luck had nothing to do with it. As soon as I knew we'd be confronting the Humongan in public, I contacted Splbrgnys and asked him to set up his film crew in Battery Park. It was my last message before my nasal processor lost the power to communicate."

"Splbrgnys?" I repeated. "You mean Steven Spielberg is a *Pant*?"

He shrugged. "You didn't think a mere Earthling could make such great movies, did you? Don't look so shocked, Devin. Where do you think he got all that alien footage for *E.T.*?"

On TV, the reporter was wrapping up my interview. "There you have it, folks. The mass hallucination turns out to be nothing more than special effects for a new Steven Spielberg film." He turned back to me. "Any idea what the movie is going to be called?"

On the screen, I watched myself flash a mischievous grin. *"Invasion of the Nose Pickers."*